THE QUEUE

Alexandra Heminsley

ORION

An Orion Paperback
First published in Great Britain in 2023 by Orion Fiction
an imprint of The Orion Publishing Group Ltd
Carmelite House, 50 Victoria Embankment
London EC4Y 0DZ

An Hachette UK Company

1 3 5 7 9 10 8 6 4 2

A CIP catalogue record for this book is
available from the British Library.

ISBN (MMP) 978 1 3987 1840 1
ISBN (eBook) 978 1 3987 1841 8

Typeset by Input Data Services Ltd, Bridgwater, Somerset

Printed in Great Britain by Clays Ltd, Elcograf, S.p.A.

www.orionbooks.co.uk

Alexandra Heminsley is a bestselling author, journalist and broadcaster. She is the author of both fiction and non-fiction, including her memoir *Running Like a Girl* and her debut novel *Under the Same Stars*, and her work has been published in fifteen countries. She spent eight years as the Books Editor at *Elle* and ten years at BBC Radio 2's Claudia Winkleman Arts Show. She regularly appears as both a co-host and guest at literary festivals and was a judge for 2011's Costa Novel of the Year Award. *The Queue* is her second novel.

Also by Alexandra Heminsley

Ex and the City
Running Like a Girl
Leap In
Some Body to Love
Under the Same Stars

For Janet, with love and admiration

Prologue

Saturday, 17th September 2022
0500 Hours

Suzie resisted the temptation to slam the front door shut as she left the house. She knew she shouldn't – it might wake the neighbours. But there was part of her which wanted to make the point: I'm up, I'm alive – getting on with things, doing my best.

Nevertheless, the temptation was resisted. She pulled the door to quietly and unlocked the car, wincing at the beep of the alarm before sitting a minute in the dark, rubbing her hands together to warm them a little before she set off. It was barely five o'clock, and she had the shortish drive to Colchester to catch her train if she was going to get a fast one to London before dawn.

She had had the television on – sound down low – while she had been packing her bag half an hour ago. The queue didn't seem to be too long. Yet. But the news reporter was saying it was only going to get busier, and the people who were there already looked freezing. Standing in the dark, bundled up in scarves and hats over padded jackets and winter hiking boots, shuffling forward slowly through the night. Was she really going to do this? Did it mean enough to her? To any of them? Suzie patted her coat pockets, double checking that her gloves were in there, and glanced across to her bag on the passenger seat.

She had snacks, drinks, a plastic mac, a phone charger, and her small make-up bag, containing a lipstick, some powder, her travel hairbrush and a small tube of hand cream she had once received in her stocking from her sister-in-law. She knew it had been a freebie with one of those deals where if you make 'two or more purchases, one to include skincare', but she liked the brand anyway. At least it hadn't been one of her jars of Laphroaig marmalade, like the year before. Suzie shuddered at the memory of 2020 – the year of hobbies. She could barely look at flour in the supermarket these days without the image of traces of congealed dough stuck to every surface in the kitchen crossing her mind.

The engine of her small Fiat came to life as soon as she turned the key. She took a deep breath. Leaving the house like this, double checking bags long before dawn, reminded her of departing for the airport. Since it had opened, almost every holiday had begun with a dawn trip to Stanstead. The night before, Colin would be up double checking that the luggage would fit in the boot – but *never* leaving it there overnight in case the car was stolen. Good god, imagine the risk! As if someone would come to this cul-de-sac, and steal this car, Suzie had always thought. The idea was laughable.

There was a part of her which knew she should have been grateful to Colin for the double, triple, and quadruple checking before each departure, his dedication to the mantra 'tickets money passport', and his love of the pale Elastoplast-coloured money belt stuffed with emergency cash hidden under his shirt. After all, they'd never missed a flight. But crikey it was stressful. She would take until day three of the holiday to unwind from the endless reminders: decant your liquids into minis, bring a reusable water bottle, pack spare underwear in a small plastic ziplock bag in case of lost luggage.

She'd give anything to have him here today though, driving her crackers.

As the car pulled out of the drive she slightly hoped there *was* something she had forgotten. Nothing major like her wallet. Just a little thing, a conversation starter so that she might get to know the people she'd be queueing near. Tissues? She couldn't remember if she had packed any – would it work better if they'd been forgotten, or if she had plenty to offer round? What if everyone around her was with friends, family, partners? She should have brought a spare sandwich to share, she realised. Even if it was just a cheese and pickle. It would have been something. A way to connect, in case she was left standing alone. Wasn't that why she was going, after all?

No, she reminded herself. This was about paying a respectful tribute to a life of duty. It was saying a formal goodbye to a face which had been there – every day, everywhere, for far longer than either of her parents had managed. On banknotes. On crockery. On stamps. She had even been born on Coronation Day, 2nd June 1953. A fact her mother liked to remind her of when she'd been a little girl, and one she'd been grateful for this summer when the shops had suddenly filled with celebratory shortbread fizz just in time for her big day.'

She felt undeniably positive once she had set off for London, driving along in the dark, all alone, the radio on her usual station. Free, even. Was it inappropriate to be feeling a little giddy at the prospect of the expedition? Maybe it was, but she didn't have to tell anyone. Yes, no one need know about this little rush of excitement, this sense of levity. She remembered breaking her arm, decades ago, and how curious she'd felt when the plaster cast was finally removed. Part fearful, suddenly aware of how exposed her fragile arm now was, but part free, mesmerised by the new lightness the limb felt without the weight of the plaster. She'd moved faster, freer, but with a fresh awareness of her own frailty. Today was similar – for the first time in ages she was going to be a part of something; she was going to be experiencing something. But what?

0500 *Hours*

It had only been a couple of weeks, but Abbie was already depressingly familiar with the small hours' slam of the flat's front door. The water in the glass on her bedside table was still rippling from the noise when she opened her eyes to see what time it was, wincing as the blue light of her phone lit up in her face. Nearly five. She put the phone face down on the table. Next to it in the half-light were a couple of make-up-soaked pads of cotton wool, and behind them was a dog-eared paperback on which sat a teetering stack of jewellery and a couple of swatches of brightly coloured fabric, the edges slightly fraying.

She had barely had three hours' sleep, but the line of emerging daylight around her thin curtains and the ongoing clack-clack-clack of her flatmates' heels on the cheap laminate hallway made sure she knew she wouldn't be drifting off again any time soon.

Next was the plastic click of the bathroom light's pull cord and the extractor fan starting to whirr. She put her head under the covers, trying to block it all out. Curled up into a ball, hugging her knees, she felt like a thirteen-year-old again, trying to avoid listening to her parents' arguments floating up from downstairs, her eyes clamped shut just in case it helped. She tried to breathe deeply, pretending she was back there, woken by the sounds of her mother getting herself ready for an early start at work. She felt the same dread, knowing that sleep was over, that the day had started without her. Just as it had been then, she knew her efforts were pointless. What had been vague mumbling a few minutes ago was now audible sentences in the hallway outside of her room. Morning was going to happen *to* her, and she could merely choose whether to participate or not.

'OMG *babe*, that's a great idea,' Annabelle's long public-school vowels were slinking under the not insignificant crack under Abbie's door.

'D'you reckon?' Maisie sounded less convinced, whatever it was they were discussing.

'Yeah, I mean, there'll be like, no one there right now . . .'

'I think I saw—'

'And we could be, y'know, totally part of it all? On the news and stuff? Like, I wanna tell my parents I did it?'

'We could even get on the news!'

'Oh babe, you're so right. Let's show our respects et cetera . . .'

Even as she tried to block out the noise, Abbie found herself grating at Annabelle's languid – yet numerous – '*baaabe*'s.

6

'We could make a cute TikTok . . . ?'

'Maisie Sullivan! You can't use the Queen for content!'

'Well it's not like the news channels don't.'

'Good point, Mais. Shall we get Abbie?'

Annabelle was still asking the question as Abbie heard the creak of her bedroom door handle turn. A second later, the silhouette of her flatmate appeared at the open door through the crack between the duvet and the bed. Abbie stayed as still as possible, desperate to seem sound asleep.

Annabelle paid scant attention to Abbie's lack of response. Why would she? Of course Abbie would want to come. Annabelle had clearly long ago discovered that this confident outlook made life look blissfully simple. It had only been a couple of weeks, but Abbie already felt herself slipping into the role of something eerily close to a supporting player, merely there to burnish Annabelle's position as leading lady of the house. It wasn't even Annabelle's flat, but as a result of either instinct, liquidity or sheer numbers on the socials, she knew she was its queen.

'Abs darling – we've had an amazing idea. We're going to go and join *the queue.*'

Abbie lay still, saying nothing. A quarter of her flatmate's face was visible through the chink of lifted duvet. A feline smile, one that knew Abbie was there, awake, awaiting instructions.

'Abs, you've got to come with us. It's like, a part of history. We're history.' Annabelle had leaned forward and was shaking her now. A hand on her shoulder, jiggling her through the duvet. The scent of cranberry juice cocktails and expensive eau de toilette used as deodorant.

Reluctantly, Abbie poked her head over the top of her covers.

'What are you talking about?'

'Get up Absicles, we're going to join the queue. You know, the *Queen* queue. Put some warm stuff on, and get, like, some snacks and shit.'

Annabelle's breath smelled sticky with booze and only one row of her false eyelashes was still sitting in place. The other had slipped, clinging to her existing lashes, creating a delicate piece of lacework. She was wearing a short black skirt, a pair of wide-diamond fishnet tights and a white shirt tied at her waist with what looked like a splash of red wine on it. It wasn't a classic mourning outfit, but it was pure Annabelle.

This plan was clearly doomed. Abbie had yet to witness either of her flatmates queue for anything, let alone commit a day to doing so without the promise of free gig tickets, luxury skincare or an exclusive seated area at the end of it. But she was curious, having spent much of the last couple of days wondering if she could go down to the river and queue alone. She had been watching the news headlines at all hours, trying to assess if it would be safe for her to simply turn up and give it ago. The previous day she'd even put together a provisional bag of provisions to take with her, only to lose her nerve at the last minute when the weather turned. Now, she had the chance to do it with company. But this company?

She ran her hands through her hair and reached for the glass of water on her bedside table.

'Are you guys for real?' she asked, not quite daring to look up. There was, after all, an outside chance that this was little more than a wind-up. Something they were going to do for an ironic selfie before heading home for a bacon sarnie.

'Of course we are babes,' came Maisie's voice from her own bedroom across the corridor. 'Don't wanna miss the national trauma dump!'

Abbie sighed as she sat up.

'Seriously? But they were saying on the socials that it takes like, a *day*.'

Annabelle whipped back the duvet cover and flicked on the main light.

'C'mon, let's do it,' she said, before turning on her heel and heading out towards her own room. 'No time like the present.'

There was a distant clank as something fell out of a kitchen cupboard, followed by the muffled sound of Maisie swearing.

Abbie sat squinting at the light, before easing her legs round to get out of bed. She was queasy at the thought of spending twenty hours in the cold watching her flatmates slowly sober up. But it had been less than a month since she'd vowed to herself that she would try and do more, be part of more, *live* more this academic year. This was just the sort of thing her parents would never have indulged in – her mum would never have had time, what with work, the gym, and her busy social calendar. Her dad would have said it was for fools and retreated upstairs. She imagined he was up there now, muttering at the TV in the grey dawn, exasperated by it all.

She wasn't in Worthing now though. She was here, in London, living the life she'd always dreamt of. Wasn't she? It had taken her years to persuade her parents that a fashion degree would not be a waste of money. That she would find useful employment from it. That a life pursuing something creative wasn't an indulgence or a passing fad. She had got her way in the end, by promising to work part-time throughout and making sure she didn't get into too much debt – a word which represented their greatest enemy.

However, the reality of her first year had fallen somewhat short of her dreams. Ensnared by the end of various remaining lockdown restrictions, much of the course had taken place remotely, her fellow students little more than faces on her laptop screen. The melting pot of inspiration and diversity she had daydreamed about had been smothered by the blizzard of new protocols, which had turned university from a non-stop party into something closer to an online speed awareness course.

Sure, she was still receiving the bare bones of the education she had so ably persuaded her parents she needed in order to make a career as a creative, but as the first year had progressed Abbie had realised that that was barely half of what she had been craving from university life. Her hopes had been for more than mere pattern-cutting and fabric-dying; as she had laid on her bed, staring at the ceiling of her family home in West Worthing and dreaming of escape, a degree in fashion had represented a door being opened to a world beyond small-town life by the sea. She wanted so much more than getting married to someone sensible, living with his parents while they saved for a deposit, and buying somewhere decent to start a family. She had *dreams*, even if her parents reared back from the word whenever it was mentioned, hearing only *danger*.

But her vision of a degree in fashion had looked less like these endless online seminars, and more like kaleidoscopic fantasies of nights out spent discussing iconic designers with like-minded makers. Or nights in with a bunch of fabric nerds who shared her eye for detail, watching old movies for inspiration and analysing every shot. Instead, meeting new people had been a logistical nightmare as much as an emotional one, leaving a young woman from the south coast feeling as provincial as it was possible to. She had quickly discovered that what passed for edgy on a day trip to Brighton's North Laine really didn't cut the mustard in the city's capital, and there were more than a few of her fellow students who were startlingly unselfconscious about letting her know.

There hadn't been anything overtly cruel, more a casual aura of indifference. After so long spent imagining this new life, these new friends, the follow requests that went unreplied to, stung almost as much as her mother's suggestion, two summers earlier, that she might find life in the big city harder than she was expecting to. The only thing worse that seeing her phone sit, zero messages incoming despite her having suggested trips to museums or galleries to her peers, was the thought that her mum might be proved right. That she might not make it through the course at all.

Annabelle and Maisie, already confident born-and-bred Londoners, were largely oblivious to all this. They paid minimal attention to the course itself, seeming more interested in 'street fashion' and endless discussions about how the algorithms of various social media worked – and thereby how to maximise their digital impact. Having grown up sixty miles away, where such luxuries as visiting Columbia Road flower market on the spur of the moment were impossible, Abbie never seemed quite able to keep up. For years, the city had existed as a hypothetical, seen only through the colourful glow of her phone. If she could just get there, she'd told herself, a life of neon creativity would unfold before her. One where her dad's never-discussed depression and her mum's highly strung ambition were not the primary forces dictating her day-to-day existence. She would talk about ideas! She would dress influencers! She would create a legacy!

Instead, she had so far spent untold hours cross-legged on her bed, still dreaming of being somewhere else. Now, in an attempt to get even closer to the action, she had taken the third room in this breezy, poorly lit Lewisham student flat when someone else from their course had dropped out. She was lucky to be in with Annabelle and Maisie, she'd told herself as she'd headed out to meet them at the end of August. She'd make the money work, and her new flatmates would introduce her to all sorts of fresh and exciting people.

The three of them had sat in a nearby cafe, Annabelle slowly sipping an oat turmeric latte, and discussed the flat. Abbie cringed inwardly as she told the waitress she actually preferred dairy milk, and hoped Annabelle, looking at her phone, hadn't noticed. The flat itself was owned by a friend of Maisie's older half-sister. It was going to be redeveloped soon, so for this year they could have it for a bargain, as long as they didn't ask for too many repairs. But it was cheap. And so close to Blackheath and Greenwich, two of the prettiest parts of London. All in all, it seemed too good to be true – a decent flat in a cool area with two girls from her course.

The reality was proving somewhat more chaotic.

It had already been a month and Abbie was still finding London life overwhelming. Desperate to fit in, but beleaguered by a sense that she didn't, she seemed to have spent much of the first two weeks scuttling home to her room to catch up on *Coronation Street*, doom-scroll what everyone else was doing and message her old Worthing mates about how great it was now that she *properly* lived here. Updates from her little brother about the gang at the skate park – somewhere she had spent last summer longing to leave behind her – now made her teary with nostalgia, scrabbling around for excuses to head back to the coast for the weekend. Was she giving up on London already, or was it giving up on her?

This life wasn't what she'd planned for herself, but she could change all that today, couldn't she? This was a chance to be someone that people at home talked about as 'probably there now that she lives in London'. She imagined herself at seventy, beginning sentences to her grandchildren with 'Back when I lived in London . . .' or 'Of *course* I queued, it was only down the road from me . . .' She still wanted to become that person, didn't she? Couldn't she?

Her bed was so warm though, and her eyes so dry. But then, as she caught a glimpse of the photos from home she had stuck around the mirror by her desk, she thought of her mother. How she'd assume Abbie would never have the tenacity to stick with something like the queue. How she'd teased her – gently, but not quite gently enough – about how she'd be hanging out with snowflakes and arty-farty types who'd never get anything done. How she'd assume Abbie wouldn't even know about a national event like this, she was so busy with her head always in the clouds.

So she ran her fingers through her hair and reached for a pair of dungarees from the heap of half-worn clothes on the chair at the end of her bed.

Of course she was going to go.

0500 *Hours*

Tim was awake before the alarm went off. He had slept lightly, as he always did when he knew he needed to be up earlier than usual. Before bed, he had laid out everything he needed for the day on his bedroom floor – every single thing from spare socks and blister plasters to the unopened crackly silver foil blanket he'd been given at the finishing line of a triathlon a while back. He'd known at the time it might come in handy one day. But he'd never dreamed that this would be the day.

As he'd turned out his light last night, he wasn't quite convinced that by the time he woke up he would actually still want to go. He was interested in the queue as a phenomenon but he wasn't quite sure if it was *for him*. He had respected the Queen from a distance, but was far from the sort of Union Jack bedecked superfan that he would warily see setting up as he cycled home via the Mall in the days before a royal wedding or a jubilee. He often took the route down towards Buckingham Palace on his way home from work, but as often as not, it would remind him of finishing the London Marathon as much as the royal family themselves.

But this felt different. The end of an era almost twice as old as himself. He didn't even remember Charles and Diana's wedding, although there was a grainy, faded photograph of him at a street party, his podgy one-year-old legs propping him up on a trestle table bedecked with red, white and blue paper bunting. Like most of the rest of the country, he and his entire living family had known nothing but this monarch, and had rarely considered life with anyone else at the top.

Then again, he had also done his reading. He knew that the empire wasn't all advances in locomotion and kedgeree for the masses. His reading group had covered William Dalrymple's *The Anarchy* last year, which had left him under no illusions about the barbarism of the East India Company. He was well aware that his assistant Kate would think he was a 'handmaiden of the empire' for even considering going. Gen Z never held back, he thought, as he folded his duvet cover carefully back and opened a window to air the bedroom.

But he also knew his mum really wanted to be there. He knew how much solace she had drawn from the Queen. Her dependability, her discretion, her kindness. All qualities he knew she prized, even more so after the last tough couple of years. Things had only just got back on their feet at the restaurant, so there was no way she'd be able to take a Saturday off. And his brother had only just had another baby, so he wasn't going to be leaving his wife with two little ones and heading to the capital. Which left Tim. Single, steadfast Tim.

Seconds later he was brushing his teeth, staring at his reflection in the heated bathroom mirror and waiting for the gentle buzz from his electric toothbrush to let him know that it was time to move from upper to lower molars. God he hated brushing his teeth. The tedium of four minutes a day staring at his own reflection. Sure, he was an OK-looking guy. But he was just so *average*. He looked like the sort of person an older woman would feel comfortable asking for directions in the street, and he knew it. But some days . . . bloody hell. He spat into the sink, watching the foaming swirls of the toothpaste trickle down the plug hole. Some days he just wanted to look like someone that one of the hot guys from the gym made a really inappropriate pass at. Or at least who women pushed their buggies across the road to avoid. Maybe one day.

But for today, he'd do what was the right thing. Once his toothbrush had buzzed to let him know his allocated two minutes of brushing was up. As soon as it was, he chucked it into the smooth concrete of the chic mug beside his sink and stepped into the shower.

Once she'd parked up at Colchester Station, Suzie checked her face in the rear-view mirror. She didn't look too bad considering the early start and the grim glare of the street lighting overhead. There was a bit more of a frizz to her hair than she'd like but the eyeliner she'd done in the dim dawn light was holding up OK. She ran a hand over her grey-blonde bob, trying to smooth what she could, then reached into her handbag to neaten up her lipstick. She used her ring finger to dab the colour on carefully, mindful to dab rather than to swipe, avoiding leaving colour to migrate up into the lines around her mouth. How did she remember these daft tips she used to read in the women's mags? She had been an absolute slave to them for years. These days, they seemed to be geared towards women with very different lives to her own.

She glanced at the spare shoes next to her bag on the passenger seat.

And would you dress like that to visit the Queen in Buckingham Palace?

She heard her mother's voice. The slight croak. The way she'd appear out of nowhere just as Suzie was giving herself a last glance in the hallway mirror before heading out. With her mother, it was never a question; she may as well have simply announced that Suzie's skirt was too short, her lipstick too bright, her eyebrows too arched. Suzie wondered what she'd think today, now that she really was off to see the Queen. Just an old lady in elasticated slacks. Mum would be devastated about Her Majesty, of course she would. But would she be proud of Suzie for making the effort, heading off to London despite the cold and the loneliness? She suspected that perhaps she would, at last. She certainly hoped so.

But would she be proud enough to forgive Suzie for wearing the comfortable shoes rather than the smarter ones? Well, she'd never know now, thought Suzie as she slid off her thin leather soled loafers and reached for the more cushioned pair she had recently bought in the sort of shoe shop she'd once swore she'd never enter. Yes, they were uglier. But – wow – were they comfy.

The train arrived bang on time and Suzie wondered if it would be busier than usual but to her surprise, she had almost an entire carriage to herself. There was a new novel in her bag, but her head was too busy to really focus on it, so she checked the headlines on her phone and watched the countryside whizz by in the dark. She wondered what was going on inside the palace, how Charles was holding up. She thought about losing her own mother only a couple of years ago, how she'd waited for it for so long and still felt hollowed out with shock when she'd realised that yes, a person could be there one minute and the next they could simply no longer exist. That had been nothing more expected, no event she could have been better prepared for, yet it had still felt like nothing more than walking off the edge of a cliff. Her eyes felt glossy for a minute. She blinked quickly, dabbing at the corner of her eye with a hanky before folding it carefully and sliding it into the pocket of her navy padded jacket.

She was quite nervous by the time she arrived at Liverpool Street. She'd caught the Tube from there hundreds of times since the move to Frinton but she still found herself nervously gripping the handrail on the stairs as she made her way to the Tube and then the overground. It was still cold enough that her breath was showing by the time she emerged above ground in the space-age splendour of Canada Water. Worried about being in central London in the dark, she had planned her arrival with daybreak, and to her enormous satisfaction, she had got it absolutely bang on. The sun was a peachy yellow glow on the horizon as she looked across the water.

It's where the logs arrived – from Canada – that's how it got its name.

Colin's voice floated by. How had he known so much about so much – and been so unselfconscious about sharing it with anyone and everyone? It had left her cringing time after time, but today she found it comforting. Without him, she wouldn't have known that just round the corner, on the way to Southwark Park, there was the blue plaque commemorating the site of Michael Caine's birth at St Olave's Hospital. She had rolled her eyes the day he'd taken her to see it, wishing they could just hurry up and get to the shopping centre, but today it left her feeling a little stronger as she turned towards Lower Road. He would have been great today, he really would. And as soon as she'd had the thought, an icy shard of guilt sliced through it. If only she'd told him the truth while she still could. How different everything might have been.

Abbie squinted into the mirror, the bathroom's overhead light casting a blueish hue over her skin. She rubbed her eyes with a flannel, trying to remove the remnants of last night's eyeliner from under her eyes. 'Last night,' she noted, was not even four hours ago. No wonder she looked grim.

She opened the bathroom cabinet to use her proper cleansing balm and saw that the lid was off, shoved to the back of the cabinet, while the balm around the tube's opening was slowing congealing to a hard plug. She dug her little fingernail in to clear it, and squirted some into her palm. Her hands were shaking with tiredness.

Get a grip, she told herself while she rubbed her face, her open hands sweeping across her face like the myriad serene women she'd watched explaining their cleansing routines time and time again. Her mum had always had too much on to take her for a girls' trip to Superdrug, to show her what sort of cleanser she might need for skin like hers. Her mate Sunnie's mum had sat her over the edge of the bath and shown her how to shave her legs – but only after delivering a solemn lecture that she didn't have to remove her body hair if she didn't want to. That she was just as beautiful either way. Abbie's mum had given her some vouchers for her birthday and told her she hoped she got something nice. It wasn't that Abbie *hadn't* got something nice, it was just that she would rather have chosen something with her mum. Instead, she had tentatively pressed a click-through link after watching ninety minutes of YouTube haul videos from young women only a few years older than her, solemnly demonstrating how to put together a 'three-step routine'. She let the hot tap run over her flannel for a few seconds, waiting for it to reach a temperature that might somehow steam her fretfulness away, before holding it to her face and counting to five. Her mum hadn't always been around to dispense advice while she'd been a teenager, but the internet had.

The door swung open and Maisie burst in, yanking the straps of her own dungarees down and flipping the lid up on the loo seat. Abbie kept the hot towel over her face, letting the steam do its bit.

It's going to be fine, it's going to be fine, it's going to be fine.

'So we could probably walk it in, like forty-five minutes, but I reckon we should just call an Uber. We'll get to Southwark Park in no time that way.'

'Sounds like a plan,' said Abbie, the cold tap now running across the flannel.

'So shall we get one on your account? I think I used an old card on mine the other day so mine won't work til I've settled up.'

'No problem,' said Abbie through the flannel. She wondered if she was flinching at the tingling of the cold water against her face or the thought of paying for this madcap plan. 'I'll just sort my face then call it.'

Five minutes later, Abbie was in the hallway watching the tiny icon of a grey car making its way to their front door while Maisie packed random bags from a multipack of crisps into a canvas bag from the bookshop in Blackheath Village. Annabelle emerged from her bedroom, her bottom half unchanged but her white shirt now swapped for a white T-shirt and loose black blazer, the sleeves rolled as if she was about to give a presentation.

'We ready girlies?' she asked as she ran a hand under her long hair to lift it up and over her collar.

'Ready as we'll ever be,' said Maisie, shaking the bag of snacks and picking up her huge steel water bottle. Annabelle raised her own bottle as if to say 'cheers'.

'Car's nearly here,' said Abbie with a pale smile, popping a very ripe banana onto the top of her own canvas bag of supplies. Already speckled with brown spots and coming a little loose at the stem, it wasn't going to take much more than a slight knock before her own snacks, lip balm, scarf and headphones were going to get generously smeared with it. She'd have to be very careful of it in the car.

Maisie headed down the narrow hallway towards the front door. Annabelle followed her, taking a final glimpse of herself in the hallway mirror, smoothing a hand over her long blonde hair. Abbie, whose path had been blocked as Annabelle paused, took a look in the mirror herself. Her wide nutty brown curls were framing her face. She had just about managed to revive their bounce where she'd slept on them, and had even had time to put some concealer and BB cream on. She pressed her lips together and smiled at herself. The car was here. The girls actually seemed like they'd sobered up. It seemed like the plan was going to work out OK after all.

It was only fifteen minutes later, as the Prius silently glided up Evelyn Street and Southwark Park loomed into view, that Abbie reached for her bag to reapply her lip balm – and realised that her bag was still on the hall table by the mirror, the banana quietly resting on top of her belongings.

As he stepped out of the shower and reached for his towel, Tim congratulated himself on remembering to change the timer on the underfloor bathroom heating before bed last night. Rubbing his hair as dry as he could, he decided that yes, it *was* worth going today. The weather forecast was good, if cold, and he really had nothing else on today apart from the autumn repotting of all his houseplants that he'd been planning for weeks. But it could wait.

It was going to take about half an hour on his bike from South Clapham, and he figured he could leave it in the shopping centre car park. Surely it would be safer there than on the street. The queue wouldn't have gone beyond Southwark Park, would it?

He ran a hand through his hair, deciding to keep be-lieving that the nascent greys at his temples would give him an air of dignity rather than aging him, and stepped into a pair of chinos. And anyway, leaving it damp would keep it looking darker a little longer. Jeans would be too tight for cycling, but he didn't want to be stuck in cycling tights and cleats for the day. Smart trainers and chinos were a happy medium, but he made sure to wear a sensible combination of thermal base layer, crisp shirt and smart merino V-neck on top. With cycling clips.

He reached into the hall cupboard to the peg next to his electricity smart meter, grabbing his rucksack and reminding himself to turn that underfloor heating off. Lightweight enough to carry everything he needed for the office most days, it was a festival of technical fabric, specifically designed webbing and expertly positioned zips and pockets. He could probably have packed it with his eyes closed, he was that familiar with each of its functions. In went a handful of protein bars, a couple of apples, a slimline aluminium Bento box full of nuts, and one of rice, peas and sweetcorn. Then he headed back to his bedroom to get a double-headed phone cable and a pre-charged spare battery pack, along with the rest of the items he had carefully laid out the night before, thinking to himself how much it looked like those police photos that are released when the Met have seized a juicy cache of drugs and weaponry. Except this was slow release complex carbohydrates and two different sizes of water-proofed maps.

The cycle itself was invigorating. He knew Brockwell Park would still be closed but chose to shimmy past it, and Ruskin Park after that. He wanted to see a bit of green, a bit of space, if he was going to be packed alongside people all day, having to move as part of a pack.

He knew the back roads in the area well, as well as which were the gnarly junctions that proved treacherous for cyclists, and which were the prettier domestic roads where there'd be little traffic until school drop-off time. At six, the most you'd be likely to see was a grey-faced father in a dressing gown, patting the back of a windy baby while staring through the white wooden shutters of a family home. Those men never made straight, married bliss look particularly appetising, thought Tim. His brother James on the other hand – with his easy confidence, his way of making everyone so proud of him when he took his son round the park for a couple of hours – made it seem like heaven. Bella would head out to brunch, or more recently pregnancy Pilates, and James would just grab a flat white, head to the swings and join the other one-handed buggy pushers in their puffy gilets, gathering admiring glances from single women as they went. A quick selfie for the grandparents and back home for the football. Or the rugby. Or the cricket.

It wasn't this part that Tim envied, but the sense of togetherness James and his little crew seemed to have. Sure, he and Bella did their fair share of bickering, especially as she reached the end of her second pregnancy and needed more help than perhaps James's schedule had envisaged. But on the whole, they moved as a unit. They never had to think in advance where they'd be at Christmas – it would be with each other. They never had to wonder about asking friends, and whether it would be overstepping the mark to suggest taking a holiday somewhere – they would all go as a family. They hadn't had a discussion about whether it would be weird to sit at home on the hastily announced bank holiday to watch a funeral – they would all be watching together.

As he approached Southwark Park, and went to cross Evelyn Street, a silent Prius tried to make it through the last second of a green light and almost clipped his back wheel. His heart rate spiked as he glanced behind him in fury at the driver. Even after all he did to avoid moments like this, Tim was still shocked by how shocked he could still be by careless driving. Lives are at stake, he'd heard himself once tell someone in the office as they'd been securing their bike. That very second, he'd heard himself, a middle-aged man on a cycling rant. God, life catches up on you fast.

Today would be different though. A moment of impulsive behaviour he was sure James and Bella would tease him about no end at Christmas time. Still, he thought, as he locked his bike, looping the plastic-coated chain around the wheels and frame then across the bike stand before hooking the D-lock through it, he was sure his mum would be touched that he was here today. She'd have loved being part of it. So, as he took a wipe from the front pocket of his rucksack, rubbed the grease from the lock off his hands, and popped it in the car park bin, he looked forward to taking a selfie to surprise her with.

A perfectly ripe banana was fastened into the webbed pocket on top of his bag. Maybe he could even offer it to someone nice later. That would really surprise his mum.

After all, today felt like the sort of day when anything was possible. It really did.

I

Southwark Park

Sunrise 6.38 a.m.

Suzie rounded the corner and realised she didn't know where the end of the queue actually was. Would it be obvious? Would there be signs? Was she even already there? In short, who was in charge and were they up to the job? Colin would obviously have looked this up already – or at the very least found some sort of forum where like-minded men would have been sharing this type of intelligence. But it was a query that Suzie was only starting to fret about as she reached the far edge of the park, the river still nowhere to be seen.

As she turned into Southwark Park itself, the atmosphere all seemed very far from the picturesque scenes on the South Bank that they'd been showing non-stop on the news. Suzie had no idea what to look for as she headed in the direction of the river, lifting a hand to protect her eyes against the sky glowing ahead of her, and hunching over her phone to locate the blue ball on its maps function. Colin hated her using it, preferring a 'real' map, preferably folded in on itself as many times as possible, and discreetly held in the inside of his palm, lest someone should spot him using it 'out in the wild' and put him at risk of a mugging. Well, he wasn't here now, but her phone was, so she spun, then spun again, trying to orientate herself on the map in the absence of any identifiable queue. What a morning. Perhaps it was finally happening, perhaps she really was losing her marbles at last.

It really was disarmingly quiet. The inherent strangeness of wandering around a London park, all alone, at dawn, suddenly hit Suzie. Was she safe? She straightened her shoulders, doing her best to look as if this were a commonplace turn of events for her, and walked towards the ornate Victorian bandstand. It reminded her of the Mary Poppins books she had read as a child, with their spindly line drawings of the nanny and her parrot umbrella, gently guiding the two Banks children through a series of escapades. The books were somehow creepier and more exciting than the movie adaptation, and she'd kept them for years, hoping to read them to her own children one day. They were still in a box somewhere up in the attic. Probably covered in dust now, despite the pristine condition she had always kept them in.

She adjusted the strap of her bag against her, feeling herself slip into the gait she often used when she approached unfamiliar situations – using the invisibility of older women in public while also trying to convey a sense of 'don't mess with me'. Eyes forward, legs strong, the quickening of her heart kept firmly within.

Twenty years ago, when the maelstrom of menopause had whipped her off her feet before spitting her out a different woman half a decade later, she had been quietly horrified by the shift in the way the world had seen her. After a lifetime of pulling her coat tight, hugging a bag to her side, keeping her gaze down as she passed construction sites or groups of men outside of pubs, she suddenly discovered she could strut by without a single head being turned. Yes, she'd felt relief, a sense of increased safety even. But also a little grief. An internal mechanism she had used for her entire adult life was no longer needed. It was as if she'd vanished.

Today, it didn't feel so reassuring. She felt older than ever and painfully alone. She started at the thud of a jogger's gait as he whizzed past her from behind, then felt a fool for having been so jumpy. Just as she was starting to fret that perhaps she had made a silly mistake in coming, getting herself swept up by the headlines, she saw a couple of young men standing by the wrought-iron bandstand in the centre of the park. Despite their age, and the fact that they were just standing there languidly chatting to each other, they still had the look of vague authority. They were wearing lanyards and hi-vis jackets, as if they'd had some sort of a briefing at a point in the not too distant past.

Suzie walked towards them, smiling with relief when

one of them extended his arm, showing her which of the paths extending from the bandstand to take.

'Queue?' he asked, as casually as if it were a permanent fixture. Suzie nodded, giving him a quick thank you. Further down the path she could see a snake of temporary railings, ready for huge numbers to zigzag along them as if waiting for a ride at a theme park. But Southwark Park remained quiet, bar the odd exercisers. And there was certainly no sense of pomp and ceremony. She kept walking, albeit hesitantly.

As she neared the river side of the park, the number of stewards increased. Bunched together in twos and threes, they seemed ready for crowds, even if there were none yet. Their tabards reminded her of Colin's stint as a Games Maker at the 2012 Olympics. Ten years ago and yet it felt like forever. She had teased him at the time, when he'd first applied to do it. Working for free! She'd been shocked he would even consider it, but he'd stuck to his guns and said he was going to be part of something historic. Years ago, he'd told her he planned to be retired by then but as it turned out, he'd still been enjoying work, so he took a sabbatical in order to play his role. His team at the office had thought it was a bit of a laugh too, until the games themselves started. He'd had the last laugh, as he so often did – he really had been a part of history. He made things happen, Colin. He always did.

She still had his shoes somewhere, the distinctive grey Adidas with the red laces. She'd never quite been able to throw them out, even when Holly had come round to help sort all his suits. She thought of them up there in the attic, in a box somewhere near the Mary Poppins books. She wondered if she would ever be able to go up into the attic again. *Just keep walking*, she told herself, like she so often had. *One foot in front of the other.* And so she did.

It was only when she reached the far side and exited the park that Suzie saw what looked to be an actual queue. At last! People in sensible anoraks and comfy shoes with small rucksacks slung across their backs, standing with backs straight, looking into the middle distance. At last, somewhere to head for. A sense of purpose. A feeling that she was doing the right thing. Her stride quickened towards them.

Abbie used her hand to feel all around her, kicking her feet to feel the space underneath the seat in front, wincing as her hand brushed against the river of crumbs between the leather seats of the taxi. She felt a lurch in the pit of her stomach as she realised that her panic was actually justified. Annabelle turned from the front seat as she felt Abbie rummaging in the pocket in front of her.

'Shit shit shit,' Abbie was whispering to herself, digging her thumbnail under the nail of her ring finger, trying to dislodge the lint, fluff and flecks of tobacco she had just snagged under there during her search.

'What's up, Abs?' asked Annabelle, her head tipped back but her eyes still forward.

Abbie squeezed her eyes shut for a second. Her eyeballs were hot against her lids, burning from lack of sleep and dehydration.

'My bag. I've left it.'

'Left it where?'

'At home. Right by the door. I put it down when I ordered the cab . . .'

'Oh shit babe. But you've got your phone, yeah?'

Abbie looked at the screen, instinctively checking her battery.

'Yes, but my food, my drink, my charger and stuff.'

Maisie gave her a quizzical look from across the back seat next to her, half spaced out, half curious as to why Abbie might have packed such essentials. The car lurched as a cyclist whizzed past them, narrowly avoiding the wing mirror as it slid between vehicles. Abbie didn't dare say anything as her phone slid off the leather between them and under Annabelle's seat. She leant forward to scrabble for that, the one thing she *really* couldn't afford to lose now.

'Don't worry, Abs, we've got you. Here, have a sip of this.' Annabelle reached round and passed Abbie her chic brushed steel water bottle. 'It'll calm you down.'

Abbie reached forward, muttering thanks, before un-screwing the lid and taking a swig, desperate for some water to calm her nerves. A second later she spluttered, clamping her mouth shut with her hand to stop herself from spitting all over the headrest in front. Warm, sweet booze shot up the back of her nose.

Vodka and Red Bull? Or something similarly sticky. Maybe even vodka and lemonade.

Jesus, Annabelle.

Abbie managed to gulp most of it down, screwing the baby pink lid back onto the bottle. She immediately ran her tongue across her teeth trying to get rid of both the taste and the sugary coating now slicked across her teeth. Her guts heaved as the car pulled to the side of the road, the alcohol sloshing uneasily on her empty stomach. She thought of her banana, perched on top of her bag in the hallway.

Time to get out, but it was only as Abbie reached to un-click her seatbelt that she saw that Maisie had nodded off, her head back, her own water bottle slipping out of her hand and dribbling onto the black leatherette seat cover.

Abbie shook her gently by the shoulder. She looked very pale. This whole expedition was turning into a disaster. There was a unpredictability to the day that reminded Abbie of her first school camping trip. She had spent weeks beforehand fretting about getting her tent up properly, only for the entire weekend to be dominated not by the drenching they had received for three hours as they trudged across the South Downs but by the inter-clique warfare that had gone on between her school friends.

They had only been twelve at the time, but some of her mates were already becoming preoccupied by romance and relationships. As some of them found boys – or even other girls – to flirt with and even kiss, others were left baffled and disinterested as the sands of friendship groups started to shift and wobble beneath them all. Abbie had been largely unbothered about snagging herself a boyfriend, but was shocked to discover how fast allegiances could crumble once certain girls had 'relationship stuff' to discuss, rather than Abbie's preferred topics of skateboarding and sewing. All those nights she had spent worrying about a leaky tent had been futile; by the time they returned, dishevelled from the Downs, her female friendships seemed to have reformatted themselves in ways that excluded Abbie from certain groups, now made up of girls bubbling with new intimacies to discuss. Invisible walls had slid up around those who had *matters of the heart* to chat about and Abbie was no longer invited behind them. When she returned to the skate park the following weekend and tried to ask some of her boy friends if they were going through similar disruption, they shrugged her off, confused.

Today, as her flatmates shrugged at Abbie's bag-less state of vulnerability, it felt somewhat similar.

Annabelle had already slammed the front passenger door behind her and was strutting into the park. Abbie was still thanking the driver, having helped Maisie shuffle across the seats to safely get to the pavement. She was painfully aware that Maisie looked – and smelled – worse for wear, and now she could see that Annabelle too was gently weaving as she made her way towards the band-stand.

Abbie pulled her denim jacket around her. The day was chillier than it looked; the autumn sun hadn't had long to warm the air in the park. She did at least have a scarf, a huge rectangle of thin olive green and pink striped wool wound elaborately around her neck and across her chest. There was a part of her wishing she was dressed more smartly, worrying that her mum and dad might see her on the news and think she wasn't being respectful. As well has her anxieties about whether she was appropriately dressed for the occasion, she was already running through a fretful mental slideshow on how she'd go to the bathroom quickly in her dungarees. Would she lose her place in the queue if she took too long? Were there loos provided along the way or would she be constantly darting in and out of cafes? And what if the dungarees got wet if they slid to the floor of a portable loo? What had seemed like a comfy, practical choice an hour ago now seemed silly.

Shut up shut up shut up, she told herself. *You're not going to need the toilet anyway, as you don't have any water.*

As they plodded across the park, Abbie spotted a few men in hi-vis tabards waving Annabelle straight past the bandstand and out towards the gates on the far side. There were mercifully few people around so far. Just a couple of cyclists in their strange Lycra babygros and some dog walkers looking as if they'd rather still be in bed. There was an older woman a few metres up ahead, bent over her phone as if it were the first time she'd ever seen one. Abbie thought of that Christmas a few years ago when she'd set her gran up with an Instagram account, and spent the whole day putting different filters on her face as she'd sat chuckling in the big armchair beside the television. Bouncy grey bunny ears. Cute puppy dog nose. A huge pair of wayfarer sunglasses. It had kept them giggling for hours as they waited for tensions to pass a little between her parents.

It was the year her mum had decided to get everything for the Christmas meal from M&S so that she would 'be spared the whole day in the kitchen', only to spend the whole day out at drinks with the neighbours. Her dad had been his usual sanguine self, laying the table wordlessly while bluffing that he was sure she'd be back before too long. Thank god for Gran, that year. Abbie wiped a tear from the corner of her eye. It was probably the chilly breeze in the park, she thought as she wiped the back of her hand on the back of her scarf.

A few steps behind her, Maisie was struggling to keep up the pace. Her eyes were watery, her gait unsteady. Abbie looked down and realised she was wearing a new pair of Dr. Martens. Oh man, no wonder her eyes were watering. She must be nowhere near having broken them in. And she'd already been wearing them out the night before. In an hour's time every step will be agony, Abbie thought. If Maisie even made it that far.

As they reached the far side of the park there were more obvious signs of the queue. People in far more sensible shoes, middle-aged folk in snug-looking anoraks and what her gran would have called 'slacks'. There were also families in matching woollen hats and scarves starting to line up behind each other, making polite, closed-lipped smiles at each other. Most people had a small rucksack, and looked very much like they were prepared for a day in the outdoors. Again, Abbie felt painfully aware that she and her flatmates looked dressed for the pub, rather than an afternoon walk across the Devil's Dyke.

Abbie watched as Annabelle strode towards the end of the queue with her characteristic confidence. She was showing no signs self-consciousness about her outfit, nor any hint of having even noticed the cold, despite her white T-shirt leaving a solid inch of flesh exposed above the line of her skirt. The blazer was lending her an air of authority. Or maybe it was the alcohol giving her swagger.

As she schlumped up to them, her shoulders drooping with tiredness after the effort of the walk, one of the straps of Maisie's canvas bag slid down, allowing three packs of crisps to tumble onto the path. She bent to pick them up, tipping further contents, including a candy-coloured disposable vape, a sausage roll and a couple of tampons, onto the path. Abbie bent to help her, her own hair falling around her face as they scrambled to gather Maisie's bits together.

By the time they had scooped everything back into the bag, Annabelle had forged ahead, reaching the end of the queue and was chatting to a woman with grey hair and a navy blue padded jacket. For a second, Abbie wondered if her flatmate had come across someone she knew, but no, this was just how she approached all social interaction: as if the person concerned was naturally delighted to be talking to her. She steeled herself to join in, determined not to let the day run away from her so soon. She was here to be a part of it, wasn't she?

'Hello,' said Abbie, speaking into an uncomfortable space somewhere between Annabelle and the woman. Behind her, Maisie had sat down on a low brick wall and was looking at her phone.

'Hi *babe*,' said Annabelle. Hearing herself called 'babe' again, and in front of this woman, made Abbie bristle, and she wasn't sure why. The woman just looked like the sort of person who'd disapprove, even though she was clearly trying not to look at them at all.

Nevertheless, Annabelle continued, unabashed.

'So guys, this is Suzie . . .' The woman nodded hello, her lips pursed, her small leather bag clamped to her side as if she expected them to grab it at any minute. Abbie was right, she clearly was summing them all up. Maisie lifted her eyes from her screen and gave the woman a limp wave. Abbie smiled back, trying her best, still wishing she looked smarter.

'It's really nice to meet you,' she said. 'I'm Abbie.' She ran her fingers through her hair, trying to lift the curls of her fringe up and away from the clamminess of her forehead. She inhaled to carry on speaking, but Suzie was already looking straight past her, smiling warmly to someone over her shoulder. She turned and saw a man unhooking cycling clips from his chinos before rubbing his gloved hands together against the chill then reaching one out towards Suzie.

'Hi, hi, I'm Tim,' he said, nodding and grinning earnestly, dropping his cycling helmet as he did. It rolled a little towards the girls, as he reached out to stop it before almost stumbling at their feet.

Abbie could see the curiosity spark in Annabelle. Her face looked not dissimilar to when she was examining the socials of someone one of them fancied, trying to glean as much as she could in the shortest time possible. She employed a steady focus that Abbie was familiar with from the metal detectorists she'd see patrolling Worthing Beach when they hit the pier early on summer mornings.

When they were kids, long before his depression, her dad was always the first up in the house. On the weekends it was their magical time together, up as soon as the sun rose in the summer. He would take her and her brother out first thing, catching the low tide before the daytrippers arrived. And there they'd be: the detectorists, scouring the shingle for lost car keys, loose change and even the odd wedding ring that might have slipped off in the cold of the waves. Abbie and her brother used to laugh at them, finding their po-faced concentration cringey. Now, she watched Annabelle trying to give nothing away as she scanned the man's look for clues as to what sort of a companion he might shape up to be.

Objectively, he was good-looking. He had the sort of

open face of someone you would willingly ask for directions. His hair was a dark blonde, cut short but not in a military way. There was more of a 1950s geek chic about it, the sort of thing you'd have to go to a certain sort of barber for – the type with pomade in vintage-style tins on a shelf at the back – rather than a high street stylist with plastic tubs of wax. She knew Annabelle would have clocked that, no matter how dishevelled the crop was by his errant bike helmet.

But there was also an earnestness to him that she knew Annabelle's almost feral ability to read and use people would have logged. As he stood up, dusting his knees off where he'd knelt to reach the helmet, then brushing his hand before finally shaking it with Suzie's, he had a nerdy sincerity that Abbie knew might instantly trigger Annabelle's most insouciant behaviour. Abbie had seen it with the barmen and bouncers who gave her a millisecond of indulgence. And she'd certainly seen it used on herself, having been somehow persuaded to cook her dinner three times in the last week alone. She could picture her now, tormenting male science teachers with nonsensical questions. God, she must have been a nightmare at school. Either way, Abbie suddenly realised boredom was one of the things she no longer needed to worry about – it was going to be fascinating watching Annabelle try to work her magic on this man, just to keep herself amused.

Maybe he'd been too hard on the twenty-somethings, thought Tim as he saw two young women introducing themselves to an older lady at what looked like the end of the queue. He'd assumed he'd be the youngest there by years, and had quite been looking forward to feeling less like the oldie in the crowd than usual. He wasn't sure when it had happened, but at some point in the last few years, he had definitely gone from being one of the youngsters at work, someone who was automatically added to the group Slack chats about after-work drinks, even if he never really attended them, to one of the elders. Worse still, to one of the ones who caused banter to dry up when he walked into the lift or the communal kitchen.

He'd never been a major participator in any of these company hijinks – he'd never had the stomach for office gossip, much less workplace romances, always fearful of giving too much of himself away, but he had never been less than thrilled to be a spectator. He was the first to giggle when new nicknames were bandied around or to provide a discreet listening ear to a female colleague who might have had her heart broken. But these days, no more. Maybe it was the new salt and pepper hair at his temples, or just that keeping his head down and getting the work done, year after year, had meant he had steadily progressed higher up the management structure of the company. But either way, he was now one of the grown-ups in the eyes of the junior colleagues.

Just his luck. But these looked like nice girls, perhaps he could learn something from them. Work out how to stay in touch with the younger members of staff, without being creepy or worse still, *cancelled*. He might even have a laugh with them.

'Hi, hi, I'm Tim.'

Stop nodding, you fool, you're going to look like a serial killer.

The three women turned to him, six eyes flickering only slightly as each of them clearly summed him up in their own way. He felt it, just as he always did, the way they tried to read him. Not threatening in his masculinity, nor overtly queer. And, hopefully, avoiding the uncomfortable middle ground of creepiness as he tried to smile warmly. The older woman adjusted her bag under her shoulder, smiling back. Well, technically it was a smile but her lips were still very closed. After a moment's hesitation, she extended her hand in return.

'Suzie,' she said. 'Nice to meet you.'

The younger women didn't extend their hands, but lifted a palm towards him. A still wave, followed by a 'hi'.

'I'm Annabelle,' said the one in the black suit jacket. She tilted her head to one side in a way that made it hard not to believe that on some level, she pitied him. 'And I'm Abbie,' said the other, a shorter, less willowy figure, lifting her hand again, before letting it limply fall to her side as she realised she'd already waved hi.

'Lovely to meet you too,' he said, as he noticed that a third, younger woman was sitting slumped on a low wall near to them. Was she looking at her phone, or was she falling asleep?

'Is she with you?' asked Tim, immediately regretting what he feared might be mistaken for nosiness.

'Yeah, that's Maisie, she's fine,' said Annabelle, who seemed to be the leader of the group, with a swish of her long blonde hair. As her head turned, Abbie mouthed 'TIRED' at him with what he suspected was a slight eye roll. 'I see!' he mouthed back, conspiratorially. Perhaps he was already making friends. But, could he smell alcohol on them? Surely not. Was he being judgmental? Why did he find talking to people twenty years younger than him so awkward? It was as if the last couple of decades had never happened, and he was back at university trying to make small talk about Radiohead when he'd have been far more comfortable discussing something to do with Malcolm Gladwell.

His thoughts were interrupted by one of the young men in tabards appearing, walking along the queue, handing out wristbands to everyone who confirmed that they were there for the Queen's Lying in State. He explained that the wristband – otherwise the same as those given out at festivals, but smartly embossed with a royal crest and the acronym LISQ – denoted what hour they'd joined the line so that they couldn't sneak forward, and so that they could temporarily leave to find toilets or to get some food. As he was finishing up his brief explanation, the people ahead started to move up a few paces. A slow, anonymous procession of sensible trainers and faces half obscured by scarves pulled up against the morning chill – they were at last moving as one.

'Gosh, I finally feel like I'm part of a queue,' said Tim, keen to break the slightly awkward silence they'd been left with as the steward had moved on to the next batch of queuers. Suzie smiled in agreement as she took a few steps to keep up with those in front. Annabelle looked at him as if he'd said something utterly nonsensical. And Abbie leant over to help her friend on the wall up and in synch with the rest of them. Behind the girls was a family – a mum, dad and two kids of about eleven or twelve.

'I'm Tim,' he said, smiling at the parents. 'And these are my new friends, Annabelle, Abbie, and . . .'

'Maisie,' said Abbie, as she gripped her friend by the elbow and led her forward to keep up with Suzie.

The father of the family said a brief hello, before the mum introduced them as the Wilsons, Rosemary and Greg, who had come down from Lincolnshire for the event.

'You must have been up early!' said Tim, realising that that might have been the reason for the husband's grim smile as he lugged what looked like a comprehensively packed picnic box forward while the queue continued to move onward. The kids – Molly and Fred – each had strawberry blonde hair, sparkling blue eyes and a smattering of freckles exactly like their mum's. In fact, Tim wondered – was it too cynical to think that the whole family looked as if they'd been cast by the government itself to look like exactly the sort of wholesome hard-working family who the nation needed to see on their news bulletins.

As they started to move away from the main road to behind the houses, the river finally came into view, and Molly and Fred audibly gasped as they finally realised where they were. The tide was high, the river full, looking like a bath that had been left running five minutes too long. Tim was surprised by how close the boats looked, sitting so high in the water, even the ones on the far side. It was turning into a stunning day though. The sun was higher in the sky now, leaving the waves twinkling in its light, and finally giving off a decent bit of warmth as they continued their shuffle forward, past the Angel pub at the edge of Bermondsey Wall and along to the Thames Path itself.

As they'd crossed the road and turned the corner, Tim had caught up with Suzie and the girls had fallen a couple of steps behind him, Maisie seeming a little dazed but the other two OK. Annabelle took a slug from her water bottle, wiping her mouth with the back of her hand and looking as if she were trying to hide a burp. Tim turned, smiling at Abbie, trying to show a sense of togetherness, but she was fiddling with her phone now too. He patted his pocket to check that his own phone was still there. What did young people find to keep constantly looking at? He'd had a few social media accounts for a while but he'd never really got into the swing of using them beyond the nifty reminders about people's birthdays. He'd never felt comfortable posting much about himself – who cared? Really?

Then he realised that he was wasting hours of his life following pet hobbies he had never thought about for years, ending up looking up train drivers as they chronicled their daily routes, detailing the specifics of their equipment, spending hours reading cabbies' blogs charting the best places for an early morning bacon butty en route to Gatwick, or clicking link after link of depressing political threads, trying to work out how and when exactly an inoffensive chap from junior school had formed such strident views about electric cars, the role of statues in universities or something else that Tim was quite sure had never bothered the guy only a handful of years ago. After a while, the emotional responsibility of being sandblasted with so much information about other people had wearied him and he'd given up, deleting the lot. Now, he had no idea when his sister-in-law's little sister's birthday was. But he also knew less about her peri-menopause, so he figured the balance of things had been restored.

He was startled out of his train of thought when he saw that Suzie had now paused and was fiddling with her wristband, struggling to get it on with her slightly shaky hands. A brisk breeze was coming off the water now that they were away from the shelter of the buildings and he could see the slim piece of orange paper flickering in the wind as Suzie tried to secure it to her wrist.

'Would you like some help?' he asked quietly,

employing the same smile he used in the office to try and show female workers that he wasn't being making a pass.

Suzie looked up at him, and suddenly looking older, a little more fragile, as the full glare of the sun hit her face, the breeze making her eyes water.

'Oh thank you,' she replied. 'My fingers just aren't quite as nimble as they once were.' She handed him the slip of paper, before pushing the sleeve of her coat back to create some clear space before extending her wrist to him. Tim picked at the backing tape on the sticky end of the wristband, regretting trimming his fingernails the night before, then unpeeled it, putting the small square of paper into the pocket of his jeans before quickly wrapping the band around her wrist and fastening it, pressing down gently on the smoothness of her inner wrist, hoping he hadn't made the whole thing seem too weirdly intimate.

'There you go, all set!' he said cheerily, his voice only sounding a tiny bit strangled at the end, before managing to try and make it sound like he had meant to clear his throat. He looked behind him, aware that he had slightly leapfrogged the three young women, and as he turned, he spotted that they were in a bit of a huddle now, giggling at each other's screens. Did *any* of them understand what they were queueing for, he wondered.

Abbie was aware of Tim watching them, and it rankled her just as much as the once-over she'd seen Suzie give them. She wasn't quite sure how she felt so convinced he was judging them, but she knew she'd been observed, and she had seen him being cheery with everyone else. Now, he'd gone quiet, preferring to help Suzie. Everyone else was chatting, why couldn't they? Were they supposed to be all funereal the whole time?

The trouble was, she was sure she knew that they looked like in Tim's eyes. She had watched as Annabelle took a swig from her 'water' bottle, and she'd noticed that she too was looking more than a little worse for wear. How much had been in that bottle, she now found herself wondering. And how long could her flatmates keep on drinking? She didn't want to think about the answers to those questions, any more than she wanted to spend any time wondering if Tim had worked out that it wasn't water in there. Either way, she just wanted to Tim to stop looking at them as if they were actually feral.

Maisie held out her wrist to her, wordlessly asking for help putting the orange band on, and as Abbie gently helped to stick it in place, she realised it was going to be *way* too mortifying to up and leave this early on, no matter uncomfortable she felt about her flatmates behaviour and the looks she was sure they were getting. She was stuck with the pair of them. At least for now.

She decided to try and lighten the mood. One of the reasons she had always got on with the two of them was because she found it surprisingly easy to make them laugh. She'd met them a handful of times in the first year, and immediately been intimidated by their urbane cool, but, as ever, diverting immediately to her usual method of playing the goofball, deploying liberal amounts of sarcasm, had worked. It's just that it came at the expense of actually making any meaningful connection. Becoming court jester had been something of a defence mechanism since she had been at school, but she'd never needed – or used – it so much as she had then. When the talk turned to their parents' second homes, casual details about teen years spent gallivanting around Camden, or plans for nights out she knew she'd never be able to afford, Abbie felt it turn on almost automatically. A wry comment implying she was above it all here, a snarky little aside about someone she knew the girls would laugh at there . . . it all added up until she was accepted as part of the group, and then part of the house. Now was as good a time as any to carry that tradition on, even if deep down she was starting to wonder if life inside this irony bubble was actually a sustainable way to exist.

'Hey girlies, you always told me East London was fashionable,' she said quietly, with one eyebrow raised.

Annabelle tittered. 'Yeah, um, Met Gala vibes, huh.'

'I mean, does anyone know if there are any navy blue gilets in London this weekend?' said Maisie, her first contribution since she'd left the cab. Annabelle tittered with glee, while Abbie looked around in case any of the numerous gilet-wearers around them had been within earshot.

'Might do some *Get The Looks*,' she said, keen to make up ground lest the girls had spotted her self-consciousness. 'GRWM kind of thing. I mean, it's a vibe.'

Annabelle snorted. Abbie hated herself for how thrilling she found it when she impressed her flatmate in any way. Objectively, Annabelle was not a decent person. Abbie knew all the buzzwords – a main dish which demonstrated how well she understood how social media and influencer behaviour worked – and she knew how to say them with just enough of a sneer, a dash of garnish to simultaneously reveal how beneath them they all knew it was supposed to be.

It was starting to feel like an alarmingly complicated way to communicate. Why did it matter so much to Abbie what Annabelle thought of her? And why couldn't she find a way not to care?

The sounds of the girls giggling felt like nails against a blackboard as the queue slowly moved along the Thames Path. The queue was clearly defined now that they were walking along the river; everyone could see into the distance to where they were headed. The queuers were on the pavement, sticking close enough together to show intention but far enough apart to allow for the fact that few friendships or introductions had been made at this stage. The other side of the road, and at some points the road itself, was still being used by the day-to-day foot passengers in the area. Parents and toddlers making their way back to their flats with the morning loaf of bread or carton of milk. Joggers on a mission to make it to the other side of the city before the crowds built. Delivery men with their brown boxes, scurrying out of vans and off bikes, as they headed up side roads and into flats, tiny gullies diverting from the main flow of the river of people heading west.

There was a pause in the onward movement, and Suzie closed her eyes, taking a breath as she tried to steady her nerves. She wasn't at all familiar with this part of the river. Even the fact she could see the Shard up ahead if she leaned towards the wall didn't quite orientate her. Looking round the curve of the water, Westminster still seemed very far away. Even Tower Bridge looked miles off, tiny, like a child's toy in the distance.

She was just thinking about how high the water was when she jumped at a black cat stalking along the wall. Almost immediately she realised it was bronze, and in that second she tripped, realised that there was a second statue of a small girl leaning against the wall. She was smiling, almost hidden by the bricks, a small seven- or eight-year-old, and had long hair pinned back in an old-fashioned style. Looking away from the water, she seemed to be facing someone she knew. Suzie found the figure slightly creepy, and tried to step round it discreetly. As she did so, she followed the child's gaze to see it was indeed looking at a second bronze statue – that of an elderly gentleman in a smart hat and small round glasses. Behind him, she now saw that there was a fourth figure – a woman in an Edwardian-style dress that reminded her somewhat of Mary Poppins. She was holding a spade, which Suzie found still more unnerving. The figures were slightly smaller than life-size, and mingled with the growing number of queuers, they felt even more disconcerting than she had found the cat.

A few steps ahead a couple of people were reading a plaque, and so Suzie stepped over to take a look herself. Wincing at the sun's glare coming off the brass, Suzie saw that it read DR SALTER'S DAYDREAM. She wanted to roll her eyes at the whimsy. People and their cats . . .

She'd never heard of this Dr Salter, and given that the girls seemed to be busy giggling amongst themselves, and that Tim chap was now looking at his fancy sports watch, she scooped her mobile phone from the pocket of her navy padded jacket and flicked the screen on to look up Dr Salter. It was going to be a long day – she might as well learn something about where she was.

It turned out he had been something of a reformer in the Bermondsey area, a good egg by all accounts, campaigning for reform of the London slums with his wife Ada, who was the woman looking out over the planting beds with her spade.

Good for them, Suzie was thinking, a little less unnerved by the statues now she knew more about them. But as she read on, she discovered that the little girl was the couple's daughter, who had died at the age of eight. Tears rose in Suzie's throat at the idea of a good person going through such a loss, but being commemorated in such a lovely, such a local way. When she had left the house this morning she'd expected to find herself learning new facts about Westminster, or even the protocol of a funeral, but she hadn't given a moment's thought to the fact that there might be history all along the river. That she might be learning about lesser known but no less deeply felt losses. Life without one's daughter, she thought, as her shoulders slumped.

She looked up and into the sun, blinking at the light to try and hide the fact that tears were about to trickle down her face. How cruel life could be to the kindest of people. The solemnity of what she was doing today fell on her like a heavy blanket, and suddenly she felt very tired, her early start catching up with her. She slid her phone back into her pocket and pushed her hands into her coat in an attempt to keep herself warm. When might they reach somewhere to buy a hot drink? she wondered.

There was movement ahead and Suzie followed the group in front of her. None of them had turned around or said so much as a hello yet – they seemed to have formed a self-contained group of their own without so much as a backwards glance. Her mood dipped again, when Tim appeared at her shoulder.

'I saw you looking at the plaque there – what a story.'

'Yes,' said Suzie, her eyes down. He seemed like a nice enough fellow, this Tim, but she didn't relish the thought of being stuck talking to him about death for the next fourteen hours. She tried to think kind thoughts. Yet again, she tried her very best. *Think of the Queen*, she told herself, as she shifted her foot, trying to move the seam of her sock where it was rubbing on the edge of the leather.

'How awful to lose a child, a little girl, like that,' he said. 'I don't know how anyone could survive such a thing.'

'Yes,' replied Suzie, her voice now quieter than ever. 'How awful.'

If only he knew.

2

Bermondsey

The queue was starting to move a bit more briskly now, snaking away from the Thames Path wall and heading into the wharves. Wow, this part of London was so bloody exciting. The childlike part of Tim remembered the thrill of reading about huge wooden ships coming in from all over the world and finding their way to inlets like these, having fought off pirates, sea storms and scurvy. To see the remnants of that London, to see the cobblestones worn smooth by those travellers, was eternally mesmerising to him.

They wove past New Concordia Wharf, St George's Wharf, Unity Wharf, once grain stores and warehouses, now luxurious converted apartments overlooking the water on one side and the chic restaurants and cafes of Bermondsey on the other. Sure, it must be lovely to live in one of them, he thought, but how much more exciting to have arrived here two hundred years ago in a ship laden with spices, cotton or rum, docking at St Saviour's feeling like a hero. What a high it must have been to finally turn into the Thames, exhausted, and see Tower Bridge at last. The thrill of making it to dry land, to your family, to the grey skies of London.

But as soon as he'd thought this, his heart thundering at the excitement of being one of those crews of adventurers opening up London and the entire country the riches the world had to offer, Tim remembered where these riches had all come from. And how. And he returned to one of his eternal loops of guilt. God, it had all seemed so much simpler at school, when they'd simply been told a ripping yarn about nutmeg, or purple dyes, or cotton, without any of the teachers mentioning the empire or how it all, well, *came about*.

School had hardly been a carnival of fun for him, but at least he had enjoyed the learning. In fact it had proved something of a sanctuary. His older brother James had started at the same South London private school a couple of years ahead of him and made it all look so easy. But then that was James, the sort of boy who everyone liked. Just enough swagger not to let the bullies try anything with him, but not so much that he was ever mistaken for one of them. Teachers liked him – he knew how to offer to help without seeming like a creep and he knew how to crack a joke in class without getting in trouble for distracting the entire group. He would run down corridors – never fast enough to get told off – with an engaging lollop, bowling invisible cricket balls into the distance. He wasn't afraid of girls, but nor did he see them as some sort of sleazy challenge. He had girl friends as much as he had girlfriends, and was sensitive enough to give out advice without mistaken for a soft touch or, worst of all at a private school in 1993, *a gay*.

So when Tim arrived two years later, most people assumed he'd be more of the same. Which proved to be an error. James's easy charm was never going to be easy to replicate, much less so in a young boy who was realising he wasn't straight but felt entirely unable to form any sort of connection with what he thought being gay meant. So he busied himself with pushing any thoughts about that to the very furthest recesses of his mind and focused on facts. Lovely, static facts. He read voraciously, non-fiction as much as fiction, taking on daft self-set challenges such as reading all of Evelyn Waugh over one Christmas holiday, or ploughing through Patricia Highsmith for an entire summer. If his parents noticed a theme to his choices of novel, they never said anything, and as his tastes outgrew theirs – and those of his peers – he stopped realising too.

The certainty of the school curriculum had proved so comforting as the nebulous concept of cool began to loom ahead of him, separating his classmates into smaller gaggles. Being James's brother only got him so far, and within a year or two he was firmly one of the nerds, sitting neatly at the front, textbooks free of doodles, glasses clean, pencils sharpened.

But back then, the exciting tales of brave sea-folk that had kept him and his chums entertained in the classroom had never mentioned complicated ideas about slavery or thievery. Tim and his friends had sat there memorising the key dates of the empire, each new fact making all these returning merchants seem so noble, especially as they went on to build public libraries, elegant railways and magnificent municipal spaces – for the good of the people!

Only in recent years had Tim come to truly understand who had really paid for those buildings, and he'd never quite got over it. History, the certainty of the past, when men were men and complicated emotions were barely mentioned, had provided so much solace for him as the jibes began and the complicated business of not just feeling like an outsider but being treated like one had begun. Now, these days he could barely think about life on the Thames without his thoughts clouding with guilt and – more than he'd like to admit – a smidgen of resentment. He hadn't stolen any bloody nutmeg, so why did he feel so crap about himself after a mere fifteen minutes of enjoying wharf-side architecture? He was quite sure not a single other person he knew would go through these endless cycles of self-recrimination. Maybe they had begun back then in the classroom? Another thought he didn't like to needle at too hard, lest he stirred an emotion too big, too scary.

Maybe it was just the people he knew. Perhaps there were others just like him who would love to wake up early on a weekend, get a coffee from one of those places that sold cold-press paraphernalia behind the counter and spend a couple of chilled out hours admiring the well-preserved wooden hatches and hoists still adorning the wharf-side buildings, while also paying an appropriate degree of respect to the fact that what was unloaded was also . . . plundered. Tim let himself daydream a little, imagining a bright Saturday like today, but as part of a couple. They wouldn't have a hangover as they'd probably just go to the gym after work on Friday then stop off for a single glass of Barolo in a cosy little bar on the way home. Catching up on their weeks, connecting again. So they'd be up early, wearing understatedly chic sunglasses, but also thinking deeply about the empire in the context of globalisation, committing to reading widely about the subject, but also laughing together at cute dogs they saw playing en route. Maybe they'd even get one one day. Harassed parents would envy their urbane calm, and by the time they'd reached London Bridge they'd turn north of the river for lunch in, maybe Covent Garden. Somewhere not too touristy, but still a little buzzy.

It would be perfect. If only he knew how to meet such a person. And how to persuade them to spend this perfect Saturday with him.

For now, he was stuck with this Saturday, and what seemed like no one to talk to at all. Suzie still looked somewhat distracted, forbidding even. She was staring around at the buildings as if trying to avoid eye contact, looking at others up ahead in the queue and occasionally checking her phone. Meanwhile, Abbie and her mates hadn't stopped taking photos and chatting among themselves. Wasn't the taller of the three cold? he wondered.

She had half her midriff on show, and those tights were barely tights at all. And now there was a growing stream of passers-by, not members of the queue but spectators of it.

It felt strange to be part of a London tourist attraction, but not much stranger than so much else that had gone on over the last week or so. Tim wished he could chat to someone about the sense of being unmoored that he'd felt since the Queen had died. His mum was genuinely devastated; there was no way he could start talking about his own feelings while she was so busy weeping. She'd never be able to comprehend the more nuanced unbalancing that Tim felt. Less grief, than a destabilising sense that the ground beneath him was shifting, irrevocably; that he didn't know how he fitted into this new world, where the Empire was now both a dirty word and our last remaining source of pride. He wanted to say it felt like a two-sided penny, but even pennies were about to start looking different.

The destabilising effect of the Queen's death had gone beyond the family though, leaving him unsure how to behave with friends and colleagues alike. His seniors at work had seemed sincere in their sadness, exchanging memories about royal weddings and silver jubilees he had no memory of, as well as expressing admiration for her steadfastness, her hard work – albeit in a way that suggested these were the right things to say in the workplace, where such attributes were very much to be acknowledged.

There had been little of that deference amongst the younger colleagues, and even some of his friends. While there were no expressions of ill will, there had been jokes within hours, and memes not long behind them. Then came rumblings about the cost of it all, with things as they were, and then – particularly in the case of the juniors in the office – a return to memes, silliness, a sort of gossipy interest in the strange new prime minister and the antics of the younger royals.

Tim, as ever, felt that he didn't fit in either camp, appreciating the sense of disconnection that the juniors seemed to be experiencing, while knowing that the old guard might have found it odd, fuddy-duddy even, that he'd turned up today. He was wary of irony, and had been for years. He knew all too well how much space it allowed for genuine cruelty under the guise of mere quipping. So he hadn't joined in with the joking, while still existing some distance from the genuine grief that others around him were feeling. But how to express that in this crowd, without upsetting or alienating anyone?

'Sheesh, some of these apartments look incredible,' he said as they passed a particularly chic set of converted warehouses, hoping to start up some more conversation with Suzie.

'Yes, very chic,' she replied. 'I remember the more modern ones being built when I worked not far from here.'

'So you're from London?' he dared to ask, having been

thrown this snippet of information and determined to make the most of it.

'Oh no, not at all. I was born in Suffolk. And I live in Frinton-on-Sea now, have done for years.'

'Aah,' said Tim, desperate for more details but anxious not to seem facetious, intrusively curious, not mournful enough. 'So . . . you commuted here?'

'Yes, I used to commute up for a few years in the eighties. Lots of building work. It seemed impossible that this would end up being a desirable area.' A pause. 'But then lots seemed impossible to imagine back then.'

Tim had no idea what she was alluding to. Her own life? Politics? The idea of Charles being king, even? He was just trying to figure out whether to push the conversation any further when some people in flats up above them opened a window and called down to the queuers.

'Hey guys!' shouted a young man with a neat beard, wearing a baseball cap. 'You need water? Breakfast?'

Someone a little further ahead shouted back 'Hell yeah!' and people around them started to chuckle, the queue at large communicating beyond the tiny groups that had formed.

'Coming right up!' said the voice, as the bloke dipped back inside the flat.

For the first time, Suzie gave Tim a genuine smile. She was an attractive woman, he realised. Her hair was in a chic bob, a mixture of soft blonde and greys. She was bundled up in layers of sensible clothing today but he imagined she had probably been rather stylish once.

'I wonder what he's up to,' she said, shrugging her shoulders a little as if to say, 'Whatever next!'

The man reappeared at the window a minute or so later, this time with a smiling long-haired woman at his side. They had cartons of juice and some small bottles of water in their arms, and started throwing them down to the crowd, shouting 'Reeeaddddy . . .' before each throw.

The crowd just ahead was in the perfect position to catch the goodies and were shouting back 'Yes!' 'Over here!' and 'Thanks guys!' as the supplies rained down.

'No worries, guys! Keep at it, you're doing great!' called back the young man, giggling with his girlfriend before heading back in and reappearing with some multipacks of crisps.

On any other day, Suzie would have found this sort of shouting and throwing bordering on disorderly. But there was a goodwill to their entire enterprise that she just couldn't deny. The young man whose flat it seemed to be had gentle eyes, the sort that turned down at the edges – one of those faces which should have looked sad but was so smiley that it looked anything but. As he dangled an arm out of the window, letting one of the crisp packets fall gently into the crowd, his strawberry blonde hair flopped forward and over his eyes.

As he turned to the woman in the window, whose back was to where Suzie was standing, she got a good look at his face and was struck by how much he looked like a young Colin. Freckled nose, floppy hair, those twinkly eyes. He was behaving not unlike a young Colin too. As she watched the man diving back into the flat for further supplies, chatting and waving to the queuers below, she thought about the first time she had met him, back when he was at university and she had just left school.

She had seen him around when they were teenagers, as he'd been a couple of years older than her at the local boys' grammar school. But then he'd headed off to the University of Manchester and she had forgotten all about him. He wasn't flash, didn't have much of the swagger of some of the lads from home who had stayed in the area, big fish in their small pond. It was the Christmas just after she'd turned nineteen that she saw Colin again, helping out behind the bar at a pub on the edge of town. She had stopped going to the pub closer to her parents since everything had happened. She had only recently come back from her summer in Wales a few months ago, having told everyone in town she'd been to stay with her cousins to take a secretarial course in Cardiff. She'd taken the course in the evenings, over autumn, in nearby Ipswich, and was looking forward to starting a proper job hunt after Christmas.

The Colin she had remembered from school was a bookish, quiet lad, someone she was really only aware of because they had shared part of a bus journey home. He'd never really spoken to her, much less engaged in any of the teasing or hijinks that some of the other lads from the boys' school did. Maggie from her class had ended up dating one of the boys she had met on the bus until well after her A levels, and there were many more who Suzie suspected had found their first boyfriend the same way.

But schoolboy Colin, while friendly enough, had always had his nose in a book. This new Colin who had returned from Manchester was altogether a different beast. No longer hiding behind his fringe, these days he was quite the character – making eye contact with each of his customers behind the bar, charming the elderly regulars and sharing a friendly wink with Suzie when her dad had been endlessly riffling through his pocket change to pay for the round. He seemed to have found not just his charm but his awareness of it, and was clearly enjoying deploying it whenever he was given the chance. 'Hi,' he'd mouthed at Suzie, making her stomach flip in a way that sat just on the right side of excitement over anxiety.

It was one of only a handful of times she had actually had a proper drink at the pub, so at the time she wasn't sure if it was the shandy or the wink that had made her wave back so coquettishly, despite all that she had so recently been through. But she did it anyway, and it felt good.

That was the Colin she had found hardest to remember during the hard times. When she'd lost herself in the nineties, and then again last year, when he'd been so ill. These days, it was the Colin that she most feared losing. He had been so kind to her, when she had been so fragile, but never at the expense of being genuinely good fun. Oh, how he had made her laugh when she thought nothing could lift her spirits.

No matter how much she wanted to disapprove of the chaos today, she knew that if Colin had been a young man today, he would have been the first to be throwing snacks at the crowd this morning. A little bit of anarchy, that's what she had liked about him. Because it had never outweighed his kindness. He really would have wanted people to have all the drinks and snacks they needed! But he'd have enjoyed lobbing them out of the window at unsuspecting grannies too.

It had been 1972 when they'd got together. She was still living at home, but he had discovered politics at university and became a bit of a rebel, always challenging people's opinions back home. Suffolk was hardly a hot bed of radical politics now, let alone fifty years ago, so it had made him stand out a bit. In hindsight, wearing CND badges on his lapel and talking about workers' rights was hardly upturning the status quo, but as far as her parents were concerned it was Bolshevik stuff. She had well and truly had her head turned – not just by his winning combination of genuinely thinking differently while managing to be sincerely kind, but by him truly showing her that there were different ways to think about or see the world.

After an exceptionally bruising twelve months, and the suffocating presence of her parents at her elbow for most of them, he felt like a breath of fresh air. When he turned up to collect her for Sunday lunch at a pub a few villages away, she wasn't just relieved to be getting out of the house, but truly interested to know what he had thought about the week's news stories, a recent profile from the weekend's papers, or talk of a movie that might be coming to Ipswich next month. She felt her horizons expanding, her heart – and mind! – open to new things after a year of feeling hidden. She would clip things out of magazines in the coffee break room on her typing course, just so she could remember to ask him about them. And when he told her, she'd listen, watching his lips move as he talked, looking ahead at the road, while her face was turned intently to his.

What made that Christmas break, and then the weekends that followed it as he dashed back and forth from university to see her, all the more intoxicating was that he seemed to have fallen as hard as she had. In fact, it turned out that Colin couldn't believe his luck when she agreed to go out with him, and then by the time he graduated, to marry him. In fact, he was so thrilled to have bagged his dream girl, that within six months of the wedding he had got himself a sensible job in order to provide for her properly, all thoughts of indefinite academia postponed. And with that, her parents had been satisfied. After some initial rumblings about his family 'thinking they were something special just because they had a lad at university', they came to see that if Colin was going to be part of the family, they could enjoy a little of the prestige themselves.

And they certainly did. The wedding wasn't glamorous,

but to Suzie's surprise, it ended up being a genuinely celebratory day, washing her memories of the last year far into
the distance. They had been to the local registry office,
Suzie in a dress her mum had made with her over the
previous month, silently taking her measurements with a
gentleness around her waist and hips that had made Suzie
tear up. After the service they'd headed to the same pub
where Colin had been working only a few months before.
A handful of Suzie's school friends came, as well as a
couple of girls from her course, as did a dashing selection
of Colin's university mates.

Everything had felt fresh, hopeful, as if the sun was
coming out after a long drizzly spring. Even her mum
ended up being charmed by Colin's dad, his same freckles
making her giggle in at least half of the wedding photos.
By the time Suzie had been sitting on the edge of the bed
in their creaky-floored B&B in Woodbridge, gingerly
taking her heels off after a whole day on her feet, she was
longing to spend the night with Colin. To let someone
love her in a way that didn't leave her jittery with self-
doubt. And to love herself that way.

At first marriage really was fun. Suzie loved the tradition of their Sunday drives up and down the Suffolk
coast. She carried on clipping bits out of these papers for
their chats, learning about politics, history and so much
more from Colin. They'd sit with warm fish and chips
on their laps, enjoying beaches that were full during the
summer and felt like they were all theirs during blowy
February afternoons. Her mind felt alive, but her body

safe, beloved, as happy curled up in Colin's lap in front of their new television as she did in more intimate moments, later in the evening.

It was this sense of being truly loved, body and mind, that meant she didn't hesitate to agree when he suggested she didn't get a job straight away, but instead to focus on starting a family. She wanted to get going as soon as possible, they both did. But, no matter how much she regretted it in later years, she just didn't tell him about before. About Wales. She tried, once or twice. But she never quite found the words, never wanted to spoil the moment. It felt cruel to tell him, when they'd been so happy, because they really had been.

She had loved having someone to cook for, having her own home to keep nice, to keep *ready*. Colin loved it too. He glowed with contentment. All his radical ideas were put on the back burner, now that they had a nest to feather and fill. He even waited until Suzie had gone to bed if he wanted to stay up listening to his Pink Floyd and Deep Purple LPs, with headphones plugged into the hi-fi. He never smoked when he was out with her, and even if he had one at work he'd change his shirt before coming home. And since that one time she told him he had fantastic legs, he took to jogging – as it had been called back then – with great dedication, determined to keep fit. Right up until last year he had kept up with his walks, counting his steps and keeping himself 'in good nick', he'd say. He would have done anything for her, and she for him. Until it started to become clear that the one thing they wanted was the one thing she didn't seem to be able to provide.

God, they had wasted so much time over the years. And now here she was, by herself, still trying to be good. As good as him.

The sticky dopamine high of making Annabelle laugh had not yet worn off. But Abbie felt queasy that she felt it at all. It hadn't taken her very long to start pointing out little details of passers-by's outfits, gently teasing them for their looks, taking fake street photography snaps and showing them to Annabelle and Maisie before basking in the sniggers of delight.

She told herself it was satire, that she was keeping an ironic distance, but rattling around in the far corners of her conscience, she knew that what she was doing wasn't kind. And she knew she was doing it to impress someone she wasn't sure was particularly kind herself.

It hadn't taken Abbie long to realise how rare a sincere compliment from Annabelle was – she was the sort of friend who made a simple statement such as 'you've lost weight' sound like a threat, an infringement. Last weekend, it had been impossible to tell if 'So you're not coming?' was Annabelle expressly forbidding her from coming to the party she and Maisie were off to, or accusing her of a great crime of disloyalty for not being ready in time. Eye contact was usually minimal unless you were a bloke, a fashion PR or a cocktail waiter, which intensified the trouble Abbie had trying to read her flatmate's moods. Most of the time, her prevailing sentiment seemed to be one of boredom – not just with Abbie, but with almost everything. So to have this time with Annabelle as a captive audience, cackling at her every quip, was leaving Abbie dizzy with pleasure.

But even then, when they were stuck in such a confined space, she was still aware of the girls – Annabelle especially – having one eye over her shoulder, keeping an eye out for something better, someone hotter, something newer. How exhausting it was, endlessly trying to move her gaze an inch or two to the left or right, continually trying to maintain position Annabelle's in eyeline. And how exhausting, she realised, it must be to be Annabelle, always watching for a bigger prize.

As the queue moved forward a little more, people from a flat up ahead were chucking cans of drink and snacks down at the waiting queuers. People were laughing and shouting up at them. Even Suzie was chuckling at the commotion while those in the queue crashed into each other trying to reach for the goodies. She'd been looking somewhat dour only half an hour ago, and Abbie had even wondered if she had been crying when they passed those creepy statues. Now she was grinning like an indulgent granny. Maybe she should try talking to her, Abbie thought. After all, she wasn't sure how long she could sustain all this banter with Annabelle.

A space cleared just as they reached the window where

the treats had been thrown from. Suzie moved forward quite quickly, Abbie assuming that she didn't want to be caught in the crossfire if people started reaching and jumping. Tim held up a hand saying he was going to 'pop off to get a cortado' shortly, and opened the space up to the girls. Moments later, the two faces appeared at the window above them, hair falling around their faces as they looked down.

'Coke?' asked the woman.

'OMG *amazing*,' replied Annabelle. 'That would be, like, the *best*.' Even Maisie had perked up and was standing now, ready to receive some treats. Just as Abbie looked up again, the couple started lobbing cans down at them.

'Be careful, ladies – they're going to be highly carbonated now,' said Tim, chuckling at the frivolity while also making sure that Suzie was standing well back. He was right to, as Annabelle's can started frothing within seconds of her opening even a crack. She felt spray on her cheek, which she wiped by lifting her shoulder to swipe across it, before crouching to open the rest of the seal as slowly as possible.

Tim offered to take Maisie's can, and opened it with the precision of a lab technician before handing it back to her. She thanked him profusely. It had only been a couple of minutes since Abbie had seen her taking a huge swig from Annabelle's 'special' bottle, and now she was gulping the fizzy drink, wiping condensation from below her mouth with the back of her hand like a long-distance athlete. For a horrible moment, Abbie thought she was going to let out a huge, gleeful belch, but she just about managed to hold it together, making a brave attempt at hiding her burps by slowing exhaling through her nose, a quiet masterpiece of pursed lips and flared nostrils.

The Coke really was ice-cold, its sugar hitting Abbie like an adrenaline shot. That same fizzy confidence that she'd already been enjoying amidst her new friends was now intensified. Maybe this was what it felt like, living in London, being in the thick of things. Living an impulsive life where no chance was left untaken to not just witness history but to *become a part of it*. Sure, Annabelle could be hard work, but maybe that was just the price that needed to be paid for this sort of life. Where escapades abounded. Where anecdotes were made. Where friendships were taken to the next level.

'No. Effing. Way!'

Abbie looked round, startled by the exclamation, to see that Annabelle was on her phone now, her voice carrying up and around the narrow brickwork and cobbles of Shad Thames. The buildings either side of them were old warehouses, several storeys high, with wrought-iron walkways running between them overhead. It felt cramped, now that the normal weekend walkers were starting to make their presence felt, passing the queuers at varying speeds. Abbie felt a momentary twinge of self-consciousness as she realised that the sound of Annabelle's conversation was no longer being carried up and away by the breeze across the river but echoing in the enclosed space that the queue had now reached.

'It's Rory!' Annabelle mouthed at Maisie, who was staring back at her with glassy eyes, her innards presumably churning. Abbie's head was moving side to side between them as if she were watching a tennis match. She had no clue who Rory was, but she was pretty sure she was about to find out.

'You're taking the piss. No, honestly you cannot be serious. All three of you?' Annabelle continued into her phone, as Maisy gripped her forearm, squealing.

'He's in the queue!' she now mouthed at the girls, a manicured finger stabbing the air in the direction they'd just come from. 'With his BROTHERS!'

Maisie turned away from her friend, her body suddenly sagging. 'I don't feel great,' she said to Abbie. Her body looked limp, a doll whose batteries were struggling for power. She put a hand out to steady herself on Abbie's shoulder.

'Oh my god, I'm coming, I'm coming right now. *Un*real.' Annabelle slammed her phone into her hand as she ended the call.

'So guys,' Annabelle looked at them both. 'I'm going to go and find Ror.'

'Belle, I don't feel great.' Maisie was indeed grey now, her face clammy, a sheen of sweat emerging.

'Did you have some of the drink, yeah? That will help.' Annabelle was no longer making eye contact with her, but rummaging in her bag, before pulling out a hairbrush and scraping it back against her roots to create volume.

'I did, but it hasn't made me feel good. I think it was too fizzy.'

'Oh babe. Look, do you want to come with me or not? They're a bit behind us, but only, like a bit. By some weird statues apparently. We can pop back here later – Abbie will keep our place. Won't you, Abs? We'll see you in a bit yeah?'

Abbie's standing in this little group was suddenly roaring into focus as Annabelle carried on speaking, while staring directly over her shoulder and into the distance. There could be no doubt – Annabelle was off to socialise, while deputising Abbie to do the actual queueing. Maisie, well, it seemed she could do what she wanted.

Abbie said nothing, waiting for Maisie's response. But none really came. A muttered 'yeah, fine, see you later', while she leaned on the immaculate brickwork of what looked like the entrance to a restaurant's kitchens.

'Who's Rory?' dared Abbie, as Annabelle dabbed at her lips with her ring finger, a sheen of gloss appearing across her mouth.

'Oh, um, yeah, he's like an old friend. Like, a family friend type thing . . . you wouldn't know him.'

'Does he want to come up here and say hi?' Abbie was surprising herself with this challenge, but something about the way she'd seen other people around them glancing at Annabelle had given her a tiny flash of confidence. That perhaps Annabelle was the one whose behaviour, well, a bit off.

'I don't think so, Abs. To be honest he doesn't

know you. So I'll just head back, catch something to eat with him. But we'll see you later, yeah?'

She'd barely finished talking when she walked away, leaving Abbie to deflate silently in the cool and calm of the queue. They had moved on a couple of hundred metres from the snack throwers now, and as they hit the narrowest part of Shad Thames, the queue seemed to have come to a temporary halt.

Abbie reached out and touched Maisie's arm, hoping to remind her that she wasn't alone, even if she was feeling somewhat jaded – and deserted. Behind her was a huge window, through which Abbie could see a couple of the large steel tables used in professional kitchens, and behind them the hobs and ovens of a very slick-looking operation. The chefs inside were in traditional whites, with some even wearing the tall white hats she associated with childhood films. A woman was rolling pastry dough on the table facing directly towards the window, folding tiny pastry cases with total focus and military precision. Abbie was mesmerised by the quiet, repetitive movements, her eyes following from rolling pin to pastry to the nimble fingers shaping and stacking again and again.

How wonderful it must be to find your calling like that, to be truly talented and putting that talent to good use. The chef brushed the back of her hand against her cheek, pushing away a tiny spec of flour, and Abbie wondered if she would ever find a way to be actually employed doing any of the activities where she felt herself immersed in that way. These days, finding a path to any sort of consistent work, let alone actual success, seemed like a dream she'd never dare let her parents know was so very distant. She longed to make clothes, not just high fashion, but beautifully, specifically cut. And she wanted to see people enjoying them, in a way that didn't simply replicate the sickly-sweet sincerity-for-sale that she saw online in influencers and models, but was also more direct, more relevant than the otherworldly proclamations of the old school glossies. But access to any job in those fields seemed reserved for the likes of Annabelle and the ease with which she moved through the world, her wide fishnets and high-held chin making her seem like the giraffes of London Zoo, peering down at the walkers on the far side of the canal. The ones who hadn't paid.

'Aaaaah, Le Pont de la Tour,' said Tim suddenly, having reappeared from his coffee mission with a small paper cup bearing the word 'WatchHouse', and what looked like a Florentine peeking out of the top of a paper bag. He peered into the windows of the kitchen. 'It's a pretty famous restaurant,' he declared, nodding like a *MasterChef* judge.

Maisie shrugged as if to say she'd never heard of it.

'It's been around for years,' he continued, undaunted. 'In fact, the first time I ever heard of it was when I first moved to London. For some reason it has always stuck in my memory that it was where Tony Blair took Bill Clinton for dinner – or maybe lunch – when he came over. And the wives! God it was exciting – New Labour!

They'd just come to power. Cool Britannia! It felt like anything was possible back then . . . didn't it, Suzie?'

Tim had leaned back to include Suzie in the conversation but she still didn't look terribly enthusiastic.

'I wouldn't go as far as to say *anything*,' she replied. 'I never trusted Cherie – she always looked like she was enjoying it all too much.'

'The nineties, though,' chipped in Abbie for the first time. 'They were, like, iconic. I would have enjoyed it.'

Suzie shot her a quick half-smile. 'Do you know, I think you would have done, my dear. There were, by all accounts, a lot of parties.'

Was that what Suzie saw when she looked at her? A party girl? Abbie shifted uneasily. She'd never seen herself as a party girl – she didn't go to enough parties for one thing, let alone enjoy that many. Again she found herself wishing that others weren't seeing her lumped in with Annabelle and Maisie, that she'd like to be there on her own terms. She could have been if only she'd had the courage yesterday, she reminded herself.

Tim concentrated on peeling the paper bag away from his treat, perhaps regretting having brought the subject up. Maisie smirked.

'But that food does look amazing,' continued Abbie, determined not to be daunted by Suzie's comment. 'I'd love to eat there.'

'Absolutely,' said Tim. 'One day . . . one day. Maybe a big birthday. My fiftieth! God I hate that that's my next big birthday. Makes me feel ancient.'

Suzie let out a little chuckle, and Abbie turned to look at her again. Tim too had his head to one side, waiting to see if Suzie was going to tell them what had amused her so much.

'If that makes you feel old,' she said with a wistful smile now, 'then how about this. My *daughter* is fifty. Fifty today, in fact.'

'Well happy birthday to her,' replied Tim, raising his coffee cup in her honour.

'Yeah, happy birthday to . . .' Abbie's voice faded away as she realised that Suzie wasn't going to supply a name. 'You're not celebrating with her?' she asked, wondering what a daughter of Suzie's might be like.

'Oh,' replied Suzie, looking at her handbag as she shifted its strap slightly. 'She doesn't live that near me.'

'Ah,' replied Abbie.

'And I was coming here, of course, paying my respects.'

'Yes, I imagine she understands how important that is to you?' Abbie felt a strange tug, unsure whether it was a desire to know more about this woman or just to impress her. Why did she need everyone to approve of her?

'Yes, yes exactly.' With that, Suzie gave her another tight little smile.

Her heart was racing, but she gave Abbie the most convincing smile she could manage. Her pulse was pounding in her throat, so much so that she could barely swallow, as she glanced around at her fellow queuers, to see if any of them had noticed the magnitude of what she'd said.

Of course they hadn't. Because for once, it wasn't a lie.

After a lifetime of lies, today she had actually told the truth. It *was* her daughter's birthday. And yes, it was her fiftieth.

It was this, and the fact that after half a century of silence, she had finally spoken the truth out loud that was making her blood race around her body as if she had just seen a fight.

But what was most surprising of all was that, as she stood there, speaking about her daughter out loud for the first time, the world had simply carried on spinning. No one was gasping. No one was pointing. In fact, they had simply continued talking, interested even, as Suzie had told these total strangers the biggest secret of her life. The one that had – time and time again – nearly broken her.

3

Tower Bridge

Whatever bottleneck had been holding them up was now uncorked. After nearly an hour in the narrow brickwork corridor outside of the Le Pont de la Tour kitchens, people ahead suddenly started moving. Suzie stumbled on a cobblestone as she tried to keep up, before righting herself and striding forward. She stretched out her legs, enjoying the little spurt of exercise as she did her best to close the gap between her and those ahead. They emerged from the high walls of Shad Thames into an open area outside of City Hall and she felt a burst of sun on her face. As if she'd turned the page in one of her childhood story books, Tower Bridge was right there, across the river ahead, its red, white and blue paint as bright as it had ever been. Now this was London.

The bridge's two towers looked like toys, building blocks from a playset that might be found in a basket in a doctor's waiting room. And, as if it were showing off to celebrate the moment, its blue painted steel suspension chains were slowly rising, the drawbridge being raised to let through an enormous tourist boat ahead. It was making its way towards them, eastwards and out of London, the faces of its passengers visible at each of the tiny windows.

'Woah,' said Abbie, a quiet voice slightly behind her, 'I didn't realise it actually did that.'

'What do you mean?' asked Suzie.

'The going up and down thing. I thought it was just from, like, ancient times.' Maisie sniggered from behind her friend.

It was the second time that girl had laughed at her friend, Suzie noted. Having added so very little to the day's proceedings, she really was in no position to be sneering at a young woman who was simply showing a bit of curiosity. She smiled at Abbie, but feared the moment had been lost in the hubbub at the edge of the river. There were police boats patrolling, families watching the bridge rise, and a sudden sense that things were very much busier than when they'd been protected by the high walls of Shad Thames.

'Seriously, I thought it was just for commemorative times, you know, things like . . . this week,' Abbie continued.

'Oh no, it's still very much a working bridge,' chipped in Tim. 'You can sail through at any time, and it's completely free – the river traffic has priority over anything crossing here.'

Suzie wanted to smirk at Tim's endless supply of general knowledge tidbits. The man could barely walk a hundred metres without thrusting another fact at them! But she'd learned the hard way that sometimes a man like that is just trying to connect. So instead of quietly rolling her eyes at Abbie, she looked on with a smile, letting their little group know she was listening, intently. Even if he was going on . . .

'And you can look up the times that the bridge will be opening. They're all online, it's really quite interesting. I did it once to impress my nephews. I got them here at a certain time, and pretended it was me, my magic zapping hands that were opening it. "Alakazam!" That kind of thing – they loved it! You should have seen their faces as the opening spans started to raise. That's what they're called – the drawbridge road bits . . .'

Suzie pretended she was still listening, but her gaze had crossed the river now, to the Tower of London, the palace with its four iconic towers. She remembered visiting as a twelve-year-old schoolgirl, not long after she had de-voured Margaret Irwin's Elizabethan trilogy. Book after book, lying on her front across her quilt every evening when she'd come home from school, her head whirling with the adventures of the Queen, and the dangers of the Palace.

She could still feel the stiff leather of her T-bar school shoes as they walked across the cool flagstones of the palace courtyard the day of that trip, her brain abuzz from the romance and adventure of those novels. It had been a day with weather just like today's; the air seemed all the fresher, being away from the classroom and the stifling rules of her strict girls' school for a few precious hours. She clearly remembered sitting on the coach on the way home, talking to her friend Maggie about how much they had loved the visit, and, as the rest of the class busied themselves with the gossip from the back seat of the bus, how much they were looking forward to taking their own children there one day.

Today, it was getting busier along the Thames as the sun rose in the sky. Families were out now, buggies and toddlers everywhere, parents running after them with water bottles, tiny woolly hats and half-eaten pastries. Regular people, just enjoying the riverside exactly as Suzie had always longed to do with a family of her own. A little girl with purple sparkly sneakers and two neat plaits walked past, pointing to the Tower with one hand as she reached for her mother's with the other. Suzie felt a familiar guilt press at her, deep inside. That guilt, alongside grief for the life she had never had, had for so long been a pebble sitting in her chest, as smooth and cold as those flagstones at the Tower.

She thought about her daughter, wondering if she had ever visited the Tower of London over the years. As a child, or perhaps even with her own children – if she had any. Her immediate instinct was to push the thought away, just as she always had when tormented by questions like these. If she didn't think about that pebble, she'd told herself year after year, maybe it wasn't there at all. But that one sentence, words she had let herself say out loud only about ten minutes ago, had dislodged something in her. It had let a chink of light in on a secret kept for so long, and now she didn't seem to be able to control her thoughts in the same way. It had simply felt too good to speak of her daughter at last. Because until today she never, ever had.

It was 1976 when Suzie and Colin lost their first baby, at nearly twenty weeks. They had barely been married a year, and it had been such a happy one. Colin had thrown himself into making their small home perfect for family life, from putting in raised vegetable beds in the garden to enthusiastically re-plastering and wallpapering each of the three bedrooms. Suzie had helped to choose the colours for each room, making sure that they were neither too blue or too pink, but just perfect for whichever baby they might be lucky enough to be blessed with. Home-making had taken up so much of that first year, then, to both of their delight, she had fallen pregnant far sooner than either of them had dared to hope.

For the most part, the pregnancy had been as easy as her first. In fact, the worst thing about it hadn't been any physical symptoms, but the constant nagging fear that a doctor, or even a midwife, might know that this wasn't the first time she had been pregnant. She had told herself when they had first got married that she'd tell Colin everything, but there had never been a moment when it seemed fair to break the spell, to let him know what sort of person she really was. Then, when she realised she was expecting, she decided that she'd have to do it sooner or later, before it got too hard.

But she couldn't do it in a doctor's appointment, not in front of a total stranger, so when the time came for each check-up she made sure that Colin needn't come, but kept careful, attentive notes about the baby's size and health at every stage. After each appointment, she promised herself she'd tell the truth when he came home from work, now that they were going to be able to start afresh. He'd come home, and she would tell him everything about the appointment, describing exactly how she felt, and even describing each and every midwife she had seen, giving them nicknames to amuse him. And he'd look so happy, taking her in his arms and telling her how proud he was of her. So she'd say nothing, in case she put a jinx on things. Anything to distract from the anxiety that she was just one well-judged question away from being found out.

Halfway, she had told herself, only days before. *Only twenty more weeks . . .*

But despite her trying to avoid a jinx, things had gone wrong very quickly after that twenty-week mark: her being rushed to the hospital in the small hours, Colin pale with worry as he followed her into the ambulance, his pyjama bottoms flapping around beneath his overcoat, shoes on without socks as he'd scrambled to get himself ready to accompany her, both of them praying that this wasn't what they dreaded it might be.

But it was. The baby was gone. And in its place an unbearable question for Suzie – had it been the worry about being found out that had caused her to lose it?

The pressure of trying to conceal the truth? Or, worse still, was it perhaps a consequence of the complicated birth she had had four years earlier? As she rolled into the papery cool of the starched hospital pillow later that day, Suzie knew that she may never get her answer, and cried silently until daylight peeked through the curtains of the ward.

The next time the lies came a little more easily. After all, it was no longer completely untrue to say 'no' when she was asked if this 'was her first'. She could explain about the miscarriage, she could talk about that one as the 'lost' baby. But as the lies flowed more easily, so did the self-recrimination. With no one to talk to, accompanied by the constant nagging fear of letting Colin down, or, worst of all, him uncovering the secrets of the summer she turned nineteen, Suzie started to turn inwards. This time, she didn't even make it to twenty weeks, the baby gone before they had reached the three-month mark.

In the years that followed, the couple walked a path familiar to many others: monthly hope and excitement, followed by another tiny grief. And with each month, the secret Suzie carried felt a little heavier, keeping the two of them a little further apart. Friends they had once felt so equal to had their own children with ease, and disappeared behind the velvet rope of straightforward family life. When they'd bump into these families out and about, the question of whether Colin and Suzie were 'trying' or would be 'next' would dangle between them like a teething toy stretched across the front of a pram.

Everyone would try to be polite, but the air would be cloudy with awkwardness.

Colin's mum would bring her all sorts of herbal teas and homeopathic tinctures, reassuring her that *the most important thing is to relax*. As if relaxing were easy when it was all that lay between you and your entire future happiness, Suzie'd think. Her own parents, meanwhile, said very little. Her mother had shed quiet tears of joy when Suzie had told her the first time that she and Colin were pregnant, dabbing at her eyes with a neatly folded lace-trimmed hanky. They had been in the living room at home, and Suzie had refused a small sherry before Sunday lunch. That same carriage clock was ticking away in the background as the penny dropped, and her father hugged her tight, almost as thrilled as Colin by the news. But when she'd lost it, they didn't visit her in hospital. A few days later, she had received a card from her mother, a small watercolour of a bunch of wild flowers on the front. There was a splash – tears? – on the ink of the envelope, and she smelled her mother's Diorella when she opened it. The words inside were no doubt heartfelt, but all Suzie really wanted was another hug, to be told it wasn't her fault, that they were proud of her nevertheless.

When advancements in fertility treatment came along, Colin and Suzie saved up and dutifully attended a handful of specialist appointments, daring to hope once again. Suzie sat through the consultations white with worry in case she was asked a compromising question in front of Colin, only to discover that her obvious anxiety merely served to make him kinder to her once they got home. He learned to cook a handful of basic healthy meals. 'Nourishment for the both of you,' he'd announce on the particularly important days, as he served her Steak Diane with a huge mound of creamed spinach next to it. He even bought her a special plate for a few custard creams, which he'd put next to her bedside for when she woke up from another round of invasive fertility procedures.

Each of these times she opened her eyes, she'd feel sick with dread – would this be the one where he wasn't there, that he'd seen the light, that he was gone? But he was always there, smiling, telling her she was doing a great job. Sometimes, it was the hope in his eyes that was the worst of all. Time and again they were told the same thing: there was no reason that they couldn't get pregnant, or stay pregnant. It was unexplained; they should just keep trying. But she became convinced that she knew what the problem was: it was a punishment.

Meanwhile, some of Suzie's friends who had waited a little longer before starting families seemed to be enjoying careers, their own money, some genuine independence. Their homes sprouted patios, conservatories, double glazing. They went on increasingly sunny holidays abroad. They joined golf clubs and took dancing lessons. When they had birthdays, they seemed to celebrate the passing of another year lived to the full. The glossy smiles of the wives seemed genuine, their husbands confident and undistracted at work.

But for Colin and Suzie, the passing of another year

just seemed a marker of more months of failure. So after a few years, far more than Suzie thought she could bear but far fewer than Colin was prepared to, Suzie persuaded her husband that perhaps it was time to give up, to stop thinking about it at all. Time to move on and enjoy their lives, to live like some of their peers. *Of course*, he said. *You're right. We* should *try adoption.*

Suzie had never imagined that this would be his response, and was at a total loss to explain to him why it was out of the question. So much that was now unsayable, so many lies that the truth would now reveal. But adoption was simply out of the question. She knew on a visceral level that she could never adopt another woman's baby. Not just because she could feel herself, from her guts to the tips of her fingernails, rejecting the prospect of being on that side of the transaction, taking the precious cargo from the mother and baby home, knowing that only a few walls away was a mother with a heart forever broken who had been told it was all for the best. But also because she knew she couldn't keep up with any more lies, and inviting in a child who had not been born to her would have been an unbearable burden to carry.

What she hadn't realised at the time, though, was that in begging not to try adoption, she was setting herself up for the biggest lie of them all. Even as the words were still coming out of her mouth, she realised that there was no turning back now. Her face streaked with tears, but not for the reason he assumed, she told him that she couldn't take it anymore, that perhaps she *didn't* want children enough after all. That they should stop. Her heart was in her throat as she waited for his response, knowing that there were now any number of ways that she might lose him as he paused, considering his reply.

But he went along with it, as he usually did with whatever she wanted. And she loved him all the more for it. Even if there was a tiny part of her somewhere that she could barely reach, much less articulate, which wanted him to shout at her, demanding that they keep trying, keep adopting, or even that she tell him the truth. But the terrible fact of it was that he just trusted her. He went along with it because he loved her and he never thought for a second that she'd tell a lie that would spiral for months, to years. And would last so much longer than even that.

So they moved on, but just as she was grieving, deep down she suspected that he was still hoping, still checking too. Each month, as she moved the discreet floral sponge bag filled with tampons from the top left of her chest of drawers and onto the cistern of the bathroom loo, he would spot it, and come downstairs to give her a silent hug. As she looked over his shoulder one sunny summer evening, staring into the back garden, she wondered if the shame would ever fade, if she'd ever feel like a good person again. Or at least one who was less lonely.

Because Colin's forbearance only seemed to highlight the darkness in Suzie's past, reminding her that the responsibility for this slow, painful tragedy lay at her feet. So each month, as she hugged him tight and prayed that he'd never leave her, she felt that cold, smooth pebble inside her pressing against her heart yet again.

An empty crisp packet whooshed past, caught by the wind and causing a toddler to shriek with excitement, snapping Suzie out of her melancholy. Suddenly, there seemed to be children everywhere. The queue was snaking back and forth around a patch of grass on the approach to City Hall. There were temporary toilets, marshals in their tabards, a new sense of formality around the queue as it became more visible. The small of Suzie's back was starting to ache, as if she'd taken a slow turn around the British Museum for an hour or two too long. She rummaged in her bag for a tissue to wipe her nose, her fingers a little stiff with cold after so long standing in the shade. She could still hear Tim rabbiting on about impressing his nieces, or was it nephews, as Abbie tittered away. How carefree these younger generations were. How many options open to them. She wondered if they'd ever be burdened by the sense of duty that her generation had been.

It was something she had always found easy to identify with in the Queen – that perception of the tracks having been laid out before them so far in advance. How could a young Elizabeth ever have fully comprehended the sudden change that the course of her life would take once she was barely into her twenties? How could young Suzie have ever imagined that one small incident – while still in her teens – would still be impacting the way she lived her life over half a century later? Her Majesty had always followed her path with such grace, despite all its surprises, whereas Suzie had long felt burdened by resentment, a worry that she'd be paying for her early mistakes forever.

She went to dab the corner of her eye, conscious that others might notice how far she had sunk into melancholy. *Get a grip, woman!* she was telling herself, when her thoughts were interrupted by Tim touching her elbow.

'Are you OK there?'

'Yes, it's just . . . well, it all suddenly feels rather real doesn't it?'

A police helicopter was almost drowning her voice out, so she leaned in to Tim, who still had a gentle hand on her arm.

'I know what you mean. It was easier to think about the whole thing as somewhat more hypothetical – just more headlines – when it was all on the other side of the television screen.'

'Exactly. And I'm not usually the sort of person who is, well, *part of things*.' Suzie looked away for a second, suddenly shy after making the admission.

'Do you know, I absolutely get what you're saying. I'm not really one for placards or flag waving or any of that malarkey normally. It's just not me.'

'Does it sound strange to say I have, sort of, butterflies in my stomach? I don't think I'd anticipated being quite so looked at . . .'

'Not strange at all, I feel just the same – which is daft because how did I think the news had all that rolling footage if it wasn't for people like them coming out and filming the people like us?'

Tim waved a hand in the direction of a foreign news crew who were walking along the crowd, looking for any Spanish speakers to interview. Suzie imagined herself on a small screen, up above the coffee machine in a cafe on a coastal holiday resort, her windswept face flickering above the Perspex display case of ice creams, the Chupa Chups by the till.

'Yes, I'm starting to think I might have underestimated how today might make me feel.'

Tim opened his mouth to answer, but was interrupted by a piercing 'Mate!' coming from just behind him in a broad Australian accent.

He'd just been wondering how Abbie could not have known that Tower Bridge still opened when he'd spotted Suzie looking close to tears. Reprieve! He'd been silently horrified that as he explained the bridge to Abbie, he was becoming someone who other *actual adults* thought of as some sort of wise old owl? People had often mistaken him for older than his years, but that had been more to do with his nerdy enthusiasm for facts and due process. But Abbie, who was proving surprisingly good company, didn't seem to find him particularly geeky. She actually seemed to be enjoying learning about where they were, and what all these buildings meant. But she did also seem to think he was some sort of nine hundred-year-old shaman.

He'd just settled into this new role, even reaching to check in on Suzie, when their new harmony was shattered by a man barrelling towards them. A man who looked alarmingly similar to a Golden Retriever wearing a leather jacket.

'Mate! Excuse me mate!' the man was calling out with an Aussie twang that reminded him of backpackers in Earls Court when he had first moved to London. An accent so broad it was almost chewy, leaving Tim longing to say the words that way himself, just to enjoy the new shapes his mouth might make.

The man bounded up to him with a grin, so full of apparent good will that Tim wondered if he was actually going to leap up on him like a puppy. He was reminded of the affable Australian dogs in a cartoon he sometimes watched with his nieces. The general air of well-meaning mayhem was enhanced by the man's hair, which was a tumble of blond, shaggy waves. The sort of thing Tim's mum had spent hours doing to her own hair in the early eighties, only this man looked as if he'd just stepped off a surfboard rather than out of a salon. Well, apart from the fact that he was bundled up in a heavy brown leather jacket over his hoodie and jeans, and was holding a paper coffee cup from the coffee place Tim had just been to. Now that he was up close, Tim could see that his eyes were very blue.

He caught himself staring, not speaking for just a beat

too long. He felt his pulse at the base of his thumb as he stood with his hands limp at his side. The man's eyes really were *very* blue.

'Mate?'

Oh god, he was actually talking to *him*.

'Hi, um, yes. How can I hel—'

'I'm sorry to bother you mate, but are these your gloves?'

Instinctively, Tim patted the pockets of his coat then jeans, despite being pretty sure he recognised the black fleece gloves in the man's hand as his own.

'Yes, er, I think they might be.' Tim looked around him, in case he'd dropped his own, and was about to claim these in error.

'I found them on the counter in the coffee shop – you were in front of me in there.'

'Oh! Oh yes, then they are mine. Yikes, thank you.'

'Epic. I am so glad I caught you. I've been queueing up ahead, and then I was standing behind you in there and you just walked out. I thought I had lost you for a minute back then!'

'No chance!' Tim's laugh caught in his throat, the noise of a lonely soprano escaping where he had intended a chummy but masculine chuckle. 'Anyway . . . Thank you so much, how daft of me. I hadn't even realised I'd left them. The coffee was keeping my hands warm.' Tim raised his own cup to show the man, as if he wouldn't believe him otherwise.

'It's great stuff in there, the real deal.'

'Absolutely.' Tim's jaw was starting to hurt, he was

smiling so much. Then, from the corner of his eye, he saw Maisie doubled over, Abbie rubbing her back. He put a hand out to touch the man's forearm, gently interrupting what he was about to say. 'Excuse me, I just need to check . . .'

The man swivelled to follow Tim's gaze. 'Jeez, is she being sick?'

'Maisie, are you OK?' Tim looked at Abbie, who turned to look up at him, her face panic-stricken.

'She suddenly said she felt really sick. She wasn't feeling great anyway, then she had that can of Coke really quick.'

'The one that was dropped out of the window?' asked Tim.

The stranger looked confused by the question, his eyes meeting Tim's, searching for some sort of explanation.

'It's a long story . . . back there . . . there was a flat on the route where they started throwing stuff at the queuers. In a good way though! You know, snacks . . .'

'Gotcha,' replied the man. Although Tim wondered if he really did.

Tim bent over to see how Maisie was. He hated moments like this, where quick, instinctive decisions needed to be made. Gut reactions! The absolute horror of it. Tim would like to have been able to run a series of tests, to summon some experts. How was he supposed to know what to do to help these total strangers – and on a day like today. He gingerly rubbed a hand on Maisie's back, hoping to hit the correct balance between reassurance and consent.

Her mouth was open, her breathing was shallow, her skin the colour of putty. He looked up again, whispering to Abbie this time. 'I don't want to be rude, but has she been drinking?'

Abbie's face flushed, her eyes darting. 'I think she has,' she said quietly. Then, with an endearing lack of guile, she looked across to check if Suzie had noticed the commotion, lest she might be looking on disapprovingly? 'Her and Annabelle hadn't really been to bed . . .' she explained, almost under her breath.

'Who the heck is Annabelle?' asked the stranger, who was still standing there, holding Tim's gloves.

Tim blinked at the man's pronunciation of heck as 'hick', before looking up and replying. 'A friend of the girls'. It's . . . another long story.'

'How long have you guys been queueing?' Tim wanted to be annoyed at the cheek of the question, but the man had a point. How were they all so enmeshed in each other's dramas already?

He unhooked his rucksack from his back and opened it on the pavement in front of him, trying to move round towards Maisie to keep her out of the range of the nearby TV crew. He started rooting through his belongings, just as Maisie started to heave. Oh god, what had this girl done? Was she going to be OK? And how was *he* suddenly in charge of her?

The stranger stepped forward, pushing his sleeve back and pulling a hair tie from his own wrist. He smoothed a large, tanned hand along Maisie's hair and tied it gently

at the nape of her neck. Despite himself, Tim was mesmerised, having to pretend that he was still rummaging
through his bag. In fact, he was barely able to tear his eyes
off the tenderness and capability in the gesture.

'There you go, sweetheart, let's keep all this out of the
way in case the worst happens.'

The man's easy composure was unnerving. Tim's hand
was shaking just searching for a protein bar. It wasn't
just the sheer awfulness of vomiting in this queue of all
queues, but the hygiene issues, the shame, the worry
about if this girl was going to be OK.

'Daa-lin, I really don't think you should be here. You
need to get to bed with a big glass of water,' the man was
saying. Tim noticed that he had taken over with the back
rubbing, his huge hand making reassuring circles against
the girl's coat.

'Do you think I should take her home?' Abbie asked
him, as Maisie tried to stand up. Tim felt the others
around them starting to stare, wondering what was going
on, if there was a problem – or at least just a diversion.

'Would you like me to come with you to get her a cab?'
asked Tim, as desperate to do something useful as he was
to get out of the glare of the rest of the queue. 'I've got
something to eat here, if . . .' he mouthed the word *alcohol*
'. . . that's the problem?' He thrust the health bar into
Abbie's hand.

'If!' chuckled the stranger. 'Mate, I'm getting tipsy just
standing here!'

Tim blushed, horrified at the thought that people

around might think their group wasn't taking the day seriously enough. The parents of the family just behind them had turned their children away, and were discreetly pointing at landmarks in the opposite direction to the commotion Maisie was making.

'Sorry . . .' Tim mouthed at the mother, who gave him smile that might have been a grimace.

Abbie looked anguished on noticing that Tim was apologising for them to the others around, then Suzie, who up until now had been staring across the river as if she was trying to pretend the whole thing wasn't happening, turned to her.

'Don't worry, dear, your place in the queue will still be here if you want to come back.' Her voice was softer than Tim had noticed before. Perhaps she just wanted Maisie out of the way as much as he did. 'No one will think any the less of you for trying to help a friend in need.'

'Do you want me to come and help you find a cab, daalin?' The man was now asking Maisie directly, as she leaned against the cool of the metal railing. 'The name's Howie, by the way.'

Maisie did not reply, instead groaning and doubling over to put her head between her legs again. Tim was unsure if she was trying not to faint or about to be sick again. Or both. Abbie was typing furiously into her phone.

'Annabelle isn't replying – she has gone back there a bit to hang out with some of her other mates.' Her eyes were darting as she admitted this, clearly mortified at having to confess on behalf of her friend's bad behaviour. 'And I've texted Maisie's boyfriend to tell her I'm sending her home. Apparently he's back at the flat now. Do you think I should go with her?'

He did not want to be the one to say so, but Tim really did think *someone* should go with her. The girl could barely stand; the safety implications were enormous. He opened his mouth to say so when Suzie stepped forward.

'Howie, excuse me. Hello, I'm Suzie.'

'Hi there, Suzie.' The man grinned that Golden Retriever grin again.

'I think we'd all be really grateful if you would help Abbie get her friend into a cab, as she obviously needs to go home. And Tim, do you think you could get Abbie a hot drink too? I'll be here, you can head straight back and find me afterwards.'

The relief!

'Great plan, thank you so much, Suzie. Are you guys OK with that?' Thank *God* someone had made a decision. Tim felt his shoulders drop an inch at the realisation that he wasn't having to be the only grown-up after all.

Maisie was nodding her head while avoiding looking directly at anyone, while Abbie was unwrapping the protein bar for her with a great sense of purpose.

There was a stillness to Suzie that Tim found reassuring, easy to comply with. He had been blundering around, thrown by the appearance of this Howie fellow, while she had played matriarch, told them all what to do. Best of all, he was deputised to getting hot drinks, which meant he could take a moment to compose himself. He hoped Howie would still be there when he got back.

'I'll be fine, Abs, honestly, I just want to go home and sleep.'

Abbie hoped this was true, but she wasn't entirely convinced. Maisie was still grey, and was hobbling in her boots, every step clearly taking an enormous amount of effort. But she did seem to be managing to hold down the protein bar that Tim had given her as they walked inland to try and find a cab on Tooley Street. Abbie glanced at her phone again with the hand that wasn't draped around Maisie's shoulders. Nothing from Annabelle, who seemed to have checked out of this expedition entirely, despite it having been her plan.

She should have known. She should have been more careful. She remembered lying on the beach with Sunnie over the summer, the sun drying their swimsuits as they lay on the sand, their feet in the water as the tide gently came in. Telling the truth was always a little easier with sunglasses on, and it was as if Sunnie herself had known this.

'So are these new flatmates good people? You know, like, be-honest-about-your-family good? Or just good fun?'

'Well I'm not planning on lying to them if that's what you mean,' replied Abbie.

'It's not what I mean.' Sometimes it took a friend who'd known you since primary school to get you to tell the truth.

'Oh you know – like, we just haven't chatted that much yet. They're literally new friends.'

'But you could call them if you were in trouble? Like how you know you can always call me? When you're in London, could you rely on them? For anything?'

'I'm sure I could, but I'm not planning to, am I?! Come on, Sunnie, we're adults now, we're supposed to need people a bit less now . . .' Abbie had felt uncomfortable, too seen. She sat up, wrapping her arms around herself despite the heat. She brushed sand off the backs of her shoulders, trying to look distracted, busy. It was as if Sunnie was throwing out lifebuoys for her; conversational inflatables for her to grab onto and admit how lonely she was finding life in London. How little she had connected with anyone. How she was barely leaving the house, so of course she'd given scant consideration to who she might call in an emergency.

But she couldn't grab on – it was too much to admit to. She'd just start this year and give it all her best show. Sunnie had sat up, lifting her water bottle and finishing the contents before stashing it down the side of her bag, picking up her skateboard and saying she had to get back for dinner.

'See you at the skate park tomorrow, yeah?'

'Of course,' Abbie replied, looking up and smiling at her friend. She was facing directly into the late afternoon sun, squinting, still not quite able to look her friend in the eye – but at least she now had an excuse.

'And you know you can call me any time, don't you? Even when you're up in London?'

'Of course.' Except she'd forgotten it. She'd much rather have been in the queue with Sunnie, even if it would have taken a lot of persuading and having to listen to a lot of her thoughts about the monarchy. The wind whistled down Tooley Street, cold in the shade of the buildings. Abbie's spine felt like ice. Brittle. Fragile.

How could she have been so daft as to have headed out for the day with those two, and in the state they were in? She had trusted them; she had assumed that if they all left together, this would be something they'd do together, supporting each other. She had imagined huddling into each other's coats against the wind, sharing stories about loved ones they missed, a blossoming sense of togetherness as they experienced a national event with an international audience. Instead, she'd been reduced to taxi monitor, then last man standing.

Howie spotted a cab rank around the back of London Bridge Station, and raised a hand.

'Here we go, ladies . . .'

A taxi driver glanced nervously over his shoulder at the group as Howie leaned towards the window to speak to him.

'We need to get this one back home, please . . .'

Abbie opened her mouth to interrupt. Shouldn't she be going with her?

'Is she alright?' The driver looked far from convinced.

'Yes mate, she's all good,' said Howie as he pushed his hair off his face, a blast of wind down Tooley Street having blown it everywhere. He crouched to look directly in at the driver. 'We've got some food in her, she's just tired really – been queueing for the lying in state.'

Maisie slid sleepily into the back seat, but the driver still looked sceptical. He'd clearly smelled her breath as she leaned forward to give him her address.

'There's a charge if you mess up the cab . . .'

'Mate, it's not going to happen. Trust me. Any problems, call.' He pulled a pen out of his pocket and scrawled HOWIE in loose capitals alongside his number across the paper cup he'd been drinking from. 'She's golden.'

'Mais – you'll be home soon. And Jamie's there.' Abbie leaned in to her. Maisie mumbled a reply, barely acknowledging her flatmate. Abbie felt Howie's hand on her shoulder.

'Thanks, pal,' he said, as he closed the back door. Then, as the cab pulled away, he looked at Abbie with a grin, broad creases around his eyes and mouth. He looked like someone who smiled a lot. 'Now then, let's get back to our queue family.'

'So you're queuing with us now, are you?'

'Well I *was* ahead of you guys, but I've spent the best part of an hour running around with a pair of gloves and helping your mate Maisie there, so I don't know how the guys I was with will feel if I suddenly reappear after all this time.'

He had a point.

'And anyway,' he continued, 'you lot are a whole heap more fun.' And with that, he bumped his shoulder against hers, giving her a nudge that seemed to imply that he'd enjoyed the chaos, rather than been put out by it.

'You're sure you can really handle another nine hours of us?'

'I wouldn't have it any other way.'

Together, they made their way back to the Thames Path, and started to walk slowly along it until they found their queue family once again.

4

London Bridge

When she'd stepped in with her suggestion, Suzie had been confident that Tim and Abbie would be able to find her, keeping their place in the queue with little problem, but as the line ahead picked up speed, passing HMS *Belfast*, then London Bridge, and then on towards the Tate Modern, Suzie started to wonder if her plan had actually been as flawless as she'd initially assumed. Well, it had hardly been a plan, more that someone had had to intervene and make a suggestion while they'd all been panicking and dithering. Which she hadn't minded doing, only now she found herself back where she'd started: queueing solo.

It wasn't too bad though, and there was a definite sense of pace now. The riverside was busy, and all chance of stopping to lean on a wall was gone now that they were all moving forward at a steady pace. But, as she placed her hands in the small of her back and leaned, trying to stretch it out, Suzie could tell that they were still hours from Westminster.

She didn't mind this moment of quiet, taking the opportunity to look at some of the queuers a little farther from her in each direction. The family behind, with the kids Fred and Molly, all seemed to be doing well. The mum had applied a layer of chalky-looking sun cream to each of the kids, before dabbing her husband's nose and the tops of his ears, playfully. They were all passing a series of statues of enormous bronze monkeys in various states of play, thoughtfulness or engagement with each other, and the kids couldn't believe their luck.

As they passed each one, Suzie was smiling, wondering what they'd be up to next time she turned around. And sure enough, there would be Fred, dangling from one by his legs, coat hanging upside down as he yelled at his sister with glee. Then there'd be another one, a big bronze marsupial mingling in with the rest of the throng, almost passing for a fellow Londoner until Molly appeared, trying to feed him the banana from her packed lunch, before Fred attempted another swing-off. Some of the others loomed over the rest of the queuers, overbearing on account of their size, people veering away as they passed. Then Suzie would turn around, and sure enough, there would be Molly, hands cupped together, giving her brother a leg up so he could wrap his scarf around the monkey's neck.

Suzie had no idea if these statues were temporary or just another thing about London that bore no resemblance to the city she had once known, but as she kept passing them, she found them increasingly charming.

Each person seemed to respond to them differently, either being startled then pretending to ignore them, or pointing up ahead with loved ones and discussing them, heads tipped to one side to get a better look. Yes, there was a twinge of loneliness that she didn't have anyone to chuckle with about them, but when *didn't* she feel a little of that these days?

Then, just as she was starting to wonder if she had lost the others for good, she felt a ripple of interest among those around her. The whites of eyes raised to look up and into the distance. Friends grabbing each other's arms to catch their attention. The low muttering of people shifting their tone to speak more discreetly to each other while achieving the opposite. Suzie scanned the area where people were looking, trying to ascertain what was going on, when a couple came out of a nearby cafe and walked a few hundred metres up ahead to rejoin the queue, eyes following them as they walked by. He was dressed in a long camel-coloured overcoat, with clunky black boots and a baseball cap pulled down low. She was in silky tracksuit bottoms and huge white trainers with a large leather jacket on top. She had a baseball cap on too, pulled down just as his was, but there was something that caught the eye about the couple – they were impeccably tanned, both his beard and her hair were glossy and neat. Their coats looked heavy, expensive. But mostly it was their manner as they walked by, eyes dipped. Celebrities . . . but who?

Suzie glanced back and saw the family behind chatting,

the mother's hands held up to her mouth in surprise? Excitement? Her husband caught Suzie's eye and smiled a little.

'Should I know who that is?' asked Suzie, leaning in towards him.

'He's from *Strictly* apparently. One of the dancers. And his girlfriend's some influencer I think.' The man gave a little shrug as if to apologise for the unreliability of his information. His wife then leaned in and mouthed the celebrity's name. And Suzie surprised herself by actually recognising the description.

'The one with the tango! On Movie Night!' she said to the woman, thrilled to have made the connection.

'*Exactly* . . .' she replied, with a glint in her eye. 'I've never been the same since!'

'Do you know I never thought that much of him when he wasn't dancing,' continued Suzie. 'But I take it all back now. Hats off to him. You never know about people do you, you just never know . . .'

The couple nodded in reply, before darting off to catch Fred who was lunging towards another perilous-looking piece of street architecture.

Suzie peered up ahead to see if the couple were still there, rummaging as she did so into her bag for an apple. She was slightly peckish now, but painfully aware that it was nowhere near lunchtime. The sudden flash of a schoolgirl memory flickered across her mind: being caught by a teacher one afternoon as she'd been crossing the local park on her way home, chomping on an apple she had kept back from breakfast as she walked. Wow, it must have been as long ago as 1969, she realised. It was out of school hours, but the teacher still felt it was her place to intervene, telling Suzie that it was 'indecorous' for a young lady to eat in public.

'Young woman, you don't want to end up being seen as unladylike,' the teacher had told her, a tiny fleck of spittle flying from her thin lips as she spoke.

Suzie had said very little in reply, but joked about it later as she'd sat in the park with her friend Caroline, their bare legs lying in the sun, resting on the early summer grass.

'She's just not coping with it all terribly well, is she?' Caroline had said.

'With what?' Suzie asked, suddenly anxious not to seem too naive in front of her new, sophisticated mate. Caroline was, after all, the sort of person who had a boyfriend with long hair.

'All of it. The changes in society. Us.' She waved her hand dismissively around the park, as if evidence of these so called 'changes in society' might actually be evident somewhere between the bandstand and the small child trying to untangle a kite with his father.

Suzie hadn't really taken on board the idea that anything profound was changing. In fact, life seemed almost stiflingly dull with her parents, neither of whom were inclined to rock the boat. Quite the opposite in fact. Suzie tried to think what Caroline could be referring to. The Queen had opened up a new Tube line earlier that year *and* got a new yacht, the *QE2*. Those were things that had excited her mum, so they could hardly be seen as a sign of the oncoming revolution. And her dad still liked to grumble about That Bloody Labour Lot over breakfast, but Harold Wilson was hardly John Lennon was he? As far as Suzie was concerned, everything in her life seemed as if it would never change.

It was only years later that she could see how much things really were changing. The thought of going to pay your respects to the Queen in a pair of trainers! It would have been unthinkable back then, and now here she was, queueing among celebrities wearing exactly that sort of get up. Even *she* was wearing her comfiest shoes, despite the moment of guilt she'd felt about leaving her smart loafers in the car at the station. Nearly seventy years old and still worrying about defying her mother, she thought. Some things would never change, no matter what that Caroline had told her.

If only it had been eating in public that had posed the real danger to her back then. Feeling like Eve herself, Suzie rubbed the apple a little against her padded jacket. Then, after checking it for fluff and dust, she took a sat-isfying first bite, for once not caring a jot what anyone around her might think. The fruit was fresh, zingy even. Far from being a 'cotton woolly' one, as her father used to say.

He'd be pleased to see that she was there today, she thought. Doing the right thing, even if she was in comfy shoes. For decades she had barely been able to look him in the eye, terrified that he would find out her secret. Then, towards the end, she had hated herself for the relief she felt about him finally dying, never having to discover the shame of what she'd done. All those years, all those conversations she had felt unable to start, just in case. What a waste. As she stood here in the sun, Suzie still couldn't quite believe that there had been no sudden crack of thunder, no recriminations from on high, no real response at all when she had told her new friends about her daughter's birthday. In fact, it had felt quite good, this clean slate. Saying it out loud. Well, some of it.

Perhaps she'd tell them about how it had been New Year 1972 when she'd fallen pregnant. There was no lie in that, after all. Maybe she'd even tell them about Eddie. How she had met him on only her third shift at The White Horse, how he'd come up behind her while she'd been restocking the fridge, gently nudging her on the hip so that she'd move to make space for him to put down the tray of glasses. She had jumped at his touch, only to wish he'd do it again the minute she saw him. He was wearing a pale yellow shirt with a wide collar, and tan flares. His waist was slim, neat even, but his chest was straining against the buttons of his shirt.

'Oops, sorry,' he'd said, shaking the water off his hand as he put down the tray and extended a palm to say hello. 'I'm Eddie. Doing weekends mostly. You Suzie?'

'Yes.' Suzie ran a hand across her forehead, hoping to smooth her hair. It had only been slightly longer than it was today. The same side-parted bob that had been with her for years, the blonde slowly turning white as the years rolled by. She had swallowed, suddenly very aware of the remnants of a packet of Chipsticks that were in her teeth as she smiled at him. 'I'm new.'

'Well, you look like you're fitting right in,' he replied, lifting fistfuls of the wine glasses they used to serve gin and tonics in. He had his hand spread like a claw picking up four at a time by the stem with a slick, professional ease, slotting them into the wooden racks alongside the spirits and their optics. She had felt the heat of his body as he leaned over her, responding by putting a hand cooled from the fridge on the nape of her neck as she stood up. His hair was almost black, cut quite short in what looked like an attempt to curb what were obvious curls sprouting out in all directions. She had a sudden urge to reach out and touch it, to see what it looked like with the damp of the condensation from her hand on it. Instead, she tugged at her red and white T-shirt, pulling it down over the waistband of her jeans, suddenly very aware that it had ridden up while she'd been bending over. The light from the back of the bar was bouncing off the newly hung glasses, the bottles she had dusted earlier, and the black of his hair.

'Thanks,' she finally replied, edging round him. 'Cos it looks like a tight squeeze.'

She'd left herself breathless at her own audacity, but to her delight he took the pun and ran with it, making references to how close they were to each other for the rest of that first shift. Their little joke, whispered to each other as they stood with their backs turned to the customers, glasses held to the optics, felt like a secret pulling them immediately close. She checked for a ring on his left hand while he was tapping away at the till, and she saw none. Her heart skipped another beat.

Pat, the pub's landlady – a fortress of a women who was thirty per cent beehive, thirty per cent bosom and forty per cent of everybody else's business – soon caught on to their giggles and raised an eyebrow at Suzie, who quickly made a reference to his wife in clumsy effort to find out if he was off limits.

'Very clever, Suzanne,' Pat had replied, without looking up from the canister of Coca-Cola she was changing under the bar. Then as she turned, she had leaned in, 'He's single. But don't get too close – he's off to college in Canada in the spring.'

Suzie thought she could hear her heart bursting through her eardrums.

And so the flirting had continued. Discreetly, of course. Or so they thought. Suzie knew that friends of her parents' popped into The White Horse, and even her dad came in on the odd Friday night to check in on her – her first job! He'd been thrilled to see her so happy, raising his old-fashioned dimpled pint glass to her silently when he caught her eye from his booth.

But it had mostly been Eddie's eye that she was catching. As she hung her red anorak on the pegs out the back when she arrived for a shift, she leaned in to see if he was already there, behind the bar. As she wiped the bar down and 'accidentally' touched the edge of his hand, resting by the tap for the Adnams. As she put the last of the chairs up on the tables at the end of the night, they would turn the jukebox on for twenty minutes of dancing while they finished evening shutdown.

And it was on one of those nights, after they had spent half an hour singing their hearts out – 'Brown Sugar', 'Proud Mary', even 'Chirpy Chirpy Cheep Cheep' – that Eddie offered to drive her home.

'But it's out of your way,' Suzie said, knowing that it was, and unsure how to interpret such an offer.

'Yes,' Eddie shrugged. 'But it's cold out there.'

'Well if it's the cold you're worried about, just get me a scarf for Christmas.' Yet again, Suzie reeled at the audacity with which Eddie made her flirt.

'Oh, I think I can do a little better than that, can't I? What have I got, thirty shopping days left? Enough for something special.'

For once, she was speechless.

'And anyway, I *want* to drive you home,' he continued, as he flicked the lights off, leaving them standing alone, at the back of the bar, in the dark.

The music wasn't off though, and as Al Green's 'Tired of Being Alone' came on, he leaned around to the stairs that led to Pat's flat upstairs and called out. 'We're heading off in a minute, Pat, all tidy down here!' She called her thanks back down, and the song played out as Eddie helped Suzie with her coat, holding it out for her to put her arms in, before facing her and doing it up. As the zip reached the top, he rested his hand on her collarbone for a second, and she dipped her head so his forefinger touched her chin. Then, at last, he leaned in to kiss her.

Suzie, who had never dared consider more than a peck on the cheek from one of the lads from the local grammar school, could not believe that this was happening to her. She buckled into his arms, finally understanding the true meaning of *swoon*, a word she clearly remembered looking up while reading a Barbara Cartland novel as a bookish twelve-year-old. Something she had never imagined might lie inside her was now awake, alive, and she never wanted the world to go back to how it used to be.

After that first kiss, she would have done anything for Eddie. Men weren't the snakes her mum so often suggested they were – why would anyone not want to live like this? It was all so exciting! Especially the day that the pub had had a power cut and the two of them had found themselves with a spare Sunday and no plans, so Eddie had driven her to Aldeburgh, where they had waited until the beach was deserted then run into the sea with their trousers and skirts off, him kissing her while she felt the wind in her hair. She had felt alive when she was with him, as if small-town life wasn't all that was on offer. The future wasn't just going to be midwifery training, a job at the local hospital and slowly congealing roast dinners at her parents' on a Sunday, while the carriage clock on the mantelpiece ticked loudly in the gaps between conversation.

Daydreams about her new future unfurled all around

Suzie like ferns in the spring. She understood the regularity of their co-ordinated shifts at the pub, plus his enthusiasm for driving her home, to mean that they were in a steady relationship, and dared to tell herself she had a boyfriend at last. Freedom was within touching distance, and she was breathless with anticipation.

All these decades later, it seemed so obvious that Eddie had never done anything to suggest he was a real partner. He knew that she knew he was off abroad soon. And with hindsight, he had never really hidden the fact that he was driving out of his way each night for a chance to smooch in the car in the dark on the way back. A smooch, and then fondle, and then after New Year's Eve, once the pub was all closed up and the snow was gently falling outside . . . so much more. He had snuck an undrunk bottle of Babycham from the bar into his big coat pocket, and they had wriggled into the back seat of his dad's Rover, drinking the sweet fizz from a couple of tin camping mugs he had in the boot. Suzie thought that that night was the beginning of the rest of her life – and in so many ways it was. As his warm hard moved up and under her corduroy skirt, finding the waistband of her tights, she had never considered that it meant anything other than Eddie's greatest demonstration yet of his passion for her.

It was certainly passion. As he unzipped his jeans and found his way on top of her while the car radio carried on playing Stevie Wonder quietly, there had been no doubt it was passion. Just not as Suzie had understood it.

She thought he was passionate about *her*, about being with her, about building a life with her – rather than simply brimming with urges of a young man in a small space with a woman who was not saying no. And to his delight, she had continued not to say no.

A few weeks later when she had realised how late her period was, then thought back to that night in the car – not to mention the many that had followed – Suzie had not even been especially scared to tell Eddie what she suspected it meant. Of course she had been nervous, but it was tinged with excitement. It was much sooner than either of them might have chosen, but this was the *start* of something, not the end, wasn't it? And she wasn't going to ask him not to go to Canada, just to suggest that she might go too. That the three of them could head off on the adventure together. Instead, he stared straight ahead, the white of his knuckles showing as he gripped the steering wheel tight.

'I'm so sorry, Suz,' he'd said quietly. 'I should have been more careful.'

She could have cried with relief at his kindness.

'Shall I ask my dad for some money to get it sorted?' he asked. The car was stationary but he was still looking straight ahead, avoiding her gaze. For a few moment or two, Suzie hadn't understood what he was saying.

'You mean . . . ?'

'Well it's legal now, isn't it? And I'm off to Canada soon. Don't want to leave you in a pickle.'

He leaned over and stroked the side of her face.

Seconds later, a tear fell down the same path his finger had taken. Suzie had never imagined that the line between kindness and cruelty might be so very slim.

'Oh,' she said, her voice hoarse. She gulped to try and hold back the sobs. 'Yes, I suppose so.'

But in the couple of weeks that followed, Eddie never mentioned anything about his dad, or what they were going to do. During their shared shifts at the pub he was chattier, more charming than ever with the punters, leaving little time for the whispered asides and giggles that she had become so used to sharing with him. At the end of the shift, he always seemed to have an excuse not to drive her home, even going so far as to call her a cab himself one night when the grim February sleet was lashing down outside. Again, Suzie reeled at how charm could be wielded like a blade, dazzling but utterly cold and unmistakably sharp.

Then one day, after not seeing him for almost a week, Suzie plucked up the courage to ask Pat when Eddie's next shift was. She daren't even look her in the eye as she spoke, slowly, deliberately peeling a beer mat apart as she waited for her answer.

'He's gone, love,' said Pat, with a shift of her bosom. 'Off to Canada early apparently.'

Suzie thought her legs were going to go from beneath her.

'He's left for Canada?' she whispered.

'Yes love, I'm sorry. I know you were soft on him.' Pat reached out her hand and rested it on Suzie's forearm for a minute. She patted it briefly, the light glinting off her long crimson nails.

Slowly, Suzie swept the tiny pieces of shredded cardboard from the bar and dropped the remnants of the beer mat in the bin. As she watched them fall, she realised the depth of her predicament. She had thought she was on the precipice of escape, only now she was more trapped than ever. It was all over. And it wasn't just her he had left behind. She stared down at the bin, blinking, hoping that no one had seen that single fat tear drop down into it.

'That's what rich kids can do, I guess,' continued Pat, who had at least had the decently not to look at her directly while she felt her entire body numb with shock. 'Bugger off when they get a bit bored.'

'Rich kids?' Suzie asked.

'Well, he didn't need to be working here, did he? His dad's a hot shot at the brewery, and a local councillor. I think the lad just wanted a job to get out of the house and away from having to spend all day talking about bloody Harold Wilson and what have you.'

'Oh, I see,' said Suzie. And suddenly so much made sense. She had never been a proper girlfriend, someone Eddie might introduce to his dad. She was the girl from the local. The bit of fun 'til he started living his real life.

When her dad was playing golf that Sunday morning, Suzie took a deep breath and told her mum what had happened. And not just what had happened, but that she knew how badly she had let her and her father down, how she knew she had to change. There, on the sofa in the front room, with the carriage clock marking every second with its incessant tick, tick, tick, she waited for her mother's response. And while she did so, she promised herself that from now on she would be good. She would be nice. She would do the right thing.

It was this moment that she had come back to over and over again for the last fifty years. And sometimes, when the loneliness of her promise had closed in around her, it had felt as if Her Majesty might be the only person in the world who could possibly understand the infinite burden of endlessly trying to do the right thing.

Oh, the absolute torture of having to choose what drinks the others might want. Suzie had just mentioned 'a hot drink' and sent him on his way, which left Tim back at the counter of WatchHouse, in front of a menu of highly specific types of coffee while realising he had no idea what anyone would want. Trying to divine their choices based on the two hours he'd known them felt like making painful judgements about them. He wasn't a psychotherapist or an astrologer, he was just a guy getting hot drinks, for heaven's sake. He couldn't go back empty-handed though, so he'd ordered an Earl Grey for Suzie, a large hot chocolate for Abbie, and then a hastily chosen almond croissant for Howie, to whom he wanted to make some sort of thank you gesture for rescuing his gloves.

He had not been so naive as to expect the day to be without emotion, but he had imagined that maybe it would be more straightforward, more obvious emotion. Last night, as he'd been preparing his kit for the morning, he'd run through the risks of coming down to the queue, and of course he had taken on board the idea that he'd spend much of the time thinking about loss. About family. About change. But at no point while he'd been deftly winding his spare charger cable ready for state storage in his rucksack had he thought he'd be prompted to think so much about his own past. Or his own loss.

As he'd stood there at the coffee shop counter, he'd remembered going to the bar as a teenager in his local pub, having gamely offered to get 'a round in' for some of the locals lads. As he'd approached the gleaming wood, the bar man – one of the lads' older brothers – standing behind it grinning, he'd felt as if he were heading to the firing squad. He had no idea what anyone wanted. And he was still legally a couple of years too young to be drinking, so there seemed to be double the pressure not to fluff it and get thrown out. With each step, he felt more keenly aware that all he really wanted was a shandy and to go home and watch the latest episode of *Prime Suspect* with his mum. But he was equally conscious that to admit that would be a red rag to a bull to those boys. It wasn't that he was properly 'out', or that they were ever truly cruel to him. It was more that by never having had a girlfriend, and by never having bothered to pretend he wanted one, some sort of deadline had passed, and his school peers just seemed to know he was queer, as instinctively as he now knew it.

At first, he'd felt relieved that there wasn't going to have to be some big dramatic moment or announcement. But as time had passed, he'd realised that by not saying anything himself, he had allowed his friends, or at least his male peers, to remain silent as well. They simply talked over him when they were discussing crushes, dalliances or full-on relationships. They simply never asked whether there was anything going on for him. Collectively, they simply never allowed space for any of them to discuss the differences between them.

It was only in recent years that Tim had come to see that the lads weren't being purposefully hurtful, and perhaps they hadn't even seen the cruelty in their behaviour. After all, this had been the 1990s – thanks to Section 28, they were all being educated in an environment where it really was illegal for schools to discuss queer lives in any way. But no matter how much he could understand it now, it had felt like cruelty at the time. That silence, that endless lonely silence, where a misordered pint could speak a thousand words, had left scar tissue for Tim. Keloid scars which never seemed to ease, social situations still prompting unpredictable anxiety in him when he least expected it. So he had tended to create as safe a life as possible around himself – swaddling his daily existence with endless facts lest he should hit an awkward silence, avoiding experiences which might prove too unpredictable, and wherever possible, staying in environments where he might not have to confront extremes of emotion. And it had worked. For a while.

Tim heard his name being called by the barista and startled himself out of his thoughts. He shook himself back to the present, thanking the staff profusely and heading back to the queue. Now he had a hot drink in each hand and the pastry in a paper bag between his teeth, and was making his way along the queue until he came to any faces he recognised. He'd been gone a good twenty minutes but the queuers seemed to have kept up a steady pace, so much so that he could not quite work out where his gang been. It was only when a child ran out, chasing a brightly crisp packet dancing in the wind that he realised the child was Fred, who had been just behind them. Working forward from him, he spotted Suzie, still alone, her face down. She looked deep in concentration, morose even. God, he hoped she liked tea.

He scuttled the remaining distance to catch her up before trying to call her name. But, with the paper bag in his mouth, it was harder than he'd anticipated.

'Hi dere! Shushie!'

She turned to look at him, her face a slow smile.

'Oh well done, Tim,' she said, reaching out to help him with his delivery. 'Let me take that.'

Tim released the pastry bag into her hand before passing her the tea, explaining that he'd got her an Earl Grey.

'Oh, you shouldn't have ...' she protested. But she looked delighted. Perhaps she was like him: just one of those people who others didn't generally go out of their way for.

'It was a pleasure,' he replied. And as she cupped her hands around it, he realised that it really was. 'How are you feeling? Not too tired?'

'I must admit the early start is beginning to catch up with me.'

'I can imagine – you came a lot further than me and my back's really starting to feel it.'

'Oh yes, it's a killer. And my feet are aching like hell, even though I'm wearing my old-lady shoes.' Suzie chuckled at him, delighted by her own description of her shoes. Tim joined in with chuckles, but only just – terrified that he might seem to be laughing *at* her.

Another police helicopter roared overhead, causing at least half of the queue to look up and watch its progress down the length of the queue towards Westminster. As Tim looked into the distance, he noticed that buildings across the river were bedecked in red, white and blue, that bunting seemed to be everywhere now that they were on the route that was making the headlines. Did it make him feel less lonely that he wasn't the only one feeling shaken by this strange last week? Or was his creeping sense that he might be feeling the wrong sorts of sad making him feel even lonelier? He wiped some damp from his eye, turning away from the helicopter and inwards to face the South Bank once again.

'It's all feeling a bit real now, isn't it?'

'Yes, until the last half hour or so, I suspect I half

thought this was just something happening on the telly,' he replied, curious at his own sudden honesty.

'It might sound silly but I almost feel like I have butterflies in my stomach. As if I'm expected to, I don't know, *do* something.'

'Yes, it's a funny sort of anxiety isn't it. But I suppose the being here is the doing something, isn't it. Paying tribute.'

'Absolutely, I *am* glad I'm here,' Suzie added. 'It's the right thing to do.'

'I do feel like half the country think we're mad though,' Tim replied, his unease at being part of the 'devoted masses' creeping up on him. 'Then again, half this country constantly thinks the other half is mad.'

Suzie chuckled. 'Precisely. It's the only thing we actually have in common with each other!'

The pair of them laughed again, the moment of unprompted and unexpected honesty mercifully passing.

'I hope Howie and Abbie are OK. Maisie wasn't looking too clever, was she?'

'She was not. She was a fool to have come at all.'

Suzie pursed her lips and stared ahead. Was she judging him for gossiping about Maisie, or making an effort not to gossip about her herself? She'd never know, because to her great relief, the sound of Howie's unmistakeable accent was now booming from behind them.

'What's up guys!' he was calling out, his arm casually slung round Abbie's shoulders. 'Young Abbie here says I'm part of your queue family now, as my spot was so far up ahead I'm not sure I can go back to join them without some tricky questions.'

Suzie smiled at them, her guard most definitely back up again. Abbie, however, looked thrilled.

'Well . . . welcome,' said Tim, holding out the hot chocolate and pastry towards them. 'Let's hope things get a bit calmer now.'

'I was just saying to Abs here that you guys seem like where the action's at, so don't get *too* boring on me . . .' The four of them shared a round of polite laughter. 'Anyway, I've got your names, and I know Abbie's a fashion student, but what do you guys do? For work and all that?'

'I'm retired now,' said Suzie, 'but only just.' Tim longed to know more about Suzie's career but as ever the moment seemed to move on before he had plucked up the courage to ask.

'And what about you, Howie? Are you a visitor to these shores?'

'Absolutely not, Timbo!'

Tim blinked very fast.

'I'm more of a Brit than the rest of you guys!' Again, Tim found himself marvelling at the way Howie seemed to actively relish his own accent. *The rest of you gooyyys.*

'I just grew up in Oz, but my ma and pa are actually pure Brits. And more than that, I used to work at the palace.'

Suzie raised an eyebrow. 'Which palace?'

'*The* palace. Big Buck House.'

'No way!' said Abbie. 'How on earth?!'

'Well it's a tale as old as time,' continued Howie. 'Aussie guy comes to London and gets a job in the service industry.'

'But at the palace? Like an actual . . . servant?' Abbie's jaw was still agape.

'It's as good a job as any,' said Howie. 'Waiting tables – ultimate edition, really.'

'*Nooooooo.*'

'Yes.' Howie was grinning again.

'What was it like?'

'It was a great job actually – I did it for years.'

'Did you meet *her*?' Thank heavens for Abbie, asking the questions that Tim would never have dared to.

'Well "meet" might be putting it a bit strongly, but yeah, we'd see her when she came to check on things, before big events and the like.'

Even Suzie was smiling now, biting her bottom lip a little as she did so. Had she noticed Abbie's disbelief at why anyone would want to work at a royal palace?

'Oh how wonderful, what an opportunity,' she said.

'You know what, it was. I met a great bunch of people and some pretty interesting visitors too.'

'Celebrities?' asked Abbie.

'More like heads of state and such, but yeah, a few celebrities.'

'Who?! Who?! Tell!' The hot chocolate had obviously hit, as Abbie was now more animated than she had been at any point so far today, all but smacking her lips at the thought of celebrity gossip.

'To be honest, the best part of it wasn't the celebrities, it was the dogs.'

'What, the—?'

'Yeah, the corgis. I got to walk them sometimes. Just take them out for a little while, into the grounds.'

'You're *kidding*.'

'I'm not kidding. They were great dogs. Couldn't have been more loved.'

Howie gave Abbie a squeeze, and she looked up at him, her eyes still like saucers. Tim felt something close to envy at their easy cuddle, Howie's broad tanned hand on her shoulder.

'I really can't believe this,' said Abbie. 'I thought it was going to be such a grim day, and now I've found you guys.'

Tim watched as Suzie shifted her gaze to Abbie. She pulled her jacket a little closer to herself, taking a little breath before she spoke.

'I don't suppose it would have been the worst thing in the world not to be having an actual party all day. After all, we *are* queuing to pay our respects to someone who devoted her whole life to serving the country . . .'

Abbie's face fell. She shifted uncomfortably, straightening her slight slouch, her inwardly turned toes.

'No, I didn't mean it like that, I just – you know, the standing around and everything.'

'It's just, I suppose we could do worse than to remember that people do go through harder things than standing around for a day,' replied Suzie.

Her voice was not hard, nor angry, but her face was

still, insistent. She was standing straight up, her feet slightly apart, indomitable, determined to be heard.

'I know, I absolutely know that. I'm sorry, Suzie, I didn't mean it to be, like, disrespectful. It's just, you know, a long time. Like, famously so – it's on the news and stuff.'

'I'm sure you didn't mean to be disrespectful, Abigail. But still. Perhaps it's a good moment to remind ourselves why we're here.'

Tim found himself instinctively staring at the pavement, in the hopes that perhaps it might open up and provide some sort of hatch for him to disappear into, the women forgetting he had ever met either of them. It wasn't that he didn't agree with the point that Suzie was making, more that he was startled that she had dared to vocalise it, especially when she'd been being so chummy only a little while ago. Poor old Abbie had just tried to do her best by her friend. He glanced up, catching Howie's eye. Should one of them say something? Try to smooth things over? And *why* was he the one blushing?

It seemed pretty clear that Abbie was turning herself inside out with shame and Suzie was also looking as if she was realising she'd gone too far. How was it possible to be surrounded by crowds, yet be enduring a silence as loud as any he'd known?

The paper cup was now cold against her hand, her hot chocolate long gone. She wanted nothing more than to vanish. To simply not be there. It wasn't just that Abbie knew she had been disrespectful, whingeing on about boring old queueing, but that she had done it in front of Suzie, who she had thought was lovely. From the minute she'd seen her, she had thought that she would probably be better off chatting to Suzie about knitting than trying to impress Annabelle, but she'd been too much of a sap to do anything about it, instead getting embroiled in Maisie's drama and now branding herself the petulant fool of the group. Ugh.

She watched as Suzie carefully tucked a strand of hair behind her ear, no longer staring directly at her but now looking forward to see where the queue was winding next. There were swarms of people everywhere now. Young families, older folk bundled up against the wind, couples heading to the museums arm in arm. And there seemed to be litter blowing everywhere in the breeze. Abbie watched as a piece of plastic wrapping was whipped up and over the wall towards the river. That poor river, she thought, it must be so full of plastic. Never mind that, she told herself, it was time to make amends.

'I agree,' she said, leaning in towards Suzie. 'And I am sorry. Here – shall I take your cup? Let me take them to the bin.'

'Thank you, dear,' said Suzie. She gave her a small smile. Enough to encourage her that they had reached a truce? Abbie took the cup, lifting the lid from her own and stacking the two of them.

'Any word from your daughter yet? Is she having a lovely birthday?'

'Yes,' replied Suzie. Her smile broader now. 'Her teenagers made her breakfast in bed, and apparently she's still there – watching the news in her pyjamas!'

'Oh good for her,' replied Abbie, her smile equally wide now that she sensed she really was forgiven. 'Tell her to look out for us on the TV – you'll have to text her if any of the news crews come along this way.'

'You're right, I shall do – good thinking!'

'I'll keep an eye out with you.' Abbie placed a hand on Suzie's arm, slightly wishing she could give the older woman a hug. She looked quite tired now out here in the breeze. 'Either way, I'm sure she's very proud of you,' she said. There, that should do it.

5

Blackfriars Bridge

This time, she really had told a lie. A string of them now.

But despite everything, in that moment it had felt like the kindest thing to do. She had been too harsh on the girl – who *had* after all been trying to help her friend, hadn't she? And poor old Abbie wasn't wrong, it *had* been a good few hours on their feet now. Hadn't she herself just been discussing it with Tim? Abbie had simply been trying to make a similar sort of chit-chat, albeit a bit dazzled by this Howie fellow's big reveal. So, Suzie now saw, she should have been kinder. She should not have brought her own melancholy, her own wallowing in memories, into things.

Colin, for all his love of business jargon – 'factors', 'eventualities', 'rationalisations' – had always reminded her of this. A deceptively empathic man, his favourite aphorism when she was letting off steam after a hard day at work was that 'we can't know what someone else's journey to today has been.' He'd say it gently, while she was grouching about how unreasonable someone had been in the warehouse, or how she felt her mum's GP wasn't paying proper attention to something, and it had wound her up no end at the time. He'd come up behind her while she was making dinner and massage her shoulders while he said it, his mouth close to her ear in what was an attempt at intimacy. But she'd find it infuriating, hunching her shoulders right up to her ears, trying to shrug him off, crunching her face up in displeasure. She'd complain about his coffee breath, or his cold hands, missing the point entirely.

How she wished he was there now, to loosen up her shoulders where they'd been hunched against the cold. To make her laugh when the blue mood started to creep up on her. He'd been right all along. Suzie just wished that she herself could have been more honest with him over the years about the journey *she* had taken to today.

'Either way, I'm sure she's very proud of you.'

If only.

Suzie yearned that, even if just for one day, even if not right until the end, Colin could have known about the moment she had eventually told her mum about Eddie and the baby. Maybe he wouldn't have been appalled, as she had feared for all those years. Maybe he would have been kind about the way that her mother's first response had been to tell her to keep the situation quiet. That she would sort things out as long as it was all kept secret – especially from her father and her grandparents. Maybe, after all, he might have held her hand as she told him about what her mother had actually meant about 'sorting it all out'. Because back then Suzie had thought that 'dealing with it' was no longer against the law – but she hadn't known that you had to get two doctors to give you permission for an abortion, and that they didn't always do that if you were young, fit and healthy. She had had no idea that she would lose a whole summer, and then so much more.

So many times Suzie had imagined the look of horror on Colin's face if she told him about the morning she left for the mother and baby home. She had never been to Wales before, but once her bump was too big to hide under loose dresses, her mum made her a packed lunch not dissimilar to today's and waved her off on the train. The journey had taken hours, her back had been stiff as a board by the time she had arrived, her hips seizing up as she tried to stand, tentatively carrying her case off the train at the small local railway station. It was early evening, and the village looked beautiful despite the warm summer drizzle. For a second she was relieved to breathe fresh air, to no longer be trying to conceal her new curves. She'd never seen anywhere so green! Then, as the taxi pulled up outside of the forbidding grey slate of the home, she remembered.

When it looked as if she and Colin wouldn't be able to have a baby of their own, when the bad news kept coming, she would lie there night after night, wrestling with how she might tell him about the way that as the pregnancy had progressed, she had longed to keep her first baby. And how her mother had closed down any discussion of the sort, making it quite clear that there was no question of that. Her father would have died of shame, she'd explained. And back then there was no financial support from the government, no childcare, no housing. Where would she have gone?

Suzie glanced over at Abbie, now hunched over her phone again. She seemed about the same age that Suzie had been that summer in Wales, but if she found herself in the same situation, the outcome would be incomparable. Suzie had waved goodbye to her family with a handful of books and a line about a summer job on a farm in the valleys. Instead, she'd arrived at the Salvation Army home and been set a daily round of general housework for the last few weeks before the baby came.

And here was Abbie going on about celebrities at the palace. She looked at the girl in her dungarees – was that a streak of pink in her hair? Oh god, she was probably judging Suzie right back. Why did the young get themselves so het up about these things that barely mattered these days? When Suzie was her age, she wasn't fretting about her social media profile. She was doing her very best to say as little as possible about her life, not to display it all out there for anyone to log on and have a good old gawp at. She was silently crying herself to sleep at night, hoping that none of her friends would ever find out how it was dawning on her that she was going to miss her baby every single day for the rest of her life, the pain nagging at her like a pulled muscle every time she tried to move forwards.

Because she did miss her daughter. When it came to it, she had been desperate to keep her, but had been told at every turn that not to give her up would have been selfish. Someone like her couldn't provide for a child, not with the welfare state, benefits and all that, the way they were back then – and then there was the shame she could have brought on her sweet parents. *She wasn't worthy*, that was the message she received back then. *Not a good girl.*

So she had got on with her chores at the home, working as a domestic really, until she finally went into labour. Then, almost immediately, the baby had been whisked away, her tiny fists barely having had time to uncurl and reach out to her. Bess. That's what she had named her. After Queen Elizabeth in her Margaret Irwin books. *Young Bess.* Her queen.

Suzie had begged to be allowed to breastfeed, but the nurses said it wouldn't be possible. Feeding the baby would be someone else's task, someone worthy of the job. No one said it out loud; the implication was enough. It was for the *real* parents. The rightful parents.

Instead, she would read her novels, her warm tears quietly splashing onto the page as she strained to hear if her baby was OK in the room next door, just out of reach. Then, once the adoptive parents had confirmed their choice of her daughter, the baby was collected, and Suzie was back on the train to Suffolk. It seemed unbelievable, when she reached home, that this could be the same life she had fitted into before. She looked down at her hands, folded in her lap as she sat in the front seat, and could not square the fact that they were the same ones which had clasped at the skin on Eddie's back fewer than ten months ago, then gripped at the metal sides of her hospital bed fewer than ten days ago. She turned them over, her nails clean, her palms white, innocent-looking. How could this be the same person? And where was Bess?

If her father had known where she had been, he'd never said. In truth, he never said much at all once she was back. As with so much else, it just left her wondering, always wondering.

Now, all these years later, the chance of anyone ever knowing about her daughter had slimmed to zero. When her mother had died a couple of years ago, so too had her secret. These days she passed through life wearing her age like a cloak of invisibility, knowing that people like Abbie would barely notice her, much less imagine that she had a past . . . secrets . . . regrets.

She looked back to Abbie. Perhaps she really did think that a day spent in a long queue was a hardship; perhaps she had not come up against much in her short life. Then again, what could she know about the things that Abbie had been through? Now she saw that instead of simply fiddling with her phone, the girl was wiping at her eyes, and now rummaging through pockets. Tim and Howie, busy in conversation, had not noticed at all.

'Are you OK, dear?' she asked gently.

Abbie pursed her lips together and nodded, her eyebrows knotted as if to say that if she opened her mouth now, she really would start sobbing. Tears were running down her cheeks. What on earth was the matter?

'Would you like a tissue?' Suzie asked, to which Abbie nodded urgently. Slowly, carefully, Suzie went into her bag and looked for her travel tissues. To her frustration, she saw that she had none, but had instead packed an old, sky blue handkerchief of Colin's. To her mild embarrassment she remembered that she had popped it in there last night, so that if she shed a tear in the Palace of Westminster and was caught on camera she'd look smart, put together, rather than scrabbling around with travel tissues.

This moment was more important though, and she instinctively handed the crisp hanky over to Abbie, who wiped her eyes with it, smearing the cotton with thick black mascara in an instant.

'I truly am sorry to have upset you,' said Suzie softly. 'It really was not my intention.'

'No, no it's not that,' replied Abbie, waving the hanky around as she spoke. 'I mean it was a *bit*, I suppose it just set me off really.'

'How do you mean?'

'Suzie, don't think I'm being rude—'

Suzie's eyebrows raised almost imperceptibly.

'Go on . . .'

'But you remind me of my own grandma. After you, well, you know – told me off – I just couldn't stop thinking about my gran.'

Suzie reached her arm out and patted Abbie's. Now that she had been given permission to cry, Abbie didn't seem to be able to stop. She was blowing her nose into the handkerchief now, huge honking blows as her shoulders juddered.

'You don't need to apologise for thinking I might be a similar age to your grandmother! I'm not so vain that I thought you had me pegged as a thirty-year-old . . .'

Abbie started to giggle. She looked so much younger now that half her make-up was gone.

'Suzie! No, this is the bit I didn't want you to be offended by – so promise me OK?'

Suzie nodded, encouraging her to go on. Abbie's smile cracked and fresh tears came. 'She's dead!' she wailed, a strange high-pitched noise which made Suzie flinch with embarrassment.

Queuers around them turned to see what the upset was. A few people ahead was a chic northern European-looking couple in almost identical padded navy blue jackets belted neatly around the waist. Suzie had noticed them earlier and noted how smart they looked, how well middle-aged people on the continent dressed. Now, they were looking on in mild but discreet horror. This was clearly not how they had imagined the Brits would grieve for their queen. The husband put his arm around his wife protectively, as if this unruly display of emotion might be catching.

In turn, Suzie put her arm around Abbie. She hadn't touched anyone like this for so long. There wasn't anyone left to hug these days. After an initial flinch at the closeness, and a little shock at herself for having made such a move, the warmth of another human felt soft. Reassuring. Lovely. She even tried not to wince at the thought of a second smear of Abbie's eye make-up ending up down the front of her own coat.

'Oh my dear, what a horrible thing to go through,' she said, stroking the mass of curls on the back of Abbie's head. 'I'm not offended in the slightest. Did she die . . . recently?'

'Four years ago . . .' came the answer.

Oh. Suzie had been expecting something a *little* more recent.

'. . . but it was honestly the worst thing that's ever happened to me. And I don't know why it's making me cry so much now. It was bad enough when the Queen died. The memories. I mean I didn't even care about her *that* much, you know, day-to-day or whatever . . .'

Suzie was acutely aware that others were catching snippets of this conversation, trying to keep an eye out so no one was upset by Abbie's somewhat frank outburst.

'. . . but it was like she was all of our grannies wasn't it? So *that's* why I wanted to come today. I was too scared to come by myself, so I ended up coming with Annabelle and Maisie, and now I've bloody been left by myself to stand in the cold, *yet again*. Thinking about Grandma Lucy *yet again*. It's just, *a lot*, y'know?'

It certainly was a lot. Suzie took a breath. And thought of Colin.

'We can't ever predict how grief is going to affect us,' she told Abbie gently, whose head was still on her shoulder.

This was another of Colin's pearls of wisdom. She remembered him writing it in a card a week or two after her father had died. He had slowly, silently passed it across the breakfast table on the day of the funeral, not even pausing to stop munching his toast. At the time Suzie had been baffled by the idea of someone writing a card to the person they shared a house, a home, a breakfast table with. Colin having to write it down had left her frustrated, borderline annoyed – why did he need to commit it to paper rather than look her in the eye and just say it? Why couldn't he hold her in the small of the night and whisper it into her ear?

It was only years later that she'd realised he had probably bought the card and written its considered message so that she could keep it. So that it could be there for her.

It felt good in Suzie's arms, it really did. She smelled faintly of the same soap that Grandma Lucy used to, making Abbie want to ask what it was so she could buy some and smell it when she felt low.

The best thing about this cuddle was the stillness, the quiet, the sense that Suzie didn't seem to need to chat. There had never been anyone since Grandma Lucy who had felt as calm as this. And there had been nothing like going round to Grandma Lucy's when she was a kid. She lived closer to the seafront than her mum and dad, in a little basement flat that she'd had for years – since her husband had died when Abbie was a baby. It felt like time stopped when you headed over there. A haven. Once Abbie was eleven or so, she was allowed to walk round there by herself and each time she did, it was an intoxicating slice of independence. Sometimes she dreamed that a busybody would stop her and ask what she was doing, just so she could reply with the delicious sentence, 'Oh I'm just popping round to Henfield Villas, by myself.'

When she got there, her heart still racing a little from the thrill of the fifteen-minute walk all alone, Abbie would walk across the smart Victorian black and white paving which led down from the immaculate white villa above, then head down the stone steps to Grandma's front door. She'd rap the big brass knocker then wait for the smile as she opened the door.

'Abigail!' she'd say, wrapping her arm round her. 'Here you are!'

Her knuckles were just starting to get a little lumpy with arthritis, but her hand never felt any different as it patted Abbie's back, making sure that first hug lasted just a little longer. That stillness felt like a sort of rest from the chaos of home, each and every time.

It always smelled amazing there. Not just clean, but fresh. Sometimes it would be because Grandma was baking something – just a handful of cookies or a loaf of bread – but other times it was the scent of her tiny herb garden balanced on the front window. Because it was a basement flat, she didn't have much a view, instead filling the windowsill that looked out onto the stone steps with pots of basil, rosemary, mint and more. By midsummer the mint would be unruly, taking up half the window, with bunches more of it in the kitchen, waiting to be used in tea, in Abbie's water glass, in anything she could think of. And by winter, once the summer's basil was used up, the rosemary would come inside to the kitchen, being snipped at when vegetables were roasted or her risotto needed what she called 'a little oomph'. At the first hint of spring there would be tiny yellow and white daffodils on the coffee table, by Easter they would be replaced by hyacinths, and later in the year there would be lilies, the orange pollen perched precariously on the stamen, ready to stain anyone who moved too fast, too frantically in Grandma's sanctuary.

And it *was* a sanctuary. Because as things became more fraught between Abbie's parents – arguments about bills, contracts and potential deals overheard from behind the flimsy kitchen door – the more she needed the escape to Grandma Lucy's. Life had felt so precarious at home since Dad had lost his job, every conversation a potential source of friction. In some ways, Abbie could tell that her mum was doing her best; it was just that doing her best didn't leave much space in her life for the things that Abbie really needed. When her dad's business had folded, her mum had picked up the slack on the work front – and as the years passed and Abbie made her way into adulthood, she really could appreciate the sacrifice and hard work that this must have taken. But for her mum it meant long hours, and constantly having to impress her boss. She seemed terrified of being one of 'those women' in the office who was always heading home early because of the kids, citing inset days as a reason not to do as much as everyone else or simply being ignored if she wasn't constantly visible, dazzling. So, under the pressure to keep things afloat financially, she never took time off over the holidays, she saved obsessively, and made sure that the house was always immaculate, that no one might ever realise how precarious things had been and still might be.

This left little time for bedside chats about boys, or periods, let along the bigger, harder to grasp subjects such as Abbie's hopes and dreams about what sort of a woman she might become, what sort of a job she might one day have, what sort of a life she might long for. She loved Abbie, there was never any doubt about that, but by the time she hit her teens, Abbie had simply stopped asking if she would be there for the school trip, or the Christmas concert. She would be too busy, wouldn't she? Somewhere along the way, her mum seemed to have interpreted the not being asked as not being wanted, letting a stalemate creep up on them.

Her dad, meanwhile, was crippled by the shame of it all, meaning he was even less keen to be one of those fun parents at the school gate. He had never really wanted to be a businessman, and had taken over his father's firm as a young man, only to discover that he was no salesman. In fact the whole experience had been an anathema to him, from the networking to the sales pitches, and it took him several years of clawing his way out of depression before he finally began work as a ranger on the South Downs, out in nature at last, doing something that he felt was genuinely useful. He might not have been great with people, but he really was great with animals and plants. It's just that that wasn't much good to a thirteen-year-old feeling increasingly lost about her place in the world.

It was during these years of loneliness and instability that Abbie cherished her visits to Grandma Lucy's flat the most. It wasn't that she was rich, or that the problems weren't still there when Abbie got home, but that Grandma's was a place where she didn't have to talk. She didn't have to pretend she hadn't heard, or that she still thought things were OK. She could sit by the oil heater, the drip-drip noise of it warming up as the opening music to *Strictly* fired up and Grandma appeared with some sausages and mash, and just let the whirring in her mind slow for an hour or two. She didn't have to explain why she wanted to leave Worthing as quickly as she possibly could. She didn't have to explain why her trainers were the knock-off ones everyone in her class knew had been in the discount store on the high street last month. She didn't have to fit in.

It was here, in the quiet of Grandma's flat, that Abbie had discovered her love of making things. It had started with watching her knit, socks magically appearing from beneath four small double pointed needles, and before long Abbie was having a go too, making hats and scarves, then jumpers – first for Sunnie's new baby brother and then for her own little brother, and at last, herself.

Then she tried sewing, saving for a sewing machine to keep at Grandma's where they would experiment together with quilt making, then fabric cutting and so much more. At first, her parents had simply been happy that she was quiet, busy, not always at the skate park where they were constantly worried she would be offered drugs, or talking to people they didn't know. (Which always struck Abbie as rather unfair, given they barely knew *any* of her friends.)

It was only when Abbie started to take it seriously, to talk about designing her own pieces, perhaps one day selling them online, and maybe even working in fashion herself, that they had started to panic. Neither of them had a problem with fashion per se. It was the prospect of their precious firstborn working in a creative field, and one with so much potential for instability, that had sent them into a spiral.

Her mum had been outright hostile to the idea, trying to close down any discussion of it when the time came for Abbie to look at what she might do for her GCSEs, A levels and beyond. Her dad was more sympathetic to her ambitions, but feared the insecurity of it all, sheepishly mentioning how troublesome he had found having to be his own boss, a constant salesman.

'I don't not want you to do it,' he had tried to explain. 'It's that I don't think you understand how hard it will be.'

They had been on a walk up to Chanctonbury Ring one late summer's evening, when they both knew Grandma was already ill, but neither of them dared to discuss it out loud. Abbie had had another exhausting argument with her mum, who was still insisting that neither of her parents were going to provide any funds if it were fashion she chose to study at university.

'It's like you *want* me to be miserable,' Abbie had declared with a slam of her bedroom door. The door was still reverberating in its frame when she realised that what she had said was probably hurtful, but she was at a loss as to how to back down. Especially when her mother responded with, 'Well that'll make two of us.'

Days like these had made the dream of London and its creative communities seem more urgent than ever. Even her dad trying to broker some sort of peace only made her frustration at his lack of self-belief feel all the keener. Surely all it would take was to dream bigger than him! To want it more! To just meet the right people!

It was this annoyance that she would try to relate to Grandma when she would inevitably end up back at hers, the two of them carefully choosing embroidery thread for the restoration of a chair they'd found at a car boot sale, or trying to figure out how to make a knitting pattern fit exactly as they wanted without interrupting the pattern. These quiet, constructive times were where her dreams felt valid. Where what the two of them were doing felt like a skill, not a pastime.

The growing shakiness in her grandmother's hands was getting harder to ignore though. So Abbie spent more time with her, trying to keep both of them distracted from what they saw coming as the illness progressed. And while the two of them busied their fingers, Grandma Lucy encouraged her to keep trying, to keep experimenting, to keep taking it all seriously – and to work from there. She taught her not to be afraid of unravelling twelve rows of Fair Isle work or to carefully unpick a piece of embroidery that turned out not to have been perfectly straight.

'Take it a stitch at a time,' she would tell Abbie, 'and wait for the beauty to reveal itself.'

So Abbie would continue, confidence restored, dreams back within reach. And the next time there was an argument she'd be back there, her canvas bag of threads with her, the two of them stitching away once more.

'Respect the craft, and it will respect you,' Grandma told her, the last time she said goodbye to Abbie, encouraging her to just keep going, and that in the end her dedication would convince her parents.

Two weeks later she was gone, and with her a beacon of hope and constancy in Abbie's life.

As the helicopters whirred overhead, now, for the first time in years – and certainly for the first time since she had moved to London – Abbie felt an echo of that stillness, that constancy, that she had once known in Grandma Lucy's arms. Despite the chatter of the crowds, the flapping of the pigeons and the endless shuffle forward of the queue itself, for a moment she felt at home in Suzie's embrace.

'Thank you so much,' she said into the fuzz of Suzie's scarf.

'You are quite alright, sweetheart,' replied Suzie.

'I imagine days like today bring out all sorts of feelings in all sorts of people – even those who think they weren't that "bothered" by the Queen.'

Abbie felt Suzie's hand stroke the back of her hair, all those promises she had made her grandma suddenly seeming a little less futile.

'I know, right? Grandma was just . . . always there. And then she wasn't. And this last week or so, it's felt kind of the same. As if the walls of everything have got a little wobbly all over again.'

'Yes, that's exactly how it's felt for me too,' replied Suzie. 'But I've had moments like these before, and they pass. I promise you, they pass. And each little one really does help you get a tiny bit stronger.'

'Oh I hope so,' said Abbie, suddenly a little shy about her outburst, slightly aware that others around them might have been listening. 'Anyway, how about that daughter of yours? Any more news since her fancy breakfast in bed?'

Suzie smiled and went to check her phone.

'I remember doing breakfast in bed for my mum one year,' Abbie told her. 'It wasn't a good breakfast – we had bits of shell in the eggs, and had cut the apple up with a normal bread knife; it was only me and my brother doing it as my dad was having one of his bad days. But she was so happy.'

'Of course she was, she would have been thrilled.'

'It's one of the last times I can remember my mum being really relaxed actually. Enough about that though – what children does your daughter have then? Are they old enough to make a decent spread?' asked Abbie, suddenly hungry for distraction outside of today, the queue, her own feelings.

'Well,' said Suzie, before taking a big breath. 'She has a boy and a girl. They're nearly teenagers now. Charlie – Charlotte – is the girl, and she's twelve. And her little brother Robbie is ten, nearly eleven. She had them quite late, you see. She had a fair bit of a struggle getting pregnant, but fertility treatments have moved on so much now, she stuck it out and she got her family.'

'That's lovely, they must love their granny.'

'Yes, they do—'

'Probably because of all the treats. I bet you're just the kind to be slipping extra chocolate sauce on their ice cream and all that!'

Suzie made a mock shocked face. 'How dare you!' She laughed, before another pause. 'I missed them something rotten the last couple of years.'

'Do they live far away then? No "socially distant" coffees on benches?'

'Yes, they're in Wales. In the most beautiful village. It's so green there that at first you can't believe it. Then you realise it rains absolutely all the time and that's why.'

'That *is* a long way,' said Abbie. 'A really long way. Did they move for your daughter's work? Or her partner's work or something?'

'Well the kids' dad, Eddie, he pushed off to Canada a few years ago. Fat lot of use he was anyway, if I'm honest.

But then Bess – that's my daughter, Elizabeth – she met . . .'

Suzie had been chatting away, more animated than Abbie had seen her all day, when she paused, looking out over the river, at the Millennium Bridge which they were just approaching. Abbie leaned in, trying to show Suzie that despite the increased hustle and flow in the area as the queue continued to move, she was still listening, interested.

'. . . Norman. She met Norman, and they settled down almost immediately. Wales was the dream, and off they went!'

'Well that sounds wonderful but it must have been a bit gutting to see them move so far. Do you miss seeing your daughter?'

The queue had paused for a minute, people bunched up a little ahead of them.

'Yes,' said Suzie, looking down. She kicked an apple core on the ground outside of the Tate Modern out of the way. 'I miss her every single day.'

Abbie was just thinking that she couldn't believe how Suzie's face had suddenly crumped at the mention of her daughter's move away when their silence was broken by a gale of laughter from Tim. He'd been chatting to Howie the entire time that the two women had been talking, and now they were roaring with laughter, Tim's arm on Howie's as if to support himself.

Abbie looked at the older woman, and asked as quietly as she could, 'Are they . . . flirting?'

Suzie frowned slightly and shrugged as if to say 'Who am I to say?' Abbie wondered if she just didn't want to gossip, or if she genuinely couldn't tell if they were flirting. Surely it was the former? Because as far as Abbie was concerned, people as far as Trafalgar Square would be able to see that the men were connected in a way that no one else in the queue seemed to be.

There was a strong chance that today wasn't actually happening, thought Tim as he looked down onto Bankside Beach, where a couple of mudlarkers were crouched in their familiar squat, eyes focused on the mulch at the water's edge. Sure, he had known it wasn't a normal day when he'd woken up this morning – that was why he had decided to come down here, after all. To be a tiny speck in one of tomorrow's headlines, tomorrow's history books. The slash across a 't' maybe, or even a full stop at the end of a footnote about the Millennium Bridge.

Instead, it felt as if something unusual was taking place in his own story. Told for so long in black and white – in thin, neat, reliable font – today it felt as if things were happening in colour. Or at least if not full-colour illustrations then line drawings, starting to move, to dance across his pages. Because today, for the first time in so long, he actually felt relaxed. He felt as if the role of him were being played by the right actor at last, instead of the endless line of uptight, unsure actors who just couldn't quite get under his skin, not properly.

And the strangest thing of all was that on the surface, nothing extraordinary seemed to have happened at all. He had just been chatting away to this Howie chap for an hour or so, while Suzie and Abbie had been deep in their own conversation, and the rest of the South Bank had buzzed around them. Because they really were on the South Bank proper now. They had passed Shakespeare's Globe, Tim briefly marvelling at how it was just there, getting on with things, as if it hadn't just existed through an entire second Elizabethan age. Then they had made their way through the crowds in front of the Tate Modern: the buskers, the ditherers, and the food stalls. The whole of London seemed to be on this stretch of the river now, everyone jostling for their spot in the national narrative.

As they'd passed the theatre and the museum, he had read the signs outside, advertising all sorts of events and exhibitions. There was so much going on in this city he had lived in forever. Had it all always been here, just sitting right here on the river, ready for the taking? The world seemed somehow to be lit differently today – things he had never noticed before now appeared just there, in front of him. There were plays he wanted to see, exhibitions he wanted to spend all day wandering around, not caring if he chatted to people or not. If he could do this; if he could get up at dawn knowing no one, and be laughing with a new friend by lunch, then perhaps the sort of life he had always imagined was just not destined for him might still be within reach.

The Tate Modern, with its imposing chimneys and dramatic entrance, looked busier than it ever had before. Just as Tim was about to remark on it, he spotted that the museum was one of the designated bathroom stops for the queuers, and told the gang that he was going to dart in to spend a penny. As he entered the low-lit chamber of the main entrance, looking down onto the children running up and down in the Turbine Hall below, he felt his heart beating, as if his blood was moving a little faster today. All these people, all these feelings. For so long these throngs of families, lovers, artists had all looked like nothing more than . . . unpredictability. Today, they were starting to look like possibility. So many first kisses must have been had against this balcony, he found himself thinking, before blushing and remembering why he had headed into the museum in the first place. But as he washed his hands in the basin, he caught sight of his own face in the mirror ahead and smiled at himself. As he did so, he had the unfamiliar sensation of liking his reflection.

Back out in the sunshine, the queue was making its way around Blackfriars Bridge, following the stone steps up and round so that people could move past the bridge without finding themselves entangled in part of the elegant glass railway station spanning its width. He caught up with his queue family, and found that his chat with Howie just picked up where it had left off. And instead of it leaving him breathless with anxiety, a metal ring tightening around his chest as he tried to find the right thing to say, he found it easy. Light, breezy even, as if someone had come into a room and opened the windows, allowing the curtains to dance in the breeze as the space filled with that which was fresh, new, a welcome change.

For the first time since his teens, he felt as if he wasn't walking in the shadow of what his peers saw as his difference. Whispered conversations in his wake had dogged so much of his teen years, and these days he sometimes found himself a little resentful that there was a barely a show on TV that didn't seem to be about coming out, being out or hanging out. When he'd been eleven or twelve, questions about crushes, whispers about kisses, and gossip about passions had left him always sitting on the edge of life. It was as if they were grains of sand beneath his skin – always there, always uncomfortable, but somehow too far away to reach, too complicated to deal with. And so, he'd taught himself not to pay heed to the discomfort, just in case it ever became worse.

It wasn't as if he didn't know he was gay. If anything, that was the one fact about himself that he was sure of – and had been since he had understood what it meant. Where so much else about him was awkward, this was the solitary fact that felt entirely normal to him, unwavering even. What had taken longer was for him to realise was that in the world's eyes that made him an outlier. At first he had imagined this difference was as commonplace, as innocuous as a difference in hair colour. But he grew older, and saw the scandalous headlines on the front of tabloids outside the Tube station. Then he watched the dramatic storylines on the soaps he used to enjoy with his mum. And then he saw the gibes on Saturday night TV shows about men with floppy wrists who spent too much time with their mothers. And he started to understand the lens through which he was being seen. At which point it had seemed easiest to just try and fit in. So he stayed quiet, observing, working out what would get him in the least trouble at school, and how to cause the least upset at home. And this in turn, left him living life without the true acceptance of having acknowledged who he truly was. People knew, of course. But not from him. Just by a process of omission. What was left unsaid had told his story, not him.

But today, watching Howie's easy charm, he started to suspect that this wasn't the only path he could have taken. For so long he had thought that if he wasn't comfortable with the flamboyance that had been deemed acceptable on TV during his youth, it was easier to say nothing. He'd never imagined that Howie's relaxed, earnest, self-ease was a path that could have been taken.

On another day, these pennies dropping might have filled him with self-recrimination. But today, there was too much going on, too much to look at, too much to consider about the fragility of life. On his way out of the museum, he'd found himself being asked about which bridge they were at by a father and son who had come down from Scotland for the day. The little boy was about ten, wearing a pair of glasses that made 'bookish' seem an insufficient descriptor. The father, clearly trying to impress his son with enough general knowledge to quench his thirst for facts. Tim had of course obliged, happy to share his knowledge unabashed, charmed by these two in an unfamiliar city, unafraid to ask strangers for help. How he wished he had had a father more like this, rather than one so happy to go along with the silence.

Now, back in the queue, Howie was entertaining him with stories about his youth as a barman in a fancy members' club, and the difference between working for celebrities and royalty. He had no shortage of anecdotes but was remarkably discreet about names. Above all, his chat never seemed like bragging, but a genuine interest in human nature. For once, Tim decided to do the same – to ask questions instead of blurting out facts. To try and genuinely connect.

'What made you come and work over here then, if working at the palace was not so much a goal as a happy career move?'

'Well you're around my age, aren't you, Tim,' he replied with a wink. 'There was nowhere cooler than London in 1997.'

'Ah – Cool Britannia,' Tim smiled, looking down at the pavement. A buggy trundled by as he paused for thought. 'In those days it felt as if the whole country and everyone who lived in it were the absolute coolest on earth. Apart from me.'

'A teenage nerd?'

'Oh absolutely. Not that I didn't love it – reading about the bands in the papers, seeing the rest of the world admire us and so on. It was just ... God, I wouldn't know what to do in a club. Didn't then, wouldn't now ...'

'You just turn up and dance, mate. Have a beer, have a laugh.'

'So I've heard ...'

'I'm only ribbing, mate.' Howie's hand landed on Tim's shoulder, as wide and as warm as a kitten.

'I'm not.'

'I hear ya. It can be bitchy out there. I mean, I loved it, when I turned up, fresh meat from the southern hemisphere. Time of my life. But then anywhere would have been better than where I came from.'

'Oh?'

'Not Oz itself. More, small-town Oz and small-town parents. It's hard to be a guy like me in a town like that. To find a ... community.'

Tim looked up.

'Ah.'

Was Howie admitting that he'd had a hard time growing up as well? That Tim wasn't the only person who had been a queer teenager in a time before social media, feeling as if he'd been born into a tribe whose language the elders hadn't taught him?

Tim watched his eyes momentarily drop. The smile lines he'd grown used to seeing over the last few hours suddenly weren't there, as Howie looked down, pensive for a second.

'Yeah,' replied Howie, looking back up at him, his face grave, 'I guess sometimes it's easier to be yourself on the other side of the world, isn't it?'

It was as if he'd taken a blow to the solar plexus. All those lonely years. And Howie had been out there too, fighting to find a way to be this warm, easy, overgrown puppy of a man.

6

Southbank Centre, the National Theatre, BFI Southbank

Suzie smiled across at the men. As *if* she didn't know what flirting looked like ... The very idea tickled her no end. How intriguing that Abbie had thought she looked so naive. Then again, maybe it was Abbie's own naivety – assuming that someone in a pair of forest green cushioned shoes might never have known the light-headedness of laughing at something utterly inconsequential, with someone who looked up to meet your eyes in perfect synch.

Just as Suzie was chuckling to herself at the thought, a flash of guilt sparked through her at the way she had continued to lie to Abbie about her daughter. It had been so shockingly easy, telling those stories about a relationship that had never existed, even if it was one she had spent more than half a lifetime dreaming of. In truth, the chat she'd had with Abbie was the most relaxed she had been all day – and it seemed to have put Abbie at ease too. In fact, it had been the most Suzie had chatted to someone – *really talked* – all year. She genuinely felt they'd connected, that Abbie had wanted to hear all about 'Bess and the kids'. But was a connection based on lies a connection at all?

The path along the river was narrowing as they passed the Oxo Tower, then the fancy gelato place next to it, and shuffled onwards towards Waterloo. Everyone around her seemed to be chatting happily now. It was past noon, the sun was high in the sky, and there was a sense that they were right in the thick of things now. No longer the straggly end of the queue, the liminal space between the truly committed and the passers-by. Now, *they* were the spectacle, even slightly barricaded off by some temporary railings. Her stiff back and aching feet were reminding her how long she'd been standing, but she didn't care. For today, she belonged, and Suzie was more sure than ever that the trip had been worth it. There was a lightness to her that she hadn't felt for years, certainly not since Colin's death.

Things slowed a little as they reached Gabriel's Wharf, and Suzie was glad of a moment's pause. Her feet were starting to feel tight in her shoes. The seams of her knee-high socks were digging in as they pressed the edge of the leather, her toes like sausages expanding in a frying pan. She wanted to sit down and slip them off, to wriggle her toes as she let the cool air help them feel a little less swollen. Her hair was an uncomfortable combination of tangled from the breeze and slightly clammy from the early start, the constant motion, the excitement of it all.

She longed to pull out her hairbrush and tidy it up but felt too self-conscious. Her mother's voice still there in the back of her mind, reminding her of what would and would not do.

There was barely a cloud in the sky now, and the lunchtime throng of families, friends and lovers was starting to gather at the various food stalls and cafes. Despite the intrinsic sadness of the reason for the queue, the crowds she could see all around seemed largely happy. She watched as a grandfather helped his grandson open the wrapper to a snack bar, the older man's fingers shaky, taking it slowly as the young boy watched patiently. Suzie had noticed them earlier – hours ago – as they had been staring intently at a map. A shard of longing needled at her heart, as she wondered if she'd ever know if she had any grandchildren of her own. How lucky Abbie's grandma had been to have her, how Suzie yearned to have a similar experience with someone – lavishing attention, ice cream, whatever they needed, on them.

A group of friends greeted each other with one huge five-person hug before they linked arms and headed towards a pizzeria in the wharf. A couple stopped to watch the river, turning to kiss each other on the lips before the woman rested her head gently on the man's shoulder. Parents lifted children up to see boats, bridges, statues as they passed. Even the solo runners, muted by their breathlessness, headphones keeping them focused, seemed content in their single-mindedness. Everyone had someone, something. And today, as she looked at Abbie, so did Suzie.

Just ahead of her, the young woman was texting her friend Annabelle, trying to figure out if Maisie was home safely, and if Annabelle was actually still in the queue with this mysterious Rory bloke she had headed off to meet. Abbie looked up from her phone at Suzie, with a shrug and a smile.

'Who knows if I'll ever hear back from her?' she said to Suzie with a smile. Suzie shrugged back.

'Maybe we won't find out until Westminster,' she told her new friend. 'But either way you're safe with us now.'

'Oh Suzie,' said the younger woman, as she nuzzled into Suzie's arm with a smile.

'Now then. How about lunch? I feel as if I've been trying to put it off for hours, and I can't hold off any longer. I don't have much, but do you want to share with me?'

'Er, yes!'

Suzie pulled her lunch out of her bag, and carefully split the sandwiches, giving half to Abbie. Once they'd finished them, she found her penknife and they stood sharing an apple, Suzie carefully shaving slice after slice from the fruit, handing every second segment to her new companion. She hadn't looked after anyone for so long, not like this anyway. There had been hospital visits, of course. But this was different, this was sharing rather than mere respite care. And after the solitude of the last couple of years, it was bliss.

As she looked to her left, she could see that the Wilsons, the young family behind them were tucking into their lunch as well, the mum dealing adeptly with the chaos of tin foil wrapping, juice boxes and half-eaten bananas being handed back to her when something more interesting came along. It looked exhausting, but oh how many years she had ached to be needed like this. Even when she was telling herself – and Colin – that she was fine, that she had moved on, that she had a career now, she would still occasionally see a mum wrangling an erratic toddler and lose herself in wondering how she would have coped with a similar situation.

Today, she was content to be shuffling along in silence, sharing her lunch with Abbie and watching up ahead as Howie and Tim shared their food too. She quietly observed as Tim pulled out a small aluminium tin, filled matryoshka-like with a variety of smaller tins. In each of them were a variety of snacks – nuts, olives, sliced avocado, and even what seemed to be sauerkraut. She watched Howie peer into the tin, reticent, sniffing at what was inside. His eyes narrowed, clearly sceptical, until Tim fished out a small fork from the side of the tin, scooped up a little, and offered it to him. There was a fumble as Howie opened his mouth to accept the food, while Tim had merely been passing the fork to him. The pickled food fell on the pavement and they both laughed, awkwardly at first, Tim running his hand through his hair as if looking for something to help him. But a seagull flew straight up from the river, perhaps looking for something as bland as a pizza crust from the restaurants behind them, only to spot and gobble up the cabbage. The men laughed together, Tim's eyes almost teary with relief. Howie broke off part of the tortilla from his own lunchbox and handed it to Tim on a napkin from his pocket, performing a daft, over the top, bow as he did so. Tim beamed, accepting it.

Beyond them, Suzie watched a woman about twenty years younger than her slide her hand into the pocket of her silver-haired partner's navy peacoat, only for him to slide his hand in too, turning to her and winking. Oh, how a moment like that had once sustained her for months. How long ago it now seemed, that she and Colin had shared moments like this, and for how long they had become lost in grief, misunderstanding ... dishonesty. She felt winded, moving her hand to her chest to steady her breath.

After one particularly hideous miscarriage, Suzie had confessed to Colin that she simply couldn't stay at home trying to relax, to be healthy, for another minute longer. She couldn't walk around the park ever again, doing her best to turn fresh air into positivity as she inhaled it deeply, passing the ornamental fountain – trying not to make eye contact if she saw someone she knew pushing a pram. She couldn't go to the bathroom one single time more only to feel too sad to wipe, scared by what she might see on the paper. She could no longer wait to hear the car in the drive, knowing she'd have to tell Colin bad news yet again. She simply couldn't carry on living as if she were the sand in an egg timer, gently gently trickling away to nothing.

So she decided to find a job. Anything to stop her from swinging her legs out of bed in the morning and having to persuade herself that 'today might be different'. She needed to be needed. By someone.

'But *I* need you,' Colin had told her. But she'd known it wasn't true.

Colin didn't need anyone. He was an uncomplicated man – yes, one who felt sad not to be a father – but who would be fine without her. Everyone loved Colin, even Reg from across the close who was in a perpetual state of ruddy-faced fury about which day the bins were collected. Even he was Colin's ally.

And of course he'd been fine when she found a job. Thrilled even. Even more so when she surprised herself, if not him, by thriving there. It was hardly a glamorous role, working for a shipping company based in Harwich but with offices in London and abroad too. She started with a basic administrative role but was organised and driven, and before long, she found herself rising up through the ranks, flushed with pride at finally being *good* at something.

She loved hearing the alarm clock, seeing the light peeking around the bedroom curtains and knowing that she only had forty-five minutes to get up and out too. Colin would make them teas while she had a quick shower, then she would get plates and toast on the table while he had his. They'd sit there listening to Derek

Jameson on the radio, before dancing round each other in the bathroom as they brushed their teeth. Colin would drop her at the office, before heading off to his.

They'd been married over ten years by then, and Suzie had thought they'd made their peace with things as they were. Colin didn't talk about babies anymore, but the silence between them was starting to grow. They had agreed companionably to put the whole subject aside, and Colin had truly been a brick about it. But the more accepting he was, the more Suzie's guilt at keeping such a secret from him curdled something inside of her. If she could just have pushed that guilt away, hidden it under some sort of emotional floorboarding the same way that her mother seemed able to never discuss the baby, perhaps things would have been easier. But Suzie couldn't do it: the better a man Colin was, the worse a woman she felt like she was. And even though she knew he didn't deserve a second of it, his decency only served to drive a wedge between them.

It wasn't that they argued, or even that she didn't love him. But as so much was left unspoken, it was as if quicksand was growing between them. A vast expanse of quicksand, and if either one of them tried to cross it, they would be in immeasurable danger, at risk of falling down, sinking, suffocated in their efforts to reach the other. She would go for months without thinking about it, then the sight of a mother tenderly wiping the graze of a child's knee would set her off. Then there'd be a fortnight of nights when she would stay up, sitting in the garden on the sultry summer evenings, watching the moon appear from behind some hazy cloud as she sipped a Bailey's and tried to find the words to tell Colin about Wales, about Eddie, about Bess. But the words never came. And so the quicksand spread.

As it spread, so did the loneliness. So, by the time her thirties were in full swing, she tried to replace the hidden bruises she carried inside with work. In a funny sort of way, their lives caught up with those of their friends who had had their babies young. They were now out from the tunnel of nappies and sleepless nights, the kids were in school and the parents were now able to enjoy nights out with greater freedom and significantly more wine. They were having fun, or at least Suzie thought they were, until her own career started to take off.

It was only when she was promoted, and ended up having to spend half the week in London, that things had changed. The starts were earlier, leaving her creeping around the house hoping not to wake him, before catching the bus to the station and then the train into London. She had been so nervous that first morning – train journeys alone had always reminded her of her lonely trip to Wales, a feeling she would never shake. But once she found her feet, she'd discovered that the job was just as satisfying as it had been back home, if not more so. It was fun, reporting back to the London lot on how things were going with the East Anglia warehouses. She learned a lot from the head office team too, and found herself even more invaluable on the days she was back in Suffolk.

Then there were the lunch breaks. The sweet rush of independence she felt for each and every one of them. At first she had been utterly disorientated, heading out of Waterloo into a mass of roundabouts and underpasses. 'CARDBOARD CITY' the headlines would blast, terrifying her in the weeks before she started there. But before long, she worked out that, as ever, it was not as fearsome as the tabloids would have had her believe. After a week or two she figured out the quickest route to the office, and by the time spring was in full bloom she had discovered that she could get to the South Bank in only five or ten minutes, and spend her hour with a sandwich watching the world go by. And there was so much world going by! The area was mostly focused on the theatres and cinemas back then, so at lunchtime it was quieter than the area ever was now, especially today.

Every couple of months she would head east and see the building work across the water at Canary Wharf, watching the gleaming new skyscrapers getting taller and taller, emerging as if out from the deep. But most days she would head to the stretch outside the National Theatre and the British Film Institute. She would find a bench and take as long as she could over her lunch – usually a sandwich wrapped in tin foil and a flask of coffee – before heading to the new second-hand book stall under the bridge. They only had a few boxes and a couple of trestle tables, setting up with a selection of hardbacks on film and theatre. It was a husband and wife team who seemed to know everyone's name, and exactly where they had laid out every single book before they packed it all up again at the end of the day.

The bench there was her favourite spot. It was quiet enough just beside the bridge to get lost in her own thoughts, wondering where her sweet daughter was and if she was well and happy. In the first few weeks after the nurses had taken her, there was a gentle trickle of letters from the home regarding the legal side of the adoption process. Sometimes, they would also include news about Bess and how she was getting along.

'She is doing very well, and it looks as if before long she will be able to sit up unaided.'

'Her family love her very much. The husband is a professional man with a good job, and the wife is a keen and proficient baker. The little one wants for nothing.'

I *love her*, Suzie would think, as she dabbed at the watermark where a tear had landed on the letter. *What if she wants for* me?

'If you could sign these final forms and then all the paperwork will be completed.'

The air felt thinner, cleaner, on this bench. As if she were at a higher altitude, where no one could find out her secrets, and she could at last breathe to the top of her lungs. And then back out again, her shoulders sagging.

A secondary advantage of that favourite spot was that it afforded her such a discreet view of the shoppers at the book stall. Week after week she would watch as the stock grew and the team made more and more sales. But it was the people who stopped, and what they picked up, that truly entranced Suzie.

On the way to the bench she would leaf through the collection of old Penguin Classics with their orange, green and purple spines. She loved reading the scandalous plot precis of the crime novels, then checking inside to see when it had first been published. Fallen women, predatory men, paternal detectives, but each with a slightly different spin, depending on the decade.

It was an otherwise unexceptional Wednesday lunchtime when she sat on her bench to drink the rest of her coffee with half an eye on the passers-by at the book stall when she felt the shadow of a man standing beside her, blocking the sun that she felt as if she'd been waiting all winter for.

'Mind if I join you?' he asked.

At first, Suzie could only see him in silhouette and her hand raised to her eyes. It was only as he sat down and his face became clear that she felt as if someone had placed a cold, tight hand on her heart and given it a squeeze. Because the man looked just like Eddie.

For a split second she had thought it really was him. He had the same short dark hair, cut in such a way that his curls were just a heartbeat away. His eyes were the same warm brown – smiling even when his mouth was at rest. And his voice, that gentle confidence . . . it was uncanny.

'Of course not,' replied Suzie with a smile. She was doing her very best to look entirely unflustered but was not sure how successful her efforts actually were. 'I'd offer you some coffee if I had a second cup.'

Again, she found herself wanting to gasp at her own cheek.

'Next time I'll bring my own,' replied the man with a smile. 'I'm Paul, by the way.'

He put out a hand, and Suzie shook it. His palm was warm compared to her own, which was cool from sitting in the shade. She felt as if even her fingertips were blushing, unable to remember the last time she had touched a man other than Colin. Instinctively, she glanced around in case anyone who knew her might be watching. But to the Wednesday lunchtime walkers the pair looked entirely innocent. They *were* entirely innocent. Two office workers taking a break on the same bench.

And they looked just as innocent the next week, when Suzie headed straight for the bench as soon as she could get out of the office. It was a bright, late-March day, the weather finally warm enough to leave the house without a scarf and gloves. The trees along the South Bank were covered in buds, heaving with potential. Easter was around the corner after a relentless winter. It had been the coldest Christmas in history apparently. It had felt like it while she had sat round her parents' dinner table with Colin, the carriage clock ticking, the conversation safe, surface-deep, stifling.

Suzie was desperate not to look as if she were hurrying as she made her way along the river. Instead, she rolled her ankle in her smart grey court shoes and winced in pain. But it was gone in a second when she saw Paul sitting there already, on 'her' bench. Still. Eyes smiling. Watching the water.

She stood up straight and smoothed her hands across the fabric of her coat and skirt.

'Well I never . . .' she said, close enough for him to hear but not so close that she couldn't back away if it had felt wrong. 'Mind if I . . . ?'

'I'd be hurt if you didn't.' He looked up at her, and in the openness of his face, she felt relief at spending time with someone she had never lied to.

She sat down next to him, settling the pleats of her smart mac as she did. He bent down and reached into the wide doctor's-style briefcase at his feet.

'I hope it wasn't impertinent of me,' he said, as he produced a small flask and two paper picnic cups.

Suzie laughed. She could hear nothing but lightness, freedom.

'You shouldn't have!' she said, as she reached into her own canvas bag for her own flask and two very similar cups. Her voice sounded like sparkling wine, bubbles racing upwards.

For the best part of a decade Suzie had taken life at a gentler pace, a lower gear. She had turned her back on anything – from friendships to holiday trips – which might be seen as slightly risky or inappropriate. Their associated consequences were simply too much for her to bear. She had tried – *so hard* – to be good. But now she found herself making a friend who had no expectations of her. Someone who saw her only as a professional woman rather than one who had failed at motherhood, and who asked nothing more of her than a bit of a chat at lunchtime.

The Bench Lunches, as the pair came to call them, became a regular thing that spring. They would meet, sitting side by side on the bench, and chat. It really was entirely innocuous. A bit of banter between two commuters who weren't proper Londoners, who each had a battered A-Z paperback in their bag most days, and who were enjoying this tiny sliver of independence in their week. A chance to slip on a different identity, away from the small towns they had both grown up in, where you were as likely to bump into your primary school teacher while picking up a prescription as you were to end up doing a prenatal class with your first boyfriend's new wife. London had space for so many versions of oneself, Suzie found herself thinking, and this one, this chatty lady who gave so little of herself away while having something funny to say about anything and everything, was a delight.

Paul didn't seem to want anything inappropriate from her, and she certainly didn't from him. It was just such a balm to be this delightful, untroubled woman, for an hour or two each week. A woman seen on her own terms, rather than through the prism of her husband, her heartache, her mistakes. A woman who made interesting sandwiches, and looked up pertinent facts about the plane trees along the South Bank. The hybrid planes of

London had started along the Embankment, she found herself telling Paul one week, assuming Colin's usual role in the relationship: the even-tempered one, the dispenser of facts. It had all been inspired by the tree-lined avenues of Paris and Berlin, she explained. The ones on this side of the river were planted eighty years after the others on the north side, which had been there since 1870.

As spring turned into summer and the plane trees grew full, they would sit sharing their coffee, and watch the book stall expand into a proper market, as they did so making up names and backstories for the browsers. There seemed to be every type of Londoner there. It was impossible to predict what any of them might do, no matter how hard they tried. The punk they assumed would be heading for avant-garde theatre books who spent a lazy ten minutes scouring the romance titles. The businessman, complete with bowler hat and briefcase who regularly returned to look at the recipe books, apparently entranced by Delia Smith's smiling face. And the couples. The endless couples, leaning into each other to look at an opened page over one another's shoulders. Suzie and Paul would fall silent then.

For months, the arrangement stayed the same. Neither of them had the other's phone number, mobile phones still something only seen a couple of miles east in the City. But each week the other was simply there, unassuming – or at least doing a wonderful job of looking unassuming – and so they'd sit and watch the world go by. Chatting about almost anything apart from their home lives, which remained tacitly, uncompromisingly undiscussed. Instead, they'd discuss politics, areas of London they did and didn't know, and how each other's respective jobs were going. Until one week he wasn't there.

Suzie was stunned, horrified even, by the despair she felt at the absence of her new friend. It was as if her new self had been whipped away, and was forcing her to reconfront the her she'd always been. She barely did a stroke of work all afternoon, including being mortifyingly distracted during a big presentation. It was a sticky August day, the sort of heat that made even your eyelids seem to sweat. Time became liquid, viscous, slipping away from her while she tried to speak to the board members, only for the rest of the afternoon to drag unbearably.

By the time she'd escaped the office and reached Waterloo to begin the trek home, she still felt as if she might cry all the way back. She couldn't face either Colin's inevitable concern or the oppressive clamminess of the Tube to Liverpool Street, so she snuck into a pub on Roupell Street that Paul had mentioned once. She knew it was daft, but it seemed like the only place she could just sit for a minute and try to understand where this bottomless sadness was coming from. She ordered a double gin and tonic and flicked listlessly through a copy of the *Evening Standard* that had been left on the grimy upholstery of the bar stool next to her. She was sure even the pages of that smelled of sweat.

The headlines were screaming about the latest political scandal. Another MP up to no good. She wondered about the mistress, if she had tried her best too. To be good. Or if it was just her who seemed to keep ending up like this. Somehow tangled up on the wrong side of good behaviour. She looked up as the door slammed. It wasn't Paul, but a giggling couple who had just left, walking past the glass front of the pub, arm in arm, heading out into the hot summer's night. How lovely for things to be so simple.

Enough. She went to the bathroom, ran her hands under the cold tap, dabbed her throat and neck, and left for home, determined not to start a new type of wallowing. Wasn't getting a job, throwing herself into a career, supposed to have healed this melancholy?

But it was hopeless. Despite six days of telling herself she wouldn't, it was barely twelve thirty the following Wednesday when she found herself slowly walking towards the bench. What had started off as 'I'll work through lunch today' had turned into 'Fresh air will help me work better', which in turn had slid towards 'Well I won't go to the bench, I'll just walk past it, in case.' And now here she was, looking for her friend like a child lost in the playground.

She didn't even need to get close to the bench to see him. He was there. But this time he wasn't still, he was craning his head all around him, looking in every direction. For her? She barely dared to hope.

I'll just walk behind the bench. To see.

He might, after all, do this with several women.

And then he saw her. He'd been looking right behind

him just as she approached, as if he'd been checking. This time, it was him who gasped.

'Suzie! You came!' His hair was damp around his hairline, his suit dishevelled.

'Of course I came. It's where I have my lunch on Wednesdays.' She resolved not to let him know how sad she'd been not to see him, lest he picked up the wrong impression. She'd be polite, honourable. A good person.

But it was too late.

'I missed you,' he said, his voice barely more than a whisper.

'I see.' Suzie sat on the bench next to him, putting her hand down on its smooth, familiar wood. It barely took him a second to move his own hand – hot, damp from his hair – and place it over hers.

There they remained in silence for a second, staring straight ahead at the creamy white colonnades of Somerset House on the north side of the river, the plane trees rustling in the breeze in front it. In that instant, she knew that her hand left there a second more would put everything she had in peril. And she had so much. Yes, there was pain, and loneliness, but there was also darling Colin. A leaf fell from one of the trees in front of them, dancing in the breeze before landing on her lap. Suzie was careful when she slipped her hand out from beneath his, her movements slow, her voice gentle. Her hand cooled in an instant as she brushed the leaf off her skirt, away from her, the air whooshing across her fingers.

'I'm so sorry, Paul,' she told him, as kindly as she could. 'We must have misunderstood each other.'

He said nothing.

'I'm happily married,' she went on, images of her and Colin on the beach reminding her that that truth was still there. 'I've been unfathomably sad, and it's nothing at all to do with you. So I'm afraid I might have led you to understand that you could be more to me than a dear friend.'

He was still looking ahead, avoiding her gaze, his hand still in the same place on the bench, where it had once been over hers. Then, it struck her – a way out of this mess! Perhaps she could tell him about Bess, about how this was at the root of her loneliness, her silly self-pity. At last, she might have someone to talk to about it.

'You have been a dear, cherished friend to me—' she continued.

But Paul stood up. Slowly, as if carrying something terribly heavy.

'I'm sorry, Suzie. I can't.' And with that he stood up and walked away.

As the summer reached its peak, and then the leaves started to brown, she never found out what that 'I can't' meant.

Was it that he had a wife or partner who had seen them, who had assumed they were embroiled in an affair? Was it that he simply didn't have it in his heart to offer friendship when there was no prospect of romance, sex, something more on offer? Or was it that he knew himself well enough to understand that there was no way he could take on details of her pain, her loneliness, when he might have been bearing so much of his own already?

She would never know. It wasn't just a time before mobile phones, but before social media, internet search engines and so much more. For a fortnight she'd felt nothing but relief that it was all over, that she had escaped without anything more intimate happening. And that she had no way of contacting him.

But sometimes, on the really bad days, she would look for him. *If he's there, he's there,* she would tell herself as she sat at her desk watching the clock hands slide past midday. *And if he's not, then that's that.* She'd just walk up and down past the spot where they'd meet, wondering where he might be. She knew, deep down, that this was transference, that she was replacing thoughts of what had become of Bess with thoughts of what had become of Paul. It was easier that way, she supposed.

Her chats with him had been a bright spark in a life of duty that she'd been on the precipice of resenting. He had let her become an imaginary self without having to make any of the actual changes that might be required to shift the melancholy, the distance she felt between her and Colin. For the rest of the summer, she felt suspended, caught in aspic, not sure what direction she could possibly turn.

Then she'd spent a week crying. Quietly, in the bathroom at home. On the train to London and then again on the way back out again. And sometimes while she was just staring out of the kitchen window, waiting for the kettle to boil and watching Colin chat to Reg at the end of the drive as they both took the bins out.

In time, she accepted that Paul had to have moved on. Either physically, out of London or at least to a different area. Or emotionally. A near miss successfully navigated. So her mind filled with the thoughts she had been seeking to laminate over. The great weight of the grief for Bess that she still carried, the guilt for letting her parents down, the loneliness in her marriage despite having a husband she truly loved.

She had to do something, anything, to remind herself that life wasn't simply happening *to* her. She urgently needed to sense that she was in control of something, that she was navigator, rather than mere passenger. So instead of using her mid-week London lunchtimes to patrol the South Bank watching the leaves start to fall, she would find one of the quiet meeting rooms in the office and embark on some investigations of her own. Her name was not on Bess's adoption certificate, the law stating that it only contained the child's name, the adopting parents' names, and the local authority who had processed the adoption. But she was determined to try to find her daughter, or at least find out how she was.

Those first couple of weeks, she had been fizzing with excitement about committing to this plan. She would wait until the big bosses had headed down to The Cut for a lunchtime pint, pretending she wanted to catch up on paperwork in the office. But the paperwork she'd produce from her bag would be the small neat wallet which held her adoption papers, and the letters from the children's home. She would creep into one of the boardrooms, closing the heavy wooden door behind her, and sliding into one of the opulent meeting chairs that always seemed to be reserved for the rooms where the men with paunches made the big decisions.

She would scour her paperwork for phone numbers, calling anything she could find, in order to discover what her options were. But it turned out things were not as simple as she had imagined. There would be no great hunt afoot. She could register her own name on the Adoption Contact Register held by the government, a move that would indicate to Bess that Suzie was contactable, willing to be reached, should she ever reach out.

But Bess was not even a teenager yet. She was years off making a decision like that, and even if and when she did, her childhood would be over. So the mourning began all over again. This time, it was the death of hope. Hope that she could make amends. Hope that she might ever forgive her parents for persuading her to do this . . . Dreaming about where Bess was and what she was doing.

Suzie sat on the bench in the drizzle on Bess's twelfth birthday. Some days, she was glad of these trips to London, these breaks from her day-to-day life. But that day, as she watched the boats full of laughing tourists heading up and down the river, she thought they might have been the loneliest of her life. They'd left her with too much time to dwell, too much space to think. Best to get on with things, to make the best of what she had, she reminded herself. But as she passed the book stall, she saw an old, bright blue hardback of *Young Bess*, that beloved Margaret Irwin novel. And, for the first time, she bought it. Just in case, she told herself, just in case.

On the train home that night, she sat slumped against the window, letting the tears meet the splashes of condensation as she stared at the endless flat familiarity of the view until she eventually fell asleep. She only just woke up in time for her stop, rushing for the last bus home with a garbled apology to Colin, who immediately noticed her red-rimmed eyes.

She told him she thought that perhaps it was to do with the plane trees along the South Bank, perhaps some sort of allergy now that they were dropping leaves. Possibly, he replied. And there are so many of them in London, he'd continued. They were imported in the 1800s, he said. The ones on the north side eighty years older than the South Bank's. They were planted in 1951, the year he'd been born.

She didn't have the heart to tell him she knew all that, and simply reassured him that she was sure things would get better soon. A promise she was making to herself as much as him. He was concerned that she was working too hard, but was happy enough in his own way. Oblivious even.

By the time the weather was cold enough for her to take a scarf and gloves on the train again, her dad had taken a turn for the worse after a recent fall, and her mum needed too much help with him. Colin was doing so well in his career that hers didn't seem to matter quite so much. She stopped going to London, taking a part-time role instead. It was for the best, she told herself.

But she had always missed the book market, which she had never been back to. Until today.

'OMG cute!' said Abbie. 'Did you guys know this was here?'

'Yes,' replied Suzie, who really was looking a bit tired now. 'I used to come here a lot when I was younger. It used to be tiny compared to this.'

'No way! Why has no one told me London has so much cool stuff? Look at it all, I bet there are some really great vintage covers there.'

'Yes, I used to love the old Penguin ones.'

'Absolute classics,' said Tim. 'Literally.'

'Maybe I should buy some, to use for work, props and stuff.'

'What do you do for work?' asked Suzie.

Abbie felt almost too embarrassed to reply. 'I'm kind of, an assistant to a content creator.'

'Goodness, I'm not even really sure I know what that means.' Suzie looked interested though. In that way that her gran used to too.

'Well, I help a fashion influencer out a couple of days a week, I sort of do it around my course.'

'That sounds like a lot of work. What kind of help is it?'

'Well, I couldn't afford not to work and study in London, and it's better experience than bar or barista work. I'm lucky really, it's kind of a dream job for so many people, and I was really lucky to get it. But it's maybe . . . not quite what I thought it would be.'

It *was* a dream job. On paper. And Abbie knew she had done really well to get the position, which was why she felt somewhat tormented not to be loving every minute. Perhaps she'd been hopelessly naive, or perhaps the woman was just a nightmare. Either way, the reality of working for Kelly Bracken, a thirty-year-old style blogger who was as obsessed with outfits comprised of endless stretchy fabrics in almost indistinguishable nude tones as she was with herself, was proving a little different from the advertisement itself.

Kelly had a rapacious thirst for the freshest aesthetic, the newest angle, the fastest turnaround, as well as an attitude to timekeeping that was baffling to Abbie. Some days her phone would be vibrating with WhatsApps before 7 a.m., as Kelly took an Uber back from Reformer Pilates, checking her messages. Other days the woman was impossible to get hold of, not online for key appointments and changing her mind about decisions she had made earlier in the week.

Abbie was only just starting to learn the grim truth that adults, including those you work for, are often winging it through their life and career just as much as any intern they hire. She didn't know if Kelly's erratic behaviour was the result of mental health issues or nothing more than pure entitlement, but her temperament made eggshells looks sturdy. Some mornings Abbie would be heading to lectures, frantically deleting 'forthright feedback' from Kelly's inbox on the bus, before she woke up and saw any of them. And others she was putting her actual course work aside to spend a morning dealing with brand requests or blagging freebie minibreaks for Kelly's next make-or-break trip away with her boyfriend.

Life as an influencer didn't seem quite as pretty when viewed from the other side of the camera. And it was certainly educating Abbie in an alternative perspective on what a career in fashion might really look like. There was very little styling to be done, and certainly no creating of her own. She wasn't developing any new skills beyond advising Kelly on what shots of her in a new brand's period pants made her look less bloated than others.

She thought of Grandma Lucy, and her consistent advice to keep going, to have faith in creating good work, and she hoped she could stick to it. Because life as it was wasn't much more fun than living in Worthing and listening to her parents squabble.

She longed to chat all this through with Suzie, to ask her advice on how to better advocate for herself, to hear about how Suzie found working in London when she was a young woman, and so much more. But the older woman really did look tired though, so she thought perhaps she wouldn't burden her with all that just now.

Suzie was staring balefully into the water. Beyond the book market, in the shade of Hungerford Bridge, – deep, swirling, agitated by all the river traffic. Sirens were louder now as they drew closer to St Thomas's Hospital. Before it, the London Eye was twinkling up ahead, the glass pods glinting in the sun. *How many secrets that river must hold*, Tim thought as he looked at Suzie. He wondered what, if anything, the mudlarkers they'd passed earlier on had found today. Oh the secrets that must pass through their hands, belched up from the ooze of the river. Some days it would be a couple of ageing Nokias, he'd read. Others it would be a glass eyeball, someone's false teeth, a discarded condom. Others, a precious coin, a rare artefact, a religious icon. How many secrets we all carry, and how varied.

Tim sighed. A dark cloud seemed to be settling above him. He didn't feel comfortable admitting it – even to himself – but despite his reservations, he'd had the time of his life today. How inappropriate that felt. He had hardly even discussed Her Majesty, really only in the context of Howie's job. But, no matter how much his hips were starting to feel stiff and his hands hot and heavy, he didn't want his time in the queue to end. Not yet, not before he had fathomed a way to keep these connections going. But the panic was starting to swell in him, just like it always did. It was as if there was a muscle he'd never developed, the knack of simply letting these people know that they meant something to him, that their lives having touched each other was of value to him. He saw himself standing up after watching TV curled up on the sofa, one foot under the weight of his body. Today, trying to express the sincerity of those emotions felt like trying to walk on that foot, tingling with pins and needles – unreliable, unpredictable, as likely to simply break beneath him as it was to simply pass.

That glumness was consuming him when distraction came in the form of a murmur from the crowd up ahead. Not only were the people in front of them, including that very chic European-looking couple, suddenly straining their necks to see what was coming, but the tourists who weren't queueing were also looking. One woman, chic in jeans, white sneakers and a Breton top, was walking along the queue itself, taking a video as she spoke, treating Tim and his fellow queuers as if they were one of London's monuments themselves. Perhaps they were, he reasoned. He knew the queuers had been the talk of the office on Friday. Curious people, he had heard one of the partners say as he waited for his coffee to gurgle out from the coffee machine. But I can't say I wouldn't do it if I had the time . . .

'Can you see what's going on?' Tim heard Abbie ask Howie, who was the tallest among them by a couple of inches.

'Looks like a camera crew,' he replied. 'Yeah, I think I recognise her off that morning show. I'm rubbish with names though.'

Tim was sure he noticed Abbie trying not to look too curious after her earlier nudge from Suzie. She wasn't doing a great job though. Howie leaned forward again, craning his neck to see over the crowds. As he did so, Tim spotted what looked like strands of yarn coming out of the top of his slouchy satchel-style bag. Suzie was looking at it too – strands of red, white and blue. For a second they caught each other's eye. But they didn't have time to say anything as within a minute, the reporters had approached their section of the queue, a couple of researchers scuttling ahead and talking to people at random, asking if anyone had any interesting stories or experiences.

They spent a few minutes talking to a mother and daughter who had flown in from Washington. Again Tim was fascinated that there were still people right there, metres from him, with stories to tell. They had caught a flight the minute they had heard that the Queen had died, the daughter was explaining. She looked about eleven or twelve, and was telling the reporters that her mum had grown up in England, that she had been at a street party for a royal wedding as a child. That she had admired the Queen all her life, especially in recent years as she too had been widowed. The girl's mother looked on, her eyes glossy with pride as her daughter spoke confidently, admiration for not just the Queen but also her own mother beaming from her. We had been saving for a trip to Paris, she explained, but the minute we heard, we knew we had to come here instead. The mother nodded, tears splashing onto her anorak as the news presenter put an arm out, resting a hand on her shoulder in sympathy.

Tim gulped, trying to contain another of these unpredictable surges of emotion. He listened in as the European couple just in front were telling the reporters about the flat who had been throwing drinks down at them, but the researchers didn't look that interested if they couldn't get footage of it.

Suddenly Abbie thrust her hand in the air.

'Excuse me! You should talk to this lady here,' she was saying, putting a hand on Suzie's back, trying to push her forward a little. The researcher peered round to listen to Abbie.

'She's missing her daughter's fiftieth birthday to be here. She's just . . . a really honourable person. You should meet her. The *Queen* should have met her.'

Tim and Howie smiled at each other. Abbie was really fighting the case for Suzie. Clearly they hadn't been the only ones making friends today.

'It's true,' said Tim, leaning forward towards the reporter, enjoying the wave of Suzie love that seemed to be building as others turned to hear Abbie. Even the couple ahead, who had seemed so quiet, so reserved all day, were nodding vociferously too now. 'She's a great lady – we've been with her since dawn, hearing about this stretch of the river back in the day.'

The researcher was now gesticulating wildly for the reporter to come over, and a reverential hush came over the crowd as Suzie appeared in front of the group. It was just like people always said, she *did* look much slimmer in real life. A cameraman appeared at her side, a huge handheld camera on his shoulder.

'Hi there, Suzie is it?' But Suzie didn't reply, only staring ahead, looking blank. 'Is this true that you're missing out on a family member's special day?'

The reporter was smiling, waiting for her answer, apparently unused to being met with silence. And it was only then that Tim noticed how pale Suzie had suddenly gone. How frail she looked. And how reluctant she now seemed to be to talk.

7

London Eye, Jubilee Gardens

A gust of wind blasted the group as they emerged from Hungerford Bridge, having stepped away from the reporter. It caught Suzie's hair on the wrong side, blowing it askew in a strange, momentary comb-over. She looked more awkward than ever, raising her hands quickly to smooth it down and gather herself. Abbie opened her mouth to apologise for her moment of excitement with the TV crew, but Suzie reached out to stop her, speaking first.

'I'm sorry – I just can't bear people looking at me, making me the focus like that. I know you were trying to be kind. But I don't want people at home thinking I came down here to get on the telly.'

'It's OK, I understand,' replied Abbie, her voice low. But she didn't really. She had been mortified at the way Suzie had frozen in front of the camera, before going pale and saying she didn't want to be on TV, but thank you, and sorry for all the trouble.

Abbie was not used to hearing people express out loud

that they didn't want to be on TV, or to be in the spotlight at all. She had spent so much of her life documenting her antics and sitting amidst others doing the same. After all, she was a child of reality TV. She'd been on her mother's knee when Jade Goody had emerged from the *Big Brother* house to cheers and boos in equal measure and enjoying a late night biscuit on the sofa, nuzzled between her parents the night that Shayne Ward was crowned winner of *The X Factor* a couple of years later. The first Christmas she could remember was the one when her mum's sister Em had come to stay. She didn't have any kids, but she did have a lot of fancy stuff – which was brilliant as far as Abbie was concerned because it meant more presents. As it turned out, this year it also meant playing with her fancy digital camera – a camera *so* fancy that it could also record and edit video.

Abbie and her brother had spent hours with it: her interviewing the gathered adults for reviews of the various festive meals, of them making their new toys perform stunts off the back of the sofa, and doing all sorts of skits and dances. If it happened, it was recorded. And it if wasn't happening, they'd have a go at setting it up.

It was later the following year – when she was six – that her mum started a Facebook page, downloading endless photographs from CD-ROMs onto the webpage, in what seemed like an endless, un-winnable competition with her Auntie Em. Whenever the kids went somewhere that would make good photos – pumpkin picking at the local farm, a ride on the seafront carousel when it opened at

Easter, a picnic at West Wittering where the wind was so fierce that their sandwiches were full of sand but Mum's hair looked fantastic – she'd take endless snaps, and upload the whole lot online to show everyone how happy she was. How happy *they* were. How well it was all going.

By the time Abbie had made it to secondary school, it had become almost de rigueur to have a mobile phone, complete with ever-improving camera. Instagram arrived hot on the heels of Facebook, then Snapchat, then TikTok. The apps just never seemed to stop coming, following her up and up as she progressed through school, social lives dictated by who had posted what, when and why. It just seemed logical to keep going when it came to college and work – it was the only life she had ever known. She wasn't always on camera – far from it – but she was always documenting. It would be pictures of a sunset, a new creation, a small patch of embroidery that she had completed to cover the hole on a vintage jumper. She was always, she now saw, observing. Even if she wasn't always in front of the camera.

So now, when she heard Suzie say 'No, thank you' to having a lens turned in her direction, she felt a kindred spirit. A glint of freedom. A whisper that perhaps she wasn't some sort of loser for not always wanting to smile towards a lens, but perhaps just a young woman with her wits about her.

Suzie, however, was still looking a little harried. Not the Suzie she had met seven hours ago.

'Would you like me to get you another cup of tea?'

asked Abbie, still a little worried about her new friend.

'I've actually got a flask here,' chipped in Tim, who was rooting around in his bag.

'No, thank you – no flask,' replied Suzie. She rummaged in her own bag for a minute, before pulling out a travel-sized hairbrush which she ran through her hair, restoring her grey bob to its former neatness. Abbie felt bashful, wanting to look away from this strangely intimate moment. But she was glad Suzie had done it – she immediately looked reassuringly neater.

Next, she watched as Suzie pulled out an old-fashioned powder compact, its gold lid swirled with an engraved design that reminded Abbie of the plate she would sometimes see communion on when she went to church with Grandma Lucy. Suzie dabbed at her nose with the powder, and then applied a deliberate slick of pale pink lipstick, dabbing at her lips gently with her ring finger. Her hand was still shaking slightly, her eyes focused on the mirror inside the compact. She reached back into her bag, fishing out her lipstick lid and clicking it onto the lipstick with a small nod of her head, then snapped the compact shut, smiling at Abbie.

'There,' she said. 'Much better.'

'I love your vintage compact,' said Abbie.

'Thank you, it's not really vintage though.'

'You're kidding! Where did you even get it? It's so cute . . .'

'From John Lewis.'

Abbie gasped.

'In the Futura Park in Ipswich.'

'No way. Wow, I'm learning a lot today.' Abbie, who had only ever bought her cosmetics online, almost always via click-through links, really was learning a lot today.

Tim, who had now finished fiddling in his own bag, produced another small, lidded tin, offering it to Suzie as Abbie peered over to see it.

'Here, it's just some almonds. But I thought they might help if you weren't feeling too great. Slow-release energy, keep you going a bit.'

'Thank you, Tim. That's very kind. I'll take a couple if I may . . .'

'Of course.'

The queue was moving again now; they were almost at the London Eye. Suzie went to open the lid of the tin of almonds, her rosy pink-painted nails immaculate as she slid them under the rim. But her still-shaky hands slipped and it fell to the pavement with a loud metallic clang.

Howie, at whose huge feet it had fallen, bent straight over to pick it up for her. He placed the tin in the palm of one hand and took the lid off with the other, like a bear cracking open a piece of fruit. As he bent over, Abbie again noticed the coloured strands of wool poking out of the bag slung over his shoulder.

'Hey Howie, what's all this?' she asked, her hand flicking at the loop of yarn that seemed to be caught on the bag's buckle.

'Oh this! Well this is my crochet, darling.'

'You're kidding, that is so sick.'

From the corner of her eye, Abbie noticed Suzie and Tim steal a glance at each other, momentarily thrown by the word.

'. . . as in good. "Sick" is good. Can we see it?'

'Of course you can, sweetie. Here ya go.'

Howie opened his bag and carefully, making sure not to tug on any ends or drop any balls of yarn, he revealed what seemed to be a half-made item of clothing. Some sort of jumper? But it looked as if it was only fit for a child.

Abbie was entranced – a fellow crafter! Someone who understood the pull of actually making something, a real thing, that you could touch, hold, stroke across your face. So often, she felt as if everyone on her course was interested in little more than a slavish devotion to being able to click on a link, an image, some 'content'. There had been nothing but two balls of wool when he had started this project and now she could see that something was emerging, coming to life like a seedling poking above ground for the first time.

'It's amazing, Howie,' said Abbie, genuinely awestruck. 'I can't believe you can do this. How did you learn?'

'YouTube, I suppose. You can find out how to do pretty much anything online can't you?'

Abbie nodded, as if this were the greatest truth of their age.

'When did you start?'

'This project? Just a couple of weeks ago. When we got the news really. But crochet in general – lockdown really.

It's super relaxing. I love it. And you know what else I love? KnitTok.'

'No way! I'm longing to get more about *that* side of TikTok, I still mostly get Matty Healy and stuff about cortisol.'

'Mixed blessings indeed.'

The pair burst into a fit of giggles while Suzie and Tim exchanged another glance, clearly convinced the pair were speaking another language altogether. They watched on with interest as Abbie continued to quiz Howie on his work, which she had now declared was 'a masterpiece'. Howie obliged by showing her how the stitches worked, how the pattern emerged and how long it had taken him so far. The group – and a fair few others around them – were entranced.

'And who is it for?' chipped in Suzie as she reached to stroke and admire the fabric. 'This stitching is immaculate!'

Tim, who had been quietly watching the reveal, looked up at Howie with a glint in his eye.

'It's for you, Howie, isn't it?'

There was a brief moment's hesitation before Abbie realised that Tim had somehow transformed between here and Tower Bridge into a man who cracked actual jokes instead of just spewing facts. She joined in with the men's laughter, giving a wide-eyed smile to Suzie, who was also chuckling to herself for a minute.

'It looks quite short though . . .' she added. 'Something for the summer holidays?'

Again, the group took a moment to make sure that they had permission to laugh, before Howie put his arm round Suzie.

'Oh you're a sneaky one Suzie, aren't you?'

She grinned. The colour was back in her cheeks.

If only he knew. If only any of them knew how sneaky she was, how sneaky she could be.

No need to dwell on it now, thought Suzie as her spirits rallied. She had taken quite a turn when confronted with the idea of discussing her daughter on national TV – what would the crowd back in Finton say? They'd think she was an absolute fantasist! But now, as she looked at her little queue family, delighting in their silly crochet jokes, she felt a strange little swell of pride. It was as if she'd known them for months – already! Abbie had really perked up since she had been with just them, Suzie noted. There's no one she would rather have shared her lunch with, and she'd tell those ghastly flatmates where to go if they turned up again. In fact, she would quite like to have the chance. They needed taking down a peg or two, the pair of them.

This unexpected surge of protective fire in her belly reminded Suzie of a summer holiday with Colin a year or two after she had stopped working in London. Those first few months after she had gone part-time were utterly miserable. It had taken all she had to get through the basics every day. Getting herself up and out on time. Smiling her way through work lest anyone ask if she were OK. Making sure the house was clean – something she'd barely thought about for over a year.

But mostly it had been all about helping her mum with caring for Dad. He had deteriorated rapidly, early onset dementia apparently relentless in its cruelty. It was heartbreaking to see him understand so little about what was happening to him, yet to understand enough to know that she and Mum were unhappy, that they missed him, and that he missed them too. Worst of all was watching her mum trying to contain her emotions, an heroic attempt to hold herself together while grief and frustration leeched out of her at every seam.

There were days when Suzie wanted to shake her by the shoulders, to scream in her face that it was OK to cry, that there was space for her to be angry, that she would be forgiven if she said out loud that this whole situation was wretched. Instead, her mother persisted with a sort of piety that Suzie found unbearable, trying against the odds to convince anyone and everyone that it was *fine*, it was just fine. Care workers, friends from the church, even Suzie herself – they all had to nod and listen as Mrs Moston spoke in her gentlest voice about how whatever they were going through, her husband was surely going through worse.

It doesn't have *to be one or the other,* Suzie wanted to yell at her.

Perhaps the hardest thing about time was how familiar

that piety was to Suzie, that long-suffering 'patience' that so often seemed like anything but. Because she'd seen it nearly twenty years earlier, as her mother had told her the hushed plans for Wales, and the home. And then again when Suzie returned to Suffolk, and rather than confront anything, or giving any single one of her emotions or experiences a name, her mother had simply smiled discreetly and pretended that absolutely everything was *fine*.

But it hadn't been fine, either time. And instead of being able to herd her complicated feelings into neatly packaged boxes, Suzie instead found them sticking to her like burrs after a long country walk. Whenever she thought she was free, she'd find another one: stuck to the ribbing of her sock, just out of sight on her shoulder, tangled in the back of her hair. All these feelings. Some days she wondered if she was the only one beset with them like this.

She certainly assumed for many years that Colin was simply letting the world wash over him, content with his little life. Corporate Colin, his friends had jokingly started to call him since he'd been promoted, and he was certainly living up to the title. His suits were getting smarter, his cars a little more expensive, and his salary was certainly improving, but there was also something so staid about him. So predictable. He was a rock while she cared for Dad, always happy to listen to her gripe about Mum or moan about the sleepless nights she'd have when she stayed over half the week, ready to help out if Dad needed anything in the small hours – which he almost always did. But this dependability seemed to highlight Suzie's own sense of her whims and passions. She spent so much of her life trying not to be impulsive that sometimes it felt impossible not to be.

What Colin didn't know was that half of the sleeplessness was due to her lying there in the dark, staring at the ceiling of her childhood bedroom, wondering what on earth had happened to Paul – and why. She'd never know, and she had to accept that. So slowly, she nursed her battered pride and bruised heart as she lay there in that room where she had first felt her baby kick all that time ago. These days she was at least glad of the solitude.

Then, the summer after Dad died, Colin announced that he was taking her on a summer holiday. And to Greece! They had dreamed of it back when they'd been newlyweds, too hard-up to go anywhere glamorous. Then when they'd been having the fertility treatment, it always seemed too risky to go. Now, they had the money *and* the time. And Colin was determined to give Suzie the full experience: the villa in Corfu with a pool and a view; the snorkelling in the blue-black sea looking for starfish and sea urchins; the nightly trips to restaurants where they'd eat endless prawns and saganaki while they watched the boats bobbing in the harbour.

It was the first time they had been abroad together since a long weekend in Paris the year they had got married. And it was certainly the first time that there had been a hint of glamour to their trip, Colin treating Suzie to a huge sunhat at the airport – and then two glasses of cava while they waited to board. For years they had crept around the Lake District hoping for a sunny day, traipsing to Cornwall in bank holiday traffic or just making day trips to Southwold or Great Yarmouth. Now, perhaps, a holiday could usher in a new era for them.

'I want this to be the honeymoon we never had,' he'd declared as they'd clinked glasses at the newly opened Stanstead Airport. Suzie had smiled back at him, and felt very, very tired.

The villa was stunning: whitewashed walls which glittered with sunlight hour after hour. An incomparably comfortable bed, decked out in immaculate linen with two neatly folded white waffly towels at the end. And a pool terrace with a view of the sunset which made Suzie feel as if she were the star of a Christmas perfume advertisement. But for the first few days, nothing seemed to quite fit. They had been apart for too long, busying themselves in the rhythms of work, care and grief, barely spending more than an hour chatting to each other, even on the evenings Suzie had been at home. They spoke over each other, then had awkward silences. For hours at a time Suzie would wonder if Colin was going to ask her if she was hiding something, then at other times he'd lose himself in an airport thriller leaving her feeling invisible, a ghost on her own holiday.

On the third night they decided to go to a bar in the village before they went for dinner. Colin had fallen asleep in the sun after having a glass of beer at lunch and his skin seemed to be glowing. He'd spent a long time in a cool shower and emerged unrepentant about his sunburn, determined to have a good evening. Suzie was wary of this mood, unsure of whether this forced jollity was sustainable on his part or if he was just making an effort on her behalf.

They'd ended up leaving a little late for dinner, and hadn't had time to stop off en route at the bar that Colin had mentioned so they'd headed straight to the restaurant. To her delight, Suzie felt herself relax the moment they walked into the tiny taverna. It was adorable – dark wood and checked tablecloths on the inside, leading straight out to the bay at the back. There were tables arranged right up to the water's edge, a trellis of vines making a canopy from the last of the evening sun overhead.

When the waiter arrived, handing over the menus, Suzie noticed with relief that they weren't the fully tacky laminated tourist versions but that they still had a couple of discreet translations here and there nevertheless. For the first time on the trip, when she raised her glass to Colin's and when their eyes met, she felt a genuine spark. Perhaps all was not lost after all.

Sunset over the bay was perfect. Suzie found the noise of the water lapping at the jetty relaxing, and didn't even mind that it made her think of one of Colin's motivational CDs, the ones she knew he sometimes listened to when he had been working late. If anything, it reminded her that he got stressed too, that he wasn't the entirely still lake that she so often believed he was.

They had a simple dinner, of the sort that she'd heard you could on the continent. Anne, who sat opposite her at work, had been to Kefalonia the previous summer and simply had not stopped banging on about 'inferior' British tomatoes ever since. 'You need them warmed by the sun,' she'd told Suzie on a particularly dreary Tuesday lunch break.

And do you know what, she'd been right. The tomatoes *did* taste as if they'd been warmed by the sun. As did the olive oil. In fact, the whole salad tasted exactly like she'd always imagined holiday food would. For the first time in years, she felt truly healthy, and as well as her newly restored vigour, she felt chic in her tan palazzo pants and linen T-shirt which she had ordered especially for the holiday. It had seemed so indulgent, as she knew someone would pass comment if she tried to wear the look on an overcast August day in East Anglia, but now vindication was hers. Even Colin didn't look too bad in his smart shorts and a crisp blue shirt. He usually looked as grey as the skies back at home, but not now – perhaps the redness would even turn to a tan in a day or two.

When she first felt his ankle brush against hers she had thought it was a cat under the table, but when she realised it was him, she didn't want to shrink away into herself, as she so often did. She leaned into it, stroking his leg with hers. It felt . . . romantic. And when a chap they'd seen earlier in the week in the town square with an armful of red cellophane-wrapped roses appeared at the side of their table, Colin did the unfathomable, and instead of batting him away, whispering that it was 'just a scam', he bought her one and presented it with a flourish. Suzie's heart skipped a beat, in a way she had thought it never would again.

On the way back to the villa, the pair linked arms and wove their way up the road from the restaurant. She loved feeling his skin against hers, warm and clean. As she nuzzled into his neck, she smelled the familiar holiday smell of the mosquito coil they had been burning on the terrace earlier. A comfortable silence fell, and Suzie sensed that Colin was relaxed too, finally enjoying his own feelings rather than trying to guess what hers might be. It was a perfect moment, a perfect evening.

When they passed the bar they'd meant to pop into on the way to dinner and saw that it was still open, she gave Colin a little nudge, whispering 'One more before bed?' with a giggle. He didn't hesitate.

The bar wasn't quite as charming as the restaurant had been, but the couple were lost in their own world by now. They sat at a corner table, talking about what else they wanted to do for the rest of the week. It was as if a spell had broken; at last enough time had passed that they could tacitly admit that the holiday was a success. They had done it – they had reconnected.

When Colin got up to go to the bathroom, Suzie sat fiddling with her rose from the restaurant. She was pretty sure all the petals would fall off the minute she took the cellophane off but she didn't care – she'd never forget the flash of passion she'd seen in Colin when he impulsively decided to buy it, and that meant so much more than the cheap flower.

'Your fella got swizzed, did he?'

She looked up. A man around Colin's age was standing at the table, looming over her. He was smartly dressed in a cream linen suit, but sweating profusely, fairly obviously drunk.

'I'm sorry?'

'The flowers – you know they see you coming don't you?'

'Oh I don't mind that, it was a lovely gesture at the time,' Suzie smiled, her instinct to placate the man kicking in. He was leering, unsteady on his feet.

'You should come and have dinner with me instead. I know all the haunts . . .'

'Oh thank you, but I'm here with my husband. He's in the bathroom – he'll be back in minute.' She waved her hand over her shoulder in the direction of the bathroom, hoping that someone else might catch her eye. She realised she was now the only woman in the bar.

'Yeah, I saw him come in. Caught the sun, did he? Why don't you come and sit with me 'til he's back – he's probably got a dicky tummy.'

'No honestly, I'm fine.' Her voice was slightly raised now, panic creeping in. What if he *did* have a dicky tummy?

'Is there a problem?'

Suzie wanted to cry with relief at hearing Colin approaching the table.

'No mate, no problem. Was just telling your missus I could show her a good time.'

'Excuse me?'

'You heard.' The man was swaying now, clearly looking to cause trouble. Suzie put her hand out to stop Colin from walking towards him. 'She looks like a right sort. She'd have a good time with me . . .'

To which Colin took a swipe at the man, sending him reeling backwards into the dark wood of the bar.

'Colin!' shrieked Suzie, who had never in her life seen one man punch another, let alone seen *Colin* punch a man.

The barman leapt out from behind the bar to help the man up.

'I'm sorry, sir, I'm sorry,' he was saying, although Suzie wasn't sure who to. The stranger was fine – the shock of Colin's blow having had far greater impact that the blow itself.

'Never mind you're sorry – what about my wife?' said Colin, undeterred, before whipping some cash out of his wallet, throwing it on the table and grabbing Suzie by the hand. 'Come on, darling, let's get out of here.'

Seconds later they were out in the street again, Suzie reeling with a combination of cheap white wine, the heat of the evening and not a little shock at the passion she had thought was long gone from grey, dependable Colin. That young man who used to argue with his parents about politics when he came home from university. The one who would spend his weekends marching for the

GLC instead of talking about regional squash tournaments. The man who had carried her heart with such care, through so much, was still a passionate one. And she could not believe her luck.

Suzie looked down at the small aluminium tin in her hand and realised that she had finished all of the almonds. She must have been hungry after all. While the crochet chat had continued, with Howie explaining that the garment was actually for one of his nephews, they had carried on with their slow walk west. They had passed the London Eye now, its gleaming glass pods twinkling as they slowly rotated in the low autumn sun, and at last Suzie could clearly see the Palace of Westminster now. For the first time, she really felt like they might be closer to the end of today's journey than the beginning.

'Thank you so much, Tim,' said Suzie. 'I'm afraid I've eaten the lot.'

'Oh Suzie, that's my pleasure. I'm glad I remembered to pack them!' he replied, genuinely relieved that his anxious packing hadn't proved overanxious, unnecessary. Made a change.

'Are those two still chatting crafts?' Suzie asked.

'They are,' he replied. 'Abbie wants to know why they don't have contestants making amazing knitted creations on *Drag Race* when they all craft such amazing outfits. And Howie has – quite rightly in my opinion – pointed out that it is much easier to stitch something together quickly if you have a machine than it is to hand-knit something.'

'Oh I love *Drag Race*,' said Suzie. 'They do make such incredible outfits.'

Tim turned slowly to Suzie. 'You watch *Drag Race*? Even I don't watch *Drag Race* . . .' It was true. He had long wondered if there was something wrong with him for finding it all a bit theatrical, so American, and now here was Suzie with her neat little pearl necklace and her elasticated slacks telling him *she* watched it?

'Well obviously I didn't always watch it. But then last year I got into the UK version – the one with the split season, the lockdown one – and I, well, I absolutely adored it. And all of them.'

'I don't know what to say.'

'You should give it a go, Tim, I reckon you'd be surprised by what you might learn. It's all about self-confidence and self-expression really, and we could all do with a bit more of those things, especially these days.'

Tim nodded, taking this new information in.

'I suppose you're right, Suzie.'

'Of course I am. And I love that they all love their mums too.'

'Everyone loves their mum, don't they?'

Suzie gave him a sad-looking smile. Perhaps she was missing her daughter, not being with her on her big day.

Abbie turned round, looking up at Tim who was standing behind her. 'You guys doing OK there?'

'Oh absolutely,' he replied. 'I've just been hearing all about how Suzie here loves *RuPaul's Drag Race*.'

'You're kidding!'

'I am not kidding.'

'As I was just saying to Tim, of *course* I love it.'

'Just when I think you can't surprise me anymore, Suzie. It's got me through some dark times, that show.'

'Do you know what, Abbie? Me too.'

'What am I missing?' asked Tim. 'It just seemed kind of cliquey and inaccessible when I watched it.' Making such a confession out loud seemed almost profane, but Abbie didn't seem shocked in the slightest.

'Yeah I know what you mean,' said Abbie. 'It takes a while to kind of get your bearings, like when you first start watching *Eastenders*, or paying attention to the news.'

'She's right,' said Suzie, with a shrug.

'But then you realise it doesn't matter if you don't always get the joke because the whole point of the show is just not worrying about fitting in. It's kind of about your duty to live your best life in the end.'

'Do you really think it's our duty to live our best life?' asked Tim, Abbie's perspective on 'duty' suddenly very curious to him.

'I'm not sure that that's what the Queen's interpretation of duty was,' added Suzie. But Abbie remained undeterred.

'D'you know what, I do. She was dutiful and loving, but she also slayed. Like, she slayed so hard.'

Tim wondered if despite it all, Abbie was actually making sense.

8

Westminster Bridge, Covid Memorial Wall, St Thomas's Hospital

After several hours of squinting into the sun, Abbie's eyes were now tight, dried out. She'd barely had any sleep last night or any water since she had reached the queue, and now the tiredness which had been creeping up on her all day had given her leaden limbs to match her stinging eyes. She thought of her little canvas bag, stuffed with snacks, water, her big sunglasses. For a moment, she wished she were curled up in bed, watching something silly on her phone under the covers. Then she remembered the flat, and her flatmates, and felt a pang of unease at the thought she was supposed to call that place home.

'Wonder if Maisie made it home OK,' she pondered aloud, as if she could mitigate the guilt she felt for being glad she was no longer queueing with her.

'Have you messaged her?' asked Howie.

'Yes, loads earlier. But now I'm down to ten per cent battery, so I'm kind of trying to ignore my phone and hope she contacts me. Do you think that's bad?'

'Here, I have a spare battery pack – you can use it.' Tim handed her the square of plastic with its attached wire. Of course he had one, of course he did.

'I wouldn't worry about her too much,' said Suzie. 'She'd just overdone it. She'll be fine.'

'Exactly,' said Tim. 'Girls like her are always fine.' He glanced away, looking as surprised by his sudden comment as she was.

'What do you mean "girls like her"?' asked Abbie.

'Oh I don't know, I suppose I was speaking out of turn a little. It's just, those two, they seemed very sure of themselves. I mean, where even is the other one?'

'Annabelle?'

'Yes, her. They just left you, Abbie. You're the one who's new to London, you're the one who was taking care of them, and you're the one who ended up being left with strangers.'

There was a queasy lurch in her guts. She knew that Tim was telling the truth. She had texted both of them, repeatedly, over the last couple of hours, but neither had replied. Had she been kidding herself she had ever fitted in in that flat? She'd thought she was giving it a decent go, that she was winning them over. This morning she had really believed that them including her in their plans had been a sign that she was connecting. Now, after nine hours without her bag and not a word from either of them, it seemed clearer that she was better connected to the friends she had met in the queue than the ones she had actually arrived with.

'Oh Tim, I don't know what to say. I can't tell if I'm embarrassed that you've kind of seen through my crappy friends or if I'm actually relieved that you have. But, they're not bad people, you know . . .'

'We know that. They never are,' Tim told her. 'They're just . . .'

'. . . they just have the insulation of wealth,' said Howie with a shrug.

Abbie looked across the river at the gold glistening on the buildings, and she knew the men were telling her the truth. Someone who knew what it was like to grow up worrying about money would not ask her to 'just pick up' a vape for them on the way home, mysteriously vanish to the bathroom when it was time to pay for the coffees or casually shirk the tab for an Uber as often those girls did. They didn't know what 'Let's just split it equally' felt like when you'd only ordered a starter and tap water as you weren't sure if you were going to get paid on time. Money meant so little to them that they had not considered that it wasn't the same for her. And she'd been too embarrassed to articulate it to them, either.

She pictured her mother, her hands scraping her hair back off her face as she opened another batch of bills, trying to figure out how to get on top of things once and for all. She thought of her father, hunched over himself at family events, ashamed to have his in-laws see the reality of how he hadn't provided for them.

'You're right, and I'm a bit ashamed now,' she said to Tim, 'that I couldn't see it myself.'

Memories of hushed conversations about 'coping' drifted back up through her memory, like the shreds of plastic twine she'd find on the beach after a high tide. All the times she had begged her parents for a puppy only to be told they couldn't afford a dog. The letters her mum would sometimes snatch from the doormat before anyone else saw them. The Friday evenings that Aunty Em had shoved a tenner in her hand 'for the weekend' when she came to visit.

Abbie could see now why her parents had been so worried about her heading to London, trying to make it in a world where job security was so scarce. It wasn't that they didn't want her to create beautiful work, or to try her very hardest to make an impact; it was that they didn't want her to feel her soul nibbled at by girls like those, with their casual confidence and their healthy allowances.

Suddenly Abbie felt completely unmoored, as if the world she had been telling herself she lived in might not ever have existed. She had been convinced that if she just kept up with the in-crowd and didn't let on, the velvet rope to the world she wanted to work in would soon be lifted for her too.

Instead, she was standing there with a bunch of people she'd known for less than a day, with a sense that she was so untethered to anything and anyone that at any moment she might just float up and away, down the river and off into the sea. What was keeping her down? And who would really care if she went? It's not as if there would ever be a queue for her if she died. There'd be no gold carriage. There wouldn't even be a corgi to miss her.

Heat rushed into her cheeks as the true weight of how alone she was in London really hit her. Of how she was trying to achieve something that she was not even sure she wanted. Her breathing felt heavier, panicked.

'Hey Abbie . . .' The familiar bear paw of Howie's hand landed on her back. 'Fuck shame.'

Abbie's eyes widened at hearing the word there, in the queue, such a solemn space. She smiled, not quite sure what to say, particularly as for the first time all day Howie really wasn't smiling. He was looking at her intently, even his eyes deadly serious.

'He's right,' said Tim. 'No one has ever, ever made a good decision driven by shame.'

'Trust us,' said Howie, glancing at Tim. Were they . . . having a moment? Abbie was sure they were. Either way, she knew that they were telling her the truth.

'You're probably right,' she said.

'They are.' Suzie had now turned to join the conversation. The queue was bunched closer together now, so they were having to huddle a little not be overheard by everyone around. But Suzie's eyes were bright, intent. She wanted to be heard. Perhaps she would have been leaning in like this anyway.

'Life happens when you're not paying attention,' she continued. 'Trust me. Even if you're lucky enough to live as long as I have, it goes by in a second. And you can waste so much time trying to avoid feeling ashamed for things you've done, you've said, you've felt, you want. Don't do it, Abbie.'

'Oh Suzie, you're so wise. I wish you were my mum. Are you sure you don't want to adopt me?'

Abbie nuzzled into the soft quilting of Suzie's coat, while the older woman stroked the younger's hair. In that moment, she really did want Suzie to do just that.

Suzie was right. But more than that, Tim could not believe that he had agreed, and agreed out loud.

He was tired of shame. Tired of pretending he didn't mind turning up at Christmas and no one asking about his love life. Tired of feeling alienated within his own community and not knowing who to talk to about it. Tired of trying to blend in at work, in the gym, on holiday, in case he made anyone uncomfortable. In case *he* made himself uncomfortable. In case he felt ashamed of who he was.

Howie made it look so easy, with his long hair, his broad shoulders and his crochet skills. He had the affable charm of someone who had spent years working behind bars, seeing people celebrating their happiest days and experiencing their darkest hours. What had Tim experienced? Spreadsheets, deadlines and petty office quibbles about whether they should be using disposable coffee pods that wasted less of the company time or should invest in an actual coffee machine and fill in the insurance forms to have all that pressurised steam in a workplace.

Suzie's little talk about how short life was had reached him where he was usually too shuttered to the world to let these anxieties in. Maybe it was just the result of having been on his feet for so long, or perhaps it was that he hadn't had much sleep last night, but today was starting to make him feel as if his heart was beating on the outside of his body, suddenly vulnerable to new sensations. Suzie's well-timed intervention to Abbie had got to him too, as if she'd been the doctor tapping his lower knee in just the spot to provoke an uninvited reaction.

How to change, though? Keeping himself steady had long been the only way to cope with a world already moving so fast that just ten minutes with the headlines could leave him reeling for the rest of the day. Was he supposed to just find a Zumba class and tell himself he was open to new experiences? Was this why he had turned up today, despite him spinning himself a yarn about family duty and honouring Her Majesty? And had he changed anything at all by coming? Or was he simply telling himself he was a part of things when in fact, as ever, he was merely playing an observer, talking to strangers about their problems, doling out food and chargers as if being helpful to other people would mean that one day he'd receive the same from one of them.

He gave a heavy sigh, and imagined himself upping and leaving the queue now, and walking away, heading south. Just keeping on until he left London, and hit the suburbs, then the hills of Surrey, the South Downs and finally the shore. He just wished he could be sitting in a cottage overlooking the sea, learning something about a rare wildflower while someone he loved – who loved him back – was making him some fresh eggs on toast.

'Look!' cried Abbie. 'That's Westminster Bridge! We are *so* nearly there now – it can't be much more than an hour or so, can it?'

'Well, the queue is actually going over Lambeth Bridge, and then back again towards the palace,' he replied, his voice heavy with tiredness. And facts. 'Westminster Bridge is just regular busy. Tourists. They're probably all looking at us.'

'Oh.' Abbie looked a little crestfallen. So he went over and put an arm around her.

'Don't worry. You've got us. And think how far we've come from where we started. We'll make it.'

Perhaps if he convinced her of this, he could convince himself. He looked up and saw Howie smiling at them. There was a tenderness in his eyes that felt like someone pressing a bruise on his heart.

'Yes, we will,' he told them. And just for a second, Tim really believed that they all would. Not just today, but beyond it.

It had been fifteen minutes ago now, but Suzie was still reeling from Abbie's comment about wishing she could adopt her. It had been a joke – hadn't it? – but it still felt too close to the bone. Did she know something? Had she figured out the lies she had been telling earlier? What had possessed her?

The memory of the fantastical tales she'd been spinning to Abbie and the gang all day left Suzie chilly, shaken a little, wishing she could just go and sit down by herself for a bit. But when they all continued their slow procession – passing straight by Westminster Bridge instead of heading over it – she had an inkling that her sense of desolation was not unique. The realisation that there was a long way to go yet seemed to have made everyone around her a little forlorn. They'd been not just standing, but moving for all this time, with no rest, no little sit-downs at all – constantly alert for the next leg of the walk. Her attention felt worn, paper thin, as if she needed some time to herself to stare into space, embracing her melancholy, before they could move on to feeling something bigger and more public-spirited.

But, just like the rest of her fellow queuers, Suzie knew that there was no way she could leave now. The whole reason they were there was to honour a woman's ability to carry on no matter what, so she could hardly come this far only to do the opposite. What was the point in queueing to commemorate someone's forbearance, their longevity, their steadfastness, if you couldn't stay on your feet for a couple more hours yourself?

Still, the atmosphere around them was changing. There was a marked increase in the police presence, and a couple of people near them were looking around, trying to figure out why. Too tired now to look ahead, Suzie watched her feet carefully as they shuffled forward; the path along the river at this point ran right alongside the wall, overlooked by the rustling plane trees outside the modern blocks of St Thomas's Hospital. Ah, so the change in mood was because they were approaching The National Covid Memorial Wall. Suzie was dimly aware of the wall, having seen a few headlines about it the previous year. But she'd largely avoided it, having reached a sort of saturation point with news coverage about the grief of others. Then, as the queuers in front took the few steps down towards the embankment facing the wall, she started to hear the sound of someone crying.

Up ahead, there it was, the wails of someone else's grief. On top of that was the noise of an increased number of news reporters and their crews. The brief shouts of camera and sound men catching each other's attention above the fray, the news reporters making phone calls and live broadcasts over the noise of boats passing, bells ringing, sirens blaring. A couple of hours ago Suzie was finding the whole day rather exciting: meeting new people, being a part of something, having a mission to complete. Now, she felt horribly exposed, vulnerable to everyone else's swirling moods and emotions as well as the increasing churn of her own.

She had, she concluded, been far too open today. And now she felt as if she were walking around with a layer of her skin missing. Things suddenly seemed precarious, unstable, as if the ground could give way beneath her at a moment's notice. Yes, she had come here to pay her respects, but she'd also been looking for a sense of community, communion even. This hubbub now, this maelstrom of emotions, this all felt like too much of it.

There was no way she would have felt this anxiety, this terrible dread that things were spiralling out of control, if Colin had still been here. Yes, he would have driven her mad all day and he would certainly have packed a mortifyingly cumbersome bag which she'd have huffed and puffed about all the way up on the train. But he'd have brought sensible things, more than a sandwich and an apple. He'd have made sure she had a hat. He'd have made sure she hadn't got this thirsty. And he'd have had no truck with that Annabelle character and the way she'd treated sweet Abbie.

If only she had appreciated these things more while he'd still been around instead of suffocating under the weight of her shame for so much of the time. Why had she wasted so much time wallowing in her past when she could have been enjoying her time with him? Oh, the hours she had spent trying to second-guess what his response might be if she ever told him about Bess, when he had always been able to surprise her – she teased him about his fastidiousness, but he'd also been a professional go-getter who was prepared to fight for her honour in a random Greek bar. Why had she not seen what she had when she still had it?

Caring for her parents, pressure at work, and even

menopause and a sense that she'd never know passion like she had with Eddie, had crept up on Suzie like a smog. By her early fifties she had been carrying the secret of her daughter for more than three decades and while the pain sometimes seemed to have numbed, what had replaced it was a hardness inside of her. Scar tissue maybe. Or a sort of calcification of her emotions, leaving her tougher, more able to deal with life's knocks, but also brittle. Her softness, her willingness to learn, to try new things, gradually ebbed away. By the time Colin approached retirement age, some days she felt her bones had been replaced with steel.

Across the river, Big Ben clanged on the hour, reminding her of the church bells that had tolled the day of that famous royal wedding in 1981. How all of London seemed to be filled with well-wishers, the mood so different from today. But it was the new king's second marriage which had truly caught her imagination. The day that Prince Charles had finally married his second bride, Camilla. The soap opera of the Diana years finally seemed to be fading, and when Suzie had watched the older couple on the steps of Windsor Guildhall that Saturday morning nearly twenty years ago, the idea of a partnership sustaining itself for so long, and despite such immeasurable odds, had seemed almost unbearably romantic. Suzie's heart had ached as she had considered the unlikely power of their romance that day, as if she were holding it in her hand, turning it over like a shell she had found on the beach.

Now, as she stood within the sound of Big Ben, she suspected that if only she had shifted her gaze from the live coverage on the television that sunny Saturday, she might have noticed that Colin still looked at her just the same way that Charles did his own bride – still unable to believe that he too had managed to marry the woman of his dreams.

Suzie's chest felt tight, sorrow not just for what she'd lost but for how little she'd appreciated it, rising like a tide around her. The day was starting to feel dreamlike, almost hallucinatory, as different memories jumbled through her mind. From the corner of her eye she saw a Chelsea Pensioner heading over Westminster Bridge and wondered if she was starting to imagine things – the London of her childhood, of her youth and of a thousand souvenir shops all starting to slide and meld into each other in this swirl of raging emotion. Hadn't they been on the news yesterday? Was this just someone in a red coat? She couldn't tell anymore, memories sliding alongside the gauzy reality of today as if they were one and the same.

One minute she could see herself and Colin, lost in the Millennium Dome, bent double with laughter at having lost their friends Richard and Caroline in the Faith zone for twenty agonising minutes. It was the most they'd laughed since New Year, Colin eventually having to grab her by the hand and find the nearest fire exit. The drama, the giggles of it all had left Suzie limp, confessing to him that she'd been reminded of the night of the Greek frisson, much to his delight.

But the next minute she could see the gorgeous country wedding of Colin's goddaughter Heather – Richard's daughter. Heather had meant so much to Colin over the years, and he had always taken an interest in her exams and hobbies and even her budding career. After Richard's sudden death a year or so before, Heather had asked Colin to give her away, and Suzie swore it was the only time she ever saw him cry.

'You have no idea how honoured I am,' he'd said. 'I honestly thought it was a duty I would never be asked to fulfil in my life.'

Suzie had felt a glug of adrenaline hit her stomach as she thought of Bess, the baby she had last seen on a drizzly day in Wales, now a young woman, perhaps getting married herself. Colin hadn't been able to give *her* away because she herself had done that long ago.

Colin had been a wreck in the week preceding the wedding itself, fretting over his speech, his suit, even his 'predicted pace' as he walked her down the aisle. Suzie had tried so hard to be thrilled for him, supportive even, but every conversation had felt like a fresh slick of sadness, lapping at her day and night. She had spent a fortune on her outfit, making a special day trip to Cambridge to get something really smart for the occasion. And she'd looked great, but she could never wear that suit again. Not because she hadn't been showered with compliments, but because she knew that beautiful butter yellow silk would always remind her of the hot, hidden tears which had splashed onto it when she had ran to the bathroom in the minutes after Colin had completed his speech.

Colin had been so deflated after the ceremony, knowing all too well that he'd never do anything similar again.

'But you were wonderful,' she told him, stroking his shoulder in bed as she curled around him despite the heat of the summer's evening. 'Richard would have been so proud.'

That night was the closest she had ever come to telling him the truth. It wasn't the first time, and it certainly wasn't the last, but it was the nearest she had ever dared to tread. And as she felt him slowly drift off to sleep, as she whispered how much she loved him in his ear, it was the time that left the deepest bruise. But then, the moment passed, the next morning the talk was back to practicalities such as beating the bank holiday traffic back to Suffolk. And by Tuesday things were back to normal. So on they'd plodded.

Suzie was snatched from her memories by Tim telling her to watch out for the steps as they followed the queue down on the west side of Westminster Bridge to walk right alongside the Memorial Wall. To her horror, she realised that it wasn't a wall of the size she had long imagined – that of a wall in a home or even a gallery – but a huge, long expanse of stone, almost the length of the Palace of Westminster, which lay on exactly the other side of the river. On it went, on and on. She really couldn't see where it ended from where she was standing.

The people around her hushed, despite the greater hubbub of non-queuers in this area. Stewards and police were keeping the queuers on the far side of the path, closer to the river, at a metre or so's distance from the wall itself. It didn't stop them from seeing it though; heart after heart after tiny red heart had been painted along the entire expanse of the wall. Five hundred metres, under the plane trees above, and inside of each one was a name, dates, messages of love.

I miss you.

I love you.

Gone too soon.

After a while, Suzie couldn't read anymore. The names, the dates, were starting to blur. Then she realised it was her eyes, welling with tears. The pandemic hadn't taken Colin, but it had meant she hadn't been able to say goodbye to him properly. And for every miserable month of those Covid years, as she became increasingly exhausted, isolated and alone, she had missed him more. Not just because he wasn't there anymore, but because there hadn't been space to say goodbye, to say all that she had wanted to him. To let him know. To let him know any of it – the baby, her love for him, the way her life was now so much greyer without him. God, there had been so many times she had called him grey – but she'd barely known back then how grey life could really become.

Had it been her duty to be happy after all, she wondered? What if she should never have worried about doing the right thing and chased her best life all along? Perhaps it was Abbie in her innocence who had turned out to be the wisest of the lot of them?

Suzie heard a scuffle behind her, and as she turned, saw that a couple of metres behind their little group someone in the queue had pulled a biro from their pocket and stepped towards the wall itself. It looked as if he was trying to add a name, a date to the wall, but that security had immediately stepped forward to stop him. He cried out, distressed, begging to reach forward with his pen. Others turned to look at first, worried, but then looked down, trying not to embarrass someone who was clearly vulnerable. Perhaps they, like Suzie, realised that he – like almost everyone there – seemed to have lost someone recently too.

At first she worried that the man was going to be removed, and after ten hours of queueing cold and hungry. But the others around him, including Howie up at the back, managed to persuade the stewards that he was fine, that they'd keep an eye on him, that he didn't deserve to be punished for something that the rest of the country had been able to do without recourse for the last year.

'Ease up, the man might never have been to London before,' she heard someone explain.

'It's not just a day trip for all of us – we've come from all over,' said another.

Suzie sighed with relief that people were defending the man, that the security staff had accepted that what people were trying to do was honourable. That they were all just trying to find a place to put their memories, their pain, their grief.

Something in the kindness of the crowd flicked a

switch in Suzie. She swallowed, looking down at her shoes. Don't cry now. It's not about you. Be respectful.

But it wasn't enough. For once, the monumental effort of trying to do the right thing simply wasn't going to be enough. And so came the tears. At first, a sob which could in isolation have been mistaken for a hiccup. But then another, and then her face was suddenly damp with tears, pouring out of her almost silently.

'My god, Suzie, are you OK?' asked Tim, putting a gentle hand on her shoulder.

'I just miss my husband,' she said. Tim looked as if he didn't know what to say. Had she even mentioned to any of them today that her husband was dead, rather than at home? But Suzie didn't care. Relative to the whirlwind of emotion inside, she now felt an almost uncanny stillness come over her. She was no longer sobbing, shoulders heaving, like she used to sometimes when Colin was at golf and she'd have a good cry about the babies they couldn't have. And she wasn't wailing like she'd seen girlfriends do when they'd found out that men had cheated on them. Instead, she was just streaming with tears, tears that no number of Colin's hankies would ever be able to help her with.

'Here, take these,' said Tim, handing her a fistful of takeaway napkins from the coffee place he'd been to earlier.

'I'm so sorry, I don't know what's come over me,' replied Suzie, dabbing at her eyes with the paper.

'You don't have to apologise,' he said. 'Is there anything

I can do? Let me get some water. Is there someone you'd like me to call for you or something?'

'Oh no, Suzie, what can we do?' piped up Abbie. 'You've been amazing today, I don't know what I'd have done without you. Here, have a hug.'

Abbie put her arms out, Suzie leant into them, her body heavy with tiredness.

'I didn't know you'd lost your husband recently, I'm so sorry, I had no idea,' said the younger woman.

'Oh, I'm being silly really,' said Suzie. 'He died well over two years ago. But we didn't have a chance to say goodbye properly, and I still miss him. I've missed him so much.'

'Of course you have . . .'

Suzie was in full flow now, tears streaming down her face, a sense of terrible relief to be letting go of what she'd been holding onto for so long.

'There's so much I wish I could have said to him,' she said, trying to wipe at least some of the tears from her face.

'Just let it go . . .' said the younger woman.

'I so badly wanted him to know about my baby,' sobbed Suzie. 'I missed her so much.'

'Of course you did.'

'And I kept it from him all that tim—'

Suddenly there was an even greater commotion up ahead – a sense of movement, the crowd straining forwards almost as one, towards something, then the noise of camera shutters.

'What is it? What's happening?' asked Abbie, standing on tiptoes, looking around to see who might know, while still keeping one protective arm around Suzie.

'I don't know, daa-lin, I can't quite see from here,' replied Howie, who, alongside Tim, had been keeping a discreet distance while the women had their conversation.

Then came whispers from a few people ahead, hastily being passed back.

It's the King.

The King? It took a second. Then Suzie realised. The new King. And Prince William, the new Prince of Wales.

They've come to see people, to thank them.

Suzie had been waiting so long to shed those tears, and now she'd been interrupted. But things were moving too fast, the crowd shifting almost as one, with no time or space for her individual grief. She felt as if she were watching events unfold, rather than a part of the crowd in that moment. Security were visible now, the queue reaching a bank of barriers ahead and then . . . there they were. The Royals. Out of their quietly expensive cars and on the pavement, chatting to people, shaking hands, saying thank you again and again – seemingly to whatever people were telling them.

Was it the almost overpowering celebrity of these people that was lending events the quality of being watched through a screen, or was it that parts of Suzie seemed to be shutting down, closing off, exhausted by the intense emotion of the day? People around her were whispering, cheering, weeping. But Suzie was dazed, blinking – staying close to the others but simultaneously not quite present. These faces were so familiar, as much a part of her life as her own family's. And yet how strange it felt to see them right there, up close, so unlike those of her own flesh and blood.

On some level it was this *moment*, this chance to personally express their condolences, that every person queueing had wished for. And Suzie was no different, having come here today to be a part of something communal, to pay tribute to something that was bigger than herself, to be a whisper in tomorrow's history books. But the intensity of the memories that the day had already brought up for her meant she didn't feel strong enough to try and lean forward into the melee. She didn't want to embarrass herself, to seem like a celebrity spotter, to be too keen. But she was also unconvinced that it was actually them. That today really was happening. That it wasn't a hallucination. A bad dream after an unnerving week.

The rest of the crowd seemed less conflicted, transfixed by the action just up ahead, the shuffle of the press now clamouring around the lucky few who were up against the barriers at Lambeth Pier. All eyes were on the action, Suzie moving almost against her will, separated briefly from the few people around her that she knew, soon finding herself at the front, her own eyes glazed, nodding, and saying yet another thank you.

'*Thank you. I'm so sorry. And thank you, Your Royal Highnesses. I know it must be a very difficult week for you too . . .*'

It was only a couple of minutes later, once the men and their team had been whisked away in their sleek, panther-like cars and the crowds had stepped back a little, that Suzie heard Abbie's voice to her left. The sun was starting to dip now. The sky was still a perfect blue but the shadows were getting longer, the stone of the wall beside the river now in shade.

'How are you feeling, Suzie?' came Abbie's now familiar voice. 'I lost you for a minute! Do you need me to get you a cup of tea or some water?'

'Much better, thank you, dear,' she replied. 'And apologies again for my little wobble.'

'Don't be daft,' replied Abbie. 'It's an emotional day isn't it?'

'It certainly is.'

'I'm glad you're OK though. But Suzie, could I ask you something, about what you said back there?'

The ringing Suzie had felt in her ears was louder now, almost more of an alarm.

'Of course,' she replied, trying hard to keep her face still, impassive. 'Fire away.'

'What did you mean about keeping something from your husband? About missing your baby? I don't want to be rude and of course you don't have to tell me, but I didn't quite understand what you were saying. When they— when we got interrupted.'

With that, Suzie felt as if she had fallen through a trapdoor and was falling, the ground simply giving way beneath her. She had not even realised it was happening at the time, but it had happened at last: her secret was out.

9

Lambeth Bridge

The ringing in her ears seemed to be louder than ever, leaving Suzie entirely unable to think. It was only as an ambulance actually passed on its way to St Thomas's Hospital that she realised the noise was internal.

Her legs were limp, jelly-like. The aching feet and dull thud in her lower back were no longer there, replaced by a hollow weightlessness. She held out her own hand in front of her, as if to check that her physical self was still there, because internally she felt as if she were spiralling through the air, nothing to catch her, nothing to grab on the way down.

But the queue was moving again, finally taking the steps back up from the embankment facing the Houses of Parliament, and onto Lambeth Bridge at last. For so long Suzie had kept herself going with the promise that they'd soon be crossing to the north side of the river, but now she was struggling to keep one foot in front of the other. There was a palpable buzz all around them, people up ahead stopping to take photographs on the bridge. It was the perfect spot, the crossing point, with Westminster, the London Eye, and the long walk they'd done behind them, bridges fading into the distance like markers on a sundial.

All Suzie could hear was Abbie's last words to her, all other thoughts crushed to the sides of her mind as if the emotional churn of the day was taking up too much internal space now – her secret was bulging and swelling after years of compression. It was threatening to take over if she couldn't think of something sensible to say in reply. And despite this, there was a small, glittering slice of her heart that was relieved to be breathing out in the open air again.

She fiddled with the strap of her handbag, waiting for the people immediately in front to clear the steps up to the bridge, making space for them to head up behind them. But the part of her that was blind with panic at being caught out and the other part, yearning for freedom like a plant reaching towards the light, were still wrestling each other internally, consuming all her attention.

The sky remained an almost impertinent bright blue, despite it being well into last hour or so of the afternoon. As Tim looked up, admiring the neat carved pine cone motifs at the end of the Lambeth Bridge, he could barely believe that the weather had been so kind all day.

He'd been prepared for near-Arctic conditions, and

now felt a little bashful about his rucksack full of spare socks, spare heat pads, and a thermal vest and snood set made entirely from recycled plastic bottles. Better safe than sorry, he tried to tell himself, but today the uninterrupted blue seemed to be mocking him a little. Teaching him a lesson that not every day needed his level of neurotic attention to detail. But there had been warnings on the news! He was just trying to do the right thing. As always, he'd just been trying to do the right thing.

He could see groups up ahead posing on the bridge, and noticed that almost without fail each of them had faces reddened from a day standing in the glare of the sun. His own face prickled with factor 50 sunscreen, a small drip of sweat having made its way from his hairline down into the corner of his eye, now causing them to water profusely. He wiped at them with a tissue, reminding himself that skin cancer would be worse than the temporary indignity of streaming eyes.

'Do you know why this bridge is painted red, and Westminster green?' he asked Howie, trying to drum up conversation, anything to break the uneasy silence that had fallen across the group.

'I'm sure you're about to tell me . . .' replied Howie, with half a smile. Was it half a smile? For a moment, Tim wondered if it was still the gentle teasing that he'd grown used to from Howie, or if the man was genuinely bored of him, sick of his endless pub quiz facts and skin-deep nuggets of British history.

'Well, the seats in the House of Commons are green, and that end of the Palace of Westminster is closer to Westminster Bridge . . . and the House of Lords is closer to this one – and its seats are red. And the carpet I think. I'm sure I remember something about the carpet changing colour between the two as well.'

Tim's voice faded away. He'd well and truly lost his nerve. The day had tired him out; he was only going to be here with these people for a couple more hours. Why should he keep trying to entertain them? To make them like him? It felt like picking at a scab, endlessly revealing that these tidbits were all he had.

'I've never really met anyone who still cared about those sorts of facts before,' replied Howie. 'It was one of the reasons I used to love working at the palace. Not because of all the fancy gold shit, and all the ancient rituals or whatever, but because you could learn so much about *people* when you looked into the details.'

Tim looked at Howie, convinced for a second that he was teasing him again. But his face, his kind, open face, was completely sincere. He had a hand up, holding his thick shaggy hair back against the wind as they reached the steps, and Tim saw that he'd caught the sun too.

'That's how I see it too. I'm sure my colleagues just think I am obsessed by pub quizzes or whatever, but it's not that. It's more that I like trying to find the order in things. Working out what sort of stone came from where or why. What sort of fabric was valuable when and why. What sort of image was important and why.'

'Except half the time in this country the answer will have something to do with plundering if you dig deep enough.'

'Yes, there is that. It gets all a bit bleak, doesn't it?'

'It does, but it also tells a story. And figuring out the story makes things all seem more—'

'Manageable?'

'Yeah, I guess so.'

'People are so . . . unpredictable. But facts, they can't mess me around – they can be put in order, and then you can find a way to manage things.'

Tim sighed. He hadn't ever really admitted to feeling this way before, not out loud at least. If he tried to talk about something like this at Sunday lunch with his family they'd tell him to lighten up and want to gossip about the Royal Family's infighting. Knowing the facts, knowing the symbols, knowing the protocols: they were what made him feel moored, not gossip about the Princes' marriages.

'I hear ya, Timbo.'

Tim's eyebrows raised almost imperceptibly at this nickname. Howie continued unabashed.

'I didn't feel like this at all until I came here. But I was alone when I turned up. Never been so far from home. And there was a funny kind of comfort in knowing bits and pieces.'

'There really is. You start to see patterns in things don't you?'

'You do, and I know what you're getting at. And it

sustained me for a bit when I first got here – maybe I'd overdone the partying a bit in my youth, you know the drill . . .'

Tim didn't, but he had a go at imagining.

'The thing is, Timothy, it can only get you so far. There's other work to be done, especially if you've had dark times.'

Tim nodded again, slower this time. Slowly, he raised his eyes to Howie, who was staring directly at him, un-embarrassed. Tim longed to look directly at someone like that, entirely sure of who he was. But how had Howie got here, if he'd had these so-called dark times. The conversation was heading into ever more uncomfortable territory.

He opened his mouth to reply, but as they hit the bright sunshine up on the bridge and he briefly overtook the women, he noticed that Suzie was really not looking very well at all. Her hair was more dishevelled than ever and her skin was grey, eyes bloodshot. Abbie seemed to be talking to her intently, stooping a little so her mouth was directly by her ear. Perhaps she hadn't noticed the look on Suzie's face. The people in front of them had paused for photographs, so he took the opportunity to turn and face the women.

'Suzie, are you feeling alright?' he asked, as gently as he could in an environment so busy.

She looked back at him, blankly. Abbie was clearly concerned, her eyes darting back and forth between Tim and Suzie. She mouthed 'I'm a bit worried' at him.

'Here,' said Tim hurriedly. 'Take one of my energy gels. It tastes disgusting, but if you're feeling tired or maybe a little wobbly, it'll perk you up.' He lifted a flap on the side of his rucksack and pulled out a tube of what looked like foil wrapping. He ripped the edge off and presented it to Suzie, all as fast as he could.

'It's glucose, just suck the gel out of the packet, they work really fast.'

Suzie still didn't speak.

What had she done? Not just with today, but with the last fifty years?

The question swirled in front of her, reality sliding a little out of view. Tim was passing her a little packet. It looked like a teeny tiny Capri Sun, and she thought of her friends who had grandchildren and how she would stock the pleasing foil packets as a treat when they were visiting, hoping that the person on the checkout thought that they were for her own grandchildren. Tim had put the pack of glucose in her hand, but she didn't seem to be able to quite grasp it. Her hands felt slack, her body so heavy, exhausted from the day and bowed by a lifetime of secrets. No more, she thought to herself. If I could just find my voice, I'd never lie again.

Tim had a supportive hand on her elbow as she moved the energy gel to her mouth and gulped at the packet, as instinctively as a baby. It tasted sticky, a chemical sort of orange that could only have come from a lab. The gloopy sugar trickled down the back of her throat, while she leaned forward and replaced the foil packet with a small water bottle.

What had she actually eaten today? A sandwich about three hours ago, and some coffee? That apple she had shared with Abbie, and maybe a bar of something at some point too? Why had she thought that would be enough? How foolish she had been to attempt this by herself. How silly she felt that just because the Queen had been through so much, she too must endure a day so physically demanding. How vain she'd been, dashing to London, trying to fit in, trying to *be* the news instead of watching it at home.

Now Abbie's hand was at her elbow, keeping her steady. How kind they were all being. How close they had all become. Then, for a second, how far away they all seemed . . .

But just as she thought her legs were buckling beneath her, the glucose hit. Her blood seemed to speed up, her fingers tingling as they came back to life, even her scalp seemed to be pulsing against the roots of her hair.

'Oh goodness, I am making a bit of a fuss today, aren't I?' she said, standing straighter now, her breathing easier, the others stepping back a little to give her space. 'And you're all being so kind to a little old lady like me.'

'Not at all,' she heard Tim saying. 'We were worried about you for a minute though.'

'Oh, look at the colour coming back into her face!' said

Abbie, with a sunbeam of a smile. 'What was in that thing!?'

Suzie smiled, screwing the lid back onto the water bottle and thanking everyone again.

'Listen up, you three,' said Howie, looming over Abbie's shoulder. 'Do you want me to take a snap of you all, while we're here?'

'Oh, go on then,' said Abbie. 'We're nearly there and once I'm home I'm worried I'll think I made the whole day up!'

'But we need you in it, Howie,' said Suzie.

'Nah, I'll be fine, let's get the shot,' he replied. Tim looked crestfallen for a second.

Suzie couldn't bear to see the look on his face, putting her arm around his and Abbie's waists as she stood between them, her back to East London, the brilliant blue sky above. She grinned at the camera, not caring if her hair looked wild or her nose pink. She really did feel better. In fact, so much better that it was as if she were approaching a sort of euphoria.

Abbie was right. When they were home in a few hours, they'd probably never see each other again. This might be her chance to end a lifetime of running from the truth and finally stand and look it in the eye. She could ignore Abbie's question and carry on just as she had done for so long, grinding forwards, getting things done, keeping up appearances. Or she could say things out loud for once – she could live a life unfettered by the secret that had already taken so much from her. Even if that life were only lived openly for an hour or two, even if it were just a glimpse before she had to head back home. She could try her hand at simply being honest.

She reminded herself to breathe. Her heart was racing, the glucose still making her slightly shaky with excitement. People ahead were now moving quickly, having reached the far side of the bridge, photo opportunity over. Suzie felt giddy, possibilities whirring and buzzing through her mind, plans she had never let herself believe might actually happen now taking on fresh urgency. But there wasn't time to stop to chat anymore, they were trotting down the steps on the north side of the bridge, leaving the water behind them. So Suzie kept up the pace, walking alongside Abbie and resting a hand on her arm briefly to catch her attention.

'Abbie, about what you asked me earlier . . .'

'Oh you don't have to explain, it's none of my business.'

Abbie was walking slightly ahead of her, leaning her head back to reply while trying to keep one eye on the road ahead. It felt like days since Suzie had seen proper traffic. The roar of the busy roundabout ahead felt deafening after hours of foot and river traffic. It was clear she could hide behind this noise, that she could use it to get away with saying nothing. Abbie had her eye on the end of the queue now; she'd lost interest in what she had to say already.

'I *do*. I mean, I want to.'

She felt less tired now, but her feet were swollen from a

day carrying her, and she stumbled on a slab of pavement as she approached the kerb.

'Honestly I was just confused, I probably got the wrong end of the stick or something,' replied Abbie, oblivious to her stumble.

'No, it's important. I want to tell the truth.'

'You're making it sound like some huge secret!'

A flick of the hair from Abbie as she turned briefly to chuckle with Suzie. Her nutty brown curls bounced as she turned back to face the road. How easily laughable she found the idea that Suzie could have a big secret.

'Abbie, sweetheart.' Suzie tugged at her sleeve to slow down a little. 'It *is*.'

Conversation was interrupted by them having to pause at the crossing as they left the bridge and made it across Millbank and passed the Horseferry Playground immediately past it. As they made their way over the roundabout at the end of the bridge there were small stretches where there was only space for them to walk single file. Abbie reached out her hand to cling onto Suzie, protecting her as they headed around the corner and towards the green.

Then, as they rounded the corner expecting to see the end of the queue, the entrance to Westminster Palace, the group's collective hearts sank. They realised that they weren't 'nearly' at Westminster Palace at all. Yes, they were mere metres from it, but on the green in front of it were endless lines of steel barriers, winding back and forth, back and forth – an indefinite queue purgatory. Suzie had only ever seen this sort of set-up at Ipswich railway station once, when she had accidentally arrived at the same time as a horde of football fans.

This was going to take a long time – another hour at least. And worst of all, the sun was going down fast, and the trees on the north side of the river were blocking the light from the entire area. They had been bathed in sunlight for the last few hours, whereas they were now standing in the early evening shade. People were huddled in like sardines, an endless, slow-moving snake of exhausted, increasingly melancholy queuers. Nowhere to rest, no way to nip off to the loo or to find a quick coffee as they had become used to on the South Bank. They were trapped, indefinitely, and it had happened just as Suzie had taken her leap of faith and started to confide in Abbie.

'Suzie, what are you talking about? Are you OK?'

'Yes, it's just . . . it's hard to get it, to say it right.'

They entered the zigzag of the queueing pen and Suzie rested a hand on the metal of one of the temporary barriers. It was icy cold to the touch.

'What I'm trying to say is that I had a baby.'

'Of course you did, Suzie, you had Bess. You've told us all about her, about how it's her birthday today. Right?'

'Well, that's not quite right.'

Abbie shot a glance at Tim, who was standing behind her. Suzie might have had a funny moment back then but she wasn't stupid, and she knew what the look meant. *Is she losing her mind?*

'Hear me out. I'm trying to explain. I did have a baby,

but not with Colin. It wasn't my husband's baby. It was *before*.'

'Oh Suzie babe, I won't judge. People do all sorts of things.'

'No, you're not listening!' Suzie suddenly raised her voice, frustrated that Abbie didn't seem to understand what she was telling her. People on the other side of the barrier were sneaking looks at them. They were packed so tightly now that people didn't want to turn and stare, but they'd still had their attention caught. There were, after all, no other raised voices around. Most people were shifting their mood to something more sombre, either exhausted or taking a moment to reflect on what was coming next. There was no other raising of voices; Suzie was alone in getting agitated. But she didn't care anymore. It was now or never. And she couldn't bear a life of 'never' for a second longer.

'Suzie, it's OK. You don't have to talk about this.' Abbie's voice was low now, trying to bring the volume down for all of them.

'But I *do*. It's been too long, you see. I've held onto this for a lifetime.'

'OK, OK.' Abbie's tone was hushed now, trying to contain the situation. Trying to protect her.

'Colin never knew, you see. No one ever knew. Bess never knew.' Suzie's head was dipped a little now, she was almost speaking into her chest, trying not to draw any further attention to herself. 'Bess *doesn't* know.'

Abbie looked at her, dipping her own face in order to

meet Suzie's gaze. She did, her pale eyes wide, listening – ready to hear but clearly still confused.

'Bess never . . . ?'

'She was adopted. I was very young. It was just what happened back then.'

'Oh Suzie.'

Tim, who she knew was right there, listening in, now bent forward himself.

'So, not even Colin knew?'

Suzie's head whipped round to look at him, startled at the way he had just asked the question outright. Her sudden surge of energy was waning fast, the optimism draining from her. In its place, a wave of grief was roaring up towards her as she looked back at Tim and mouthed 'no'.

She watched her knuckles whiten as she gripped the steel barrier, using it to steady herself as they wound further and further into the steel snake of barriers. They were no longer on the edge of the zigzag, but were surrounded now – the only way out would be to be lifted out.

'No,' she said, aloud this time. 'He never knew. I lied to him for nearly fifty years.'

As she saw the look on Tim's face, she wondered if she had made the worst mistake of her life, unravelling decades worth of secrets – and for what? To impress some strangers who had bought her a coffee?

Standing in the shade had been an enormous vibe shift. Abbie suspected that if it hadn't been so difficult to get out from this grim steel snake of queuers, half of them would have upped and left. She was cold now, properly cold, for the first time all day. Her back ached from standing all day, her hair felt lank, sore at the roots, and the inside of her mouth tasted of hours-old coffee and yesterday's Cava. She wanted to be at home in her childhood bedroom, with her dad making her beans on toast downstairs and the title music for *Lord of the Rings* drifting up from the family TV.

She no longer wanted to be here, trying to work out what on earth was going on with Suzie. First she was blurting out things about her past, then trying not to explain, then desperate to explain but making no sense. What was the big deal if she had had a baby before she was married? No one judged that kind of thing anymore – half her friends' parents had never got married in the first place.

There was a part of her that couldn't stop wondering – why would you lie? Why didn't she just tell Colin? But mostly she wanted to tell Suzie to cheer up, to explain that things had changed, that today was not about the mistakes of the past. Tim was joining in the questions now, and it only seemed to be stoking Suzie's anxiety.

'There you go, you see. That's why I never told anyone. To avoid looks like that.'

Abbie wasn't sure that Tim looked like much at all, beyond baffled. If anything, he was probably trying to be polite, to make a genuine effort at understanding.

'What look?' asked Tim.

'Disappointment. A look that says you thought better of me.'

'Suzie, I hardly know you at all. I am just a bit worried about you – you seem to be getting quite upset.'

'Don't worry, Tim. It's not the first time I've been told I'm behaving irrationally.'

Tim stood open-mouthed, amazed by the sudden sharpness of Suzie's tongue. Howie took a brief step closer to him, as if in solidarity with him during this awkward moment.

'Suzie,' Abbie said, 'I honestly don't think Tim is trying to make any sort of point. We just want to help.'

Suzie gave a heavy sigh. The queue shuffled forwards, little by little.

'It's a bit late for help though. Everything's done. Colin's gone, Bess is gone, and I'm still here, having messed it all up. I suppose I feel very . . . regretful.'

Why was she being like this? Suzie was the coolest grannie she'd ever met, who had treated her like a proper adult all day – something even her own flatmates rarely did – and now turned out to have been more interesting than any of them had given her credit for . . . and she was ashamed of it?

'Suzie, please, this is daft. You're not the one whose life is over. We can turn this around!'

'Abigail, please don't tell me what is or isn't daft. I know what I've done. I know about the lies I've told.'

'They weren't lies, they were fantasies! They were barely white lies! I can completely understand why you might want a day where you told some strangers that what you wished was true, was true. Please, consider us – or at the very least me – a safe space.'

Suzie's face crumpled.

'Oh Abbie,' she said, her face now crumpling, almost aging before her eyes. 'Thank you. But it's not just today, is it? It's all the lies before today too. My darling Colin. All that wasted time.'

Her voice was breathy, almost a whisper now. Tim was leaning in, his arm round her as she hunched over, looking smaller than she had at any time all day.

'Suzie, you can't change the past. But you've still got a life to live. There are things you can do. You can even make yourself contactable if you want to, if your daughter ever wants to find you.'

'Oh I've done all that. Years ago. Nothing. Nothing! I don't even know if she's still alive,' said Suzie, as a tear sat on the edge of her eye, glinting as a shard of light came through the trees.

'Well *you* are,' said Abbie. 'And you have to make the most of that time. We all do.'

'She's right,' said Tim, looking over at Abbie with a

smile. For the first time in a long while, she actually felt a little proud of herself.

'Now then,' she continued, more confident than ever. 'We're going to be here for quite a bit longer. And we're not going to have you leaving London feeling this way. Would it help if you told us about your daughter? From the beginning? So that some of us might properly understand, even if no one else ever has?'

Tim's face was betraying some mild alarm at this suggestion, but Howie was beaming.

'That's a fantastic idea, Abs,' said the Australian with a nod. 'We'll listen. Bear witness if you like.'

And so she did. There, in the shadow of the Palace of Westminster, with people all around her nursing their own regrets, private sorrows, aching hearts, she told them everything. From the way Eddie had looked at her over the bar to the fear she had felt as she had arrived in Wales, to the years and years of unspoken pain that had grown around her like rings on a tree as she tried time and again not to let her parents down, not to let Colin down, not to let her daughter – wherever she may now be – down.

She explained to them how different things had been back then, how no one person had forced her towards adoption but the situation had seemed to present only one option. Then, as the queue moved steadily forwards and the chill in the air grew, she told them what it had done to her to try and be a particular sort of person when society had already labelled you another. And they listened.

Abbie, Tim and Howie listened to her pain, and her desire and her loneliness, watching the artichoke layers of a life peel away, each more plump, more full of spirit than they ever could have imagined.

Abbie must have stood behind women like Suzie a million times in supermarket queues, waiting to board trains, and at the pharmacy. And she had never imagined that any one of them might ever have lived a life so rich, so full of passion. Nor, by the looks of things, had Tim or Howie, whose eyes were now also shiny with tears.

Up ahead, they could see that the end of the line was actually finally approaching. The final walk into the Hall was very close. People around them were starting to abandon anything they no longer needed or would be permitted to take through the tight, airport-style security. There were huge trestle tables set up for people to leave unopened food and drink to be taken to local food banks. Apples, sandwiches, packets of crisps were mounting up as people realised their new life of infinite queueing was coming to a sudden end. People were abandoning excess clothing, hand cream, lip glosses, all so that they could pass into the Hall to pay their respects as unencumbered as possible.

Suzie tipped almost everything out of her bag and slipped the strap across her body. With nothing in her hand or under one arm for the first time in forty years, she felt weightless, giddy, at odds with the air of solemnity around them.

Maybe they'd judge her, maybe they had just been indulging her all this time as a way to entertain themselves during a long boring queue. Maybe they really had been listening as intently as they looked as if they had been. And maybe she would never know which it was. But she had done it. She had told the truth.

They left the steel barriers behind them and moved across the final stretch of lawn to the luggage scanners. And as they waited for the people in front to remove their bags and dump them in the black plastic tubs ready for scanning, Suzie turned to her new friends.

'Life's short, you know,' she told them. 'Even one as long as Her Majesty's goes by in a flash. You think it's just something old people tell you, and then one day you look in the mirror and there's a face you barely recognise staring back at you and it's yours, wishing you'd told more people you loved them when you had the chance.'

Tim was fiddling with the toggle on his rucksack, apparently trying to avoid eye contact. She gave him a prod in the chest.

'I mean it, you know. It isn't just something old people say because they're lonely. It's something we say because it's true.'

10

Palace of Westminster

Suzie was right. Of course, on some level he had known it all along, but it had taken today to make him *feel* it.

It had felt important, bearing witness to a life so different to his own. Indeed, it *was* important. Now, as they gathered themselves to enter the Palace of Westminster, he could see that that had been so much of what today was about: creating a space not just to think about the Queen, although they had all discussed her throughout the day, but to pay testament to their own grief – all of it.

Tim had found it so easy over the years to look around at other lives and in them see only what he didn't have. Focusing on that which he didn't dare reach for, or that which he felt others saw as different in him, had been the simpler path to take. The idea of being part of some sort of minority had never sat easily with him – he hadn't asked for it, he wasn't well suited to standing out, and he was someone who tended to resist change rather than embrace it, let alone advocate for it.

But he had always known that society had put him

somewhat on the edges of things, and trying to ignore it had only ended up making him think about it more. Today, seen from the perspective of Suzie's experiences, what unspoken sadness Howie was carrying, and even what the veteran he had quietly been watching all day as he queued in his uniform must have seen – had made his own problems feel very different.

We are all bearing something, he realised. Especially after these last few years. We'd lost not just friends and family members, but time and experiences. There were newborns that had grown up unkissed by grandparents, sitting up and playing with their own chubby toes by the time they met half of their loved ones. There were final goodbyes that were never said, or at best transmitted digitally. And there were childhoods which would now and forever bear the scars of experiences, explanations and repercussions that they should never have had to deal with. To stop and think, to pay tribute to what sadness – and what hope – each of us carries, had been important. Not just important, but the very reason why Tim and so very many others had made it to Westminster this week.

But as much as it was important, it was nerve-racking. As Tim watched Suzie patting down her hair and tidying herself up, he realised that even at nearly seventy years old, there was still time for fresh starts and new approaches. So there was no way he couldn't reach for that same optimism, to not make a grab for life even in his early forties. He had to use today as a catalyst for change, he knew he had to. But how? And . . . alone?

The queue was quieter now, as they approached the security scanners at the entrance to Westminster. Abbie and Suzie were up in front of him, the younger woman's hand in the small of Suzie's back, protectively guiding her along, making sure she didn't get jostled by the crowds as the space to stand narrowed. Slowly, steadily, while as the volume around them fell as expectations rose, they had their bags scanned, moving forwards, until at last they were indoors. And then, before they had a chance to get their bearings, they were there, in Westminster Hall, at the very centre of Westminster.

Tim spent a lot of time alone, and he was used to quiet. But this, as he stood at the top of the stone steps at the entrance to the hall, was a different sort of silence. It felt like an active silence, more than the absence of the usual chit-chat and bustle that one might hear in the entrance to any other of the city's great monuments. This absence of noise was people paying tribute with their silence, using it to say what words couldn't. It was purposeful, deliberate, a silence that felt like a roar.

As they approached the hall, there wasn't a single one of them who hadn't known all day that this was where they were heading, but now that they were here, the mood had suddenly felt forbidding to Abbie. It was as if she had only just received some bad news, rather than known it all along. People were so tired now, they'd travelled so far, stood in the sun for so long, trying to keep their energy up; but here, on the threshold of Westminster Hall, the energy was shifting entirely.

Time seemed to slow down a little, people moving steadily, deliberately, keen not to make sudden noise or disrupt the peace of others. She glanced behind to Tim, and ahead to Suzie as they turned towards the hall itself. It looked enormous, but the scene managed to be both formal, staged, and uncannily intimate. The huge wooden beams overhead seemed almost cosy, folksy, but the quieter clack of smart shoes on the flagstone floor was near military in the silence.

They stood for a second at the top of the steps down towards the hall itself, taking in the scene which was both familiar from the rolling news coverage and like nothing she had ever encountered before.

Without thinking, Abbie reached forward and put her hand out to Suzie, taking her by the arm. She held on as they stepped gingerly down into the hall, following the line of the rope cordons and the people who had been queuing all day. As she took Suzie's arm she felt the woman lean into her, protective, something halfway between a cuddle and an attempt to have Abbie walk alongside her for support. The three sets of steps felt almost endless, Abbie anxious not to fall or let Suzie fall. They clung onto each other, silently following the rest of the queue.

They made their way behind the European couple they had been following all day. The man handed his wife a neatly folded tissue as they approached the coffin, draped in the Royal Standard, surrounded by the Queen's guardsmen. As the couple paused, their heads bowed, so Suzie and Abbie stopped too.

Abbie took Suzie's hand in hers, relieved to feel the warmth of her flesh, to let her know that she was there – no matter what she had been through today. She felt Suzie give it a quick, reassuring squeeze, and the two of them walked forward, towards the catafalque.

It was only a couple of seconds, but as they stood there, Abbie felt as if she had grown up more today that she had in the last year. For once, she had seen something through, instead of fretting about the friends who had disregarded her or losing her nerve when she felt alone. Grandma Lucy had been right – she could do this. She could make something, she could leave a legacy. And above all, as she looked down at Suzie's hand, she wasn't alone, even in the unlikeliest of places.

Suzie's head was bowed now, her eyes closed for a second or two. Then, quietly, she stepped away, moving on. Abbie placed an arm around her and suddenly felt absolutely bereft at the thought that they'd be saying goodbye to each other soon.

As he stepped down the three sets of steps and towards the catafalque, Tim's head was swirling with the facts about Westminster Hall that he had spent so much of last

night reading about. Built nearly a thousand years ago . . .
survived a huge fire during World War II . . . surrounded
by walls six feet thick . . . He was scurrying for his usual
place of refuge in an intense emotional moment, gathering facts and longing to share all this information with
someone. The silence felt almost oppressive, making him
panic that he'd fall and disrupt the peace.

Up ahead he watched Abbie and Suzie, holding hands
now, heads bowed in thought and respect. As he did so,
he stumbled momentarily on the crease between two
flagstones, almost tripping and catching the back of
Suzie's coat. He righted himself, took a huge breath, and
as he looked up, he saw Howie at his side, mouthing 'You
OK?' at him. He nodded, embarrassed, as they were now
mere steps from the catafalque.

A heartbeat later he was standing in front of it, his
head bowed, promising not just to himself but a god he
wasn't sure he believed in and a queen he knew to be dead,
that he would make the very most of his life. That he had
wasted enough time hiding. That the time was now.

And as he did so, he felt Howie's hand, his little finger,
brush against his own. The gesture wasn't intrusive, but
it was unmistakable. And it made him want to stay there
forever, next to this man who had already taught him so
much, even on a day when he'd been so beset by self-
reflection. In that instant, as they stood, still, peaceful,
paying tribute to a life of service, Tim felt closer to Howie
than he ever had done to anyone. And instead of running
from it, the long-familiar nag of anxiety gnawing at him,

he chose to let it happen. To stand there a blink longer. To let himself believe that he deserved it.

Within seconds it was all over. The queue was still moving behind them, more mourners ready to pay their respects. Back up the steps at the opposite end of the hall they went, and a minute later they were once again out in the open air. Only now it was no longer blazing sunshine, but the peachy pink sky of a sunset.

Tim felt something close to homesick, desperate to hold onto not just the intensity of the moment they had just experienced but these people themselves. People were making their way to the Tube, walking away back over the South Bank on foot, and hopping onto buses as soon as they could. But others were stepping out onto Westminster Green, sharing phone numbers and making calls, figuring out what to do next. Letting instinct take over for once, Tim seized the chance to walk over to Westminster Green when the traffic lights turned green, and to his delight, the rest of their little group followed him, busy talking among themselves.

'Shall we go to Westminster Bridge? The green one?' he suggested. 'We had to walk straight past it on the other side when we were queueing but we could go and take a proper group photograph, something to remember the day by now that we're, maybe, a little calmer? We deserve a second shot. Even the light feels warmer than it did before, on Lambeth Bridge.'

'Good shout,' said Howie with a smile. 'This is a sunset I don't want to forget.'

Had he forgotten what had happened in there? Had he even noticed it at all? Tim's breath stuck in his throat for a second at the very thought.

'Oh Tim, I'd love that,' said Suzie. 'Will you come too, Abbie?'

'Of course! I mean, I'd come anyway but I have nowhere else to be – turns out Annabelle went home hours ago and she's only just bothered to text me.'

'Abbie! You poor thing.' Suzie looked genuinely shocked.

'Don't let them get to you,' added Howie. 'It takes time to find your people sometimes. And *they* are not yours.'

'He's right,' Tim chipped in. 'It's taken me a while to find mine too, but I think I may have found a couple today.'

'Well now, I'm the oldest so I obviously know the most about this,' said Suzie, her eyes twinkling with mischief. 'But Abbie, they're both right. You don't have to have it all sorted yet. We're all works in progress. You just have to concentrate on who you are and what you want. And to that end, shall you and I go and find somewhere to have something to eat after this photo? Please, let me treat you.'

'I'd love that,' replied Abbie. 'I really would.'

The four of them made their way onto the bridge, with Howie arranging them with the river behind and the pink of the sunset gently fading right behind their heads. Just as he was waving his hand, trying to nudge them slightly closer together so that he could fit himself into the photo too, a stranger approached and asked if they'd like him to take a photo of all four of them.

'I'm not really part of the original group,' replied Howie, a response which Tim suspected was aimed towards them as much as to the passing stranger.

'Of course you are!' cried Suzie. 'Isn't he, Tim?'

'I should say,' he replied, his face beaming, his hand beckoning to Howie to join the group.

'No problem,' said the stranger. 'Could one of you hold this for me though?'

The four of them looked at the man's extended hand and saw that he was holding out a dog lead, on the end of which was a small, strawberry blonde dog. A corgi.

'Oh my god!' yelped Abbie. 'How gorgeous! What's their name?'

'She's called Alba,' replied the man, handing her the lead.

The corgi waddled towards her, as she grinned at Howie. 'You're the expert,' she said. 'Do you want to hold her?'

'She's all yours,' replied Howie, as Abbie bent down to pet her.

'You can pick her up if you'd like,' the stranger said. 'She's quite old now, very sweet-natured.' And so she did, lifting Alba into her arms as she stood between Suzie and Howie, grinning into the camera.

The four of them nuzzled into each other, laughing as their new friend directed them, heads the right heights. Tim and Howie at the back, arms around each other, heads almost imperceptibly tipped towards each other, with Abbie and Suzie in front, petting Alba. A perfect shot of a single moment.

The group thanked the man profusely as he handed the phone back to Howie and headed into the distance, Alba's fluffy bottom wiggling along beside him. The four of them exchanged numbers, excited to see the photos, before realising that they had no idea where they were all heading now.

Tim's stomach lurched as he hugged Suzie and Abbie goodbye, half filled with dread at the thought of the day ending. Abbie had draped herself over Howie, excitedly arranging a knitting night with him next week, and enthusiastically taking him up on his offer to introduce her to some friends who worked in the costume department on a string of West End shows. And Suzie had given Tim a tight squeeze, making him promise to keep in touch, 'no matter *what else* happens'. She had said those last few words with a brief wink followed by a quick glance at Howie. And as she hugged him a second time, she whispered 'go for it' into his ear, before patting the back of his hand.

So as he watched them walking off towards the South Bank, having decided to get some food near to the book market, he remembered the promise he had made to himself only half an hour ago, inside the Palace of Westminster. So he turned to face Howie, looked him dead in the eye and said, 'So, shall we go and get a drink?'

'Absolutely,' he replied. 'I thought you'd never ask.'

With that, the two of them walked back off the bridge and north from the river, heading towards Covent Garden. He could collect his bike later. Maybe even tomorrow.

It was dark by the time Suzie got on the train home, exhausted after the long day and the warm bowl of pasta she'd had with Abbie. When she glanced at her phone, she saw that Howie had set up a little WhatsApp group for the four of them, posting the photos from Westminster Bridge.

There they all were, Suzie with her arm around Abbie, who was holding Alba, and Tim at the back with his arm around Howie. In one of the shots, he was clearly stealing a glance at his new friend, and Suzie noted with interest that Howie had included this in the images he'd chosen to send. At first, Suzie felt a twinge of shame for the huge smiles they all had, as if they'd spent a day at a theme park. Then, as she turned her phone off and stared out of the window, she realised she had spent enough of her life feeling guilty.

It had not been the day she had expected, but it had been the day she needed, and she suspected it was the same for all of them. She had sat in that restaurant with Abbie, watching her demolish a bowl of tiramisu while they chatted about whether Tim and Howie were going to end up together by the end of the evening, and for the first time a cloud of thoughts about Bess had not put a moment of joy in the shade.

She would wait, probably for the rest of her life, wondering if she would ever hear from her daughter. But she would no longer do it with shame. For that, she had waited long enough. This morning, she had thought a twelve-hour queue would feel endless, but as her train pulled into the station she could see that the real wait had taken place long before. Now it was time to live, and to do it with her whole heart.

Acknowledgements

First and foremost, thank you to my agent Sophie Lambert, who did not flinch when an author she had only just taken on sent a weekend email which began 'Maybe you'll think I'm bonkers, but . . .' and instead saw the potential in my idea. All of the encouragement and guidance has been more than appreciated!

And thank you to my editor Charlotte Mursell, Snigdha Koirala and the team at Orion for not just agreeing with Sophie's faith in the idea, but then defying the glacial pace of publishing to get this novel into print this year. No novel is merely one person's work, but especially not this one, and it has been a privilege to be part of your team.

On a personal level, thank you to the Jersey Street Queers for all of the support while I was writing the book. Food, sympathy, a second home across the city, and the knowledge that L was always, *always* happy when I was busy writing. Nicky, Kel, Issie and Ella: you slay!

I also owe a huge thank you to my brother for walking

the walk and talking the talk with me on a very chilly January day. And to my mother who quite rightly considers herself *The Queue*'s granny. She was its first reader, and without her I could not have done it, so she is quite right. Here's to the first Fish Club novel!

Credits

Alexandra Heminsley and Orion Fiction would like to thank everyone at Orion who worked on the publication of *The Queue* in the UK.

Editorial
Charlotte Mursell
Snigdha Koirala

Copy editor
Laura Gerrard

Proofreader
Clare Wallis

Audio
Paul Stark
Jake Alderson

Contracts
Dan Herron
Ellie Bowker

Design
Tomás Almeida
Joanna Ridley
Charlotte Abrams-
    Simpson
Rachael Lancaster

Editorial Management
Charlie Panayiotou
Jane Hughes
Bartley Shaw